ELTING MEMORIAL LIBRARY NEW PALTZ

3 2913 00078 6745

DARE ME

D1166815

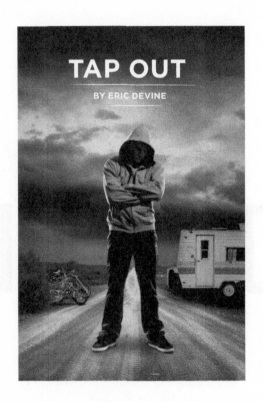

Also by Eric Devine
TAP OUT
RUNNING PRESS TEENS

DARE ME

ERIC DEVINE

Elting Memorial Library
93 Main Street
New Paltz, New York 12561-1593

RP|TEENS
PHILADELPHIA · LONDON

Copyright © 2013 by Eric Devine

All rights reserved under the Pan-American and
International Copyright Conventions

Printed in the United States

*This book may not be reproduced in whole or in part, in any form or
by any means, electronic or mechanical, including photocopying, recording,
or by any information storage and retrieval system now known
or hereafter invented, without written permission from the publisher.*

Books published by Running Press are available at special discounts
for bulk purchases in the United States by corporations, institutions, and other
organizations. For more information, please contact the Special Markets
Department at the Perseus Books Group, 2300 Chestnut Street, Suite 200,
Philadelphia, PA 19103, or call (800) 810-4145, ext. 5000,
or e-mail special.markets@perseusbooks.com.

ISBN 978-0-7624-5015-2
Library of Congress Control Number: 2013937586

E-book ISBN 978-0-7624-5080-0

9   8   7   6   5   4   3   2
Digit on the right indicates the number of this printing

Cover designed by Joshua McDonnell
Interior designed by Frances J. Soo Ping Chow
Edited by Lisa Cheng
Typography: Adobe Garamond, Agenda, Akzidenz Grotesk,
Memphis, and Just Me Again Down Here

Published by Running Press Teens
An Imprint of Running Press Book Publishers
A Member of the Perseus Books Group
2300 Chestnut Street
Philadelphia, PA 19103–4371

Visit us on the web!
www.runningpress.com/kids

For those with the will to dare
and the courage to accept the consequences

CHAPTER 1

There is no doubt that one of us will die. I'm not hoping for it, just considering the probability: three of us, ten stunts, each "death defying." At least that's the plan: spend senior year completing one dare a month. Why? So we're legends by the end.

Ricky's driving and he looks at me, rocks his head to the music blaring, and says, "Ready, Ben?"

As if there's any answer I can give but yes. I know how it works. He looks in the rearview. "John, ready?"

John gives a thumbs-up and gets the camera into position. "On you, Ben." He slides out of the rear window.

I turn and look. Nothing but cornstalks and pavement, blue sky and puffy white clouds. Perfection. I focus on that image and the stillness, the quiet. If I don't, I'll chicken out. My mind's already filling with scenarios for how this will end badly. But school starts tomorrow, and I agreed to this, however it goes.

I pull the ski mask over my face and slide out the window.

The wind whips even though Ricky's only going like thirty miles per hour. I can't hear what John's saying. His mouth's moving, but it's like being in a dream, all background noise, nothing real. He jacks his thumb into the air, an obvious sign for me to get on the roof. I take a deep breath, steady my elbows, and push myself up.

My feet tingle and my heart hammers, but I keep going. I grab the roof rack and pull and am flat on top. The wind pours over me now, but the space around my face is calm. Unreal.

"Let's do it." John's words are faint, but they're enough to propel me. I grip the rack and slide my feet beneath me. Ten seconds. All I have to do is stay on my feet and count.

I stand but wobble and have to sit back down on my heels. Shit, maybe I *can't* do this. No matter how much I convince myself. I look over at John for help, forgetting that the camera is on me. There's nothing he can do. This is all mine. I'd love nothing more than to crawl right back in the window, but it would be on film, and Ricky would never let me hear the end of it. Just like before.

I've decided that's not what *I* want, so I swallow, take another breath, and ease my way up.

I rock again, but only slightly. John raps on the roof to let Ricky know I'm up, and Ricky lets out a scream. I spread my arms and yell along with him because this is fucking insane. The road stretches before me, and one false move and I'm part of it. But Ricky's smooth, and it's like I'm on a skateboard without the rumble beneath my feet.

A car comes from the other direction and Ricky honks. The driver looks up and sees me and I look down at him and for a second our eyes meet. In his, pure panic. His mouth is dropped and his skin is paper-white. But then he's gone and my heart is racing and it's been ten seconds. I let out one more scream and tuck back to the roof rack.

John smacks the car again to let Ricky know I'm done, and I hear muffled cheering from within. I smile. It's big and hurts my cheeks and my eyes water from the wind, but this is the most alive I've felt in forever, exactly like Ricky said we would. One dare down, nine to go.

—

When I went to bed at 2:00 a.m., there were thirty-five views. I woke up at 7:00 and there were thirty-seven. I just checked my phone and we're up to a whopping fifty. Ricky talked about these videos being "the best senior prank ever" because they'll last all year. I had to agree to the brilliance of the uniqueness. He also said that we'll be "larger than Jesse Holmes" and his crew. I don't know about that. One look at those guys, and it's obvious they own our school. Handsome, suave, athletic. Considering either hopeful outcome, fifty views aren't going to do jack.

John rolls up to my locker. "I'm still wrecked from yesterday. I kept dreaming about it. Woke up screaming."

I picture John in his bed, all wound up in his sheets, screaming into the night. Doesn't surprise me. He's always had nightmares. Scared the hell out of me the first time he slept over in fifth grade. "You've got a month before the next one. Try to relax."

He shakes his head and doesn't say anything, but I know what he means. This isn't our thing: trouble. That's Ricky's territory. But we're only visiting, right?

We walk toward the cafeteria and go as unnoticed as usual. I watch the clusters and wonder what the hot girls are discussing, the übergeeks, the Bible-thumpers. I remember Ricky's words: *This is how we make our mark. You've seen all the stupid dares kids are doing. Cinnamon eating and vodka in the eye. Not us. We're going balls out and will leave here legends.*

Yet day one of senior year feels like we never left. Classes have been exactly as I expected. *I'm Mr./Mrs. so-and-so, and this class will be difficult. You are a senior, so I'm not holding your hand. Here's your first assignment.* And off we go.

John and I grab trays and get served the miserable offerings and head to our table. Ricky's already there.

"Hey, John, don't trip!"

Ricky laughs at his own joke and chews on a French fry.

"You hit that pothole on purpose?" John sits but doesn't touch his food.

"That's one way of looking at it. Or maybe you wanted to end up on the windshield. Crying." Ricky smiles. "Guess we'll never know, huh?"

"I wasn't crying," John mumbles into his food.

He was totally crying, but who cares? It was good footage. Well, for our purposes.

I take a bite of the hamburger. "You think maybe the low numbers are because of the distortion?"

Ricky takes a sip of his drink. He looks calm, like this is all part of his plan. "We need the masks and the blurring so we don't get in trouble. No faces, no identity match. We've been through this." He leans in. "Don't worry, I got this. Plan B, the old-fashioned route."

"What are you going to do?" I ask. I don't know how many times I've asked him this question. For all of high school, the answers didn't include me. Until now.

Ricky laughs. "Ben, don't worry, I'm going to make a PSA. You like those, don't you?" He climbs onto the table and I kind of hate him.

"Shit," John whispers.

Ricky looks around, smiling and waving. Some kids point. Others swear at him. But in a moment everyone is watching. He opens his mouth.

"Ladies and gentleman of the senior class, today is the beginning of our last year at this institution." His voice is steady and thick and he pauses for the cheers that accompany anything about seniors. "It could be just another year, the same as the last and the one before, where we hope for something exciting to actually happen, but it never does. Or, we can make a decision. We can decide to make that excitement a priority." He pauses dramatically and I wince. "That's what *someone* here has done."

The room murmurs and students look around at one another. I'm trying not to think of all the ways this could get us into trouble, but the infractions scramble my head.

"Do yourselves a favor," Ricky continues, "check out 'Brookwood High Senior Year Dare Number One' on YouTube. It seems like someone here has a plan for the year. Hopefully, you'll see it and feel like I did: pumped. Hopefully it will get you excited for this year. Hopefully it'll give you something fun to watch instead of just stalking one another on Twitter." Ricky thrusts his fist into the air and nods his head while looking around the room. He's gone too far. Most of the kids stare, while others start cracking jokes. A teacher motions for him to get off the table, and in a moment his big scene is over and people are back to their lunches. I'm quietly relieved.

"That was impressive," John says, as Ricky gets down from the table.

Ricky's jaw is set and his shoulders are pinned, and it seems he doesn't know where to look or what to say. His PSA failed, like the video. Maybe he's realizing that his ideas suck. This is nothing new, but the way he seems to feel about it is. I take another bite out of the hamburger, and it's like putting my mouth around a sponge.

—

The rest of the day flows as before, irritating and uncomfortable, like a tag still in my underwear. I manage to zone out long enough in econ to feel as if I'm not even in the room, but floating somewhere. This is what gets me by. I think too much, worry too much. But it's not like I can stop. Success comes from seeing the next turn before you're there. At least that's what my dad says. So I try to detach and think. But I'm having trouble today. Maybe it's the dare. Maybe it's being back at school. One class isn't enough to figure it out, so I'm going to blame it on the weather.

It's still too warm for school. When the last bell rings, it feels more like we're leaving for the year rather than just beginning.

"I'm taking a nap. Today was terrible. Not at all what I expected." John slaps his feet across the sidewalk as we walk.

"Yeah, it could have been better. I've got work now, too."

"Thought you weren't staying on once school started?"

I was going to quit. My parents would rather I focus on school, anyway. And it's disgustingly hot in there. But my boss, Chuck, is cool, and I like delivering, even though reeking of pizza sucks.

"Yeah. The money's good, and I should start saving for next year."

John stops walking. "Next year?"

"You know, college?"

His face clears. "Oh, right."

I love John and all, but lately he's like a telephone pole: tall, thick, and only useful for one purpose. Fortunately for him that purpose is basketball, and because of it, scholarships. He will most likely get redshirted for his freshman year because of his grades. If he weren't so dumb, he might have known enough not to hang with me. He could have been popular. Maybe that's why I never worry about him, our friendship. His loyalty is like a dog's.

"Hey, check it." He points across the street and I follow his finger. Danielle Thompson, top Mean Girl, is laying into her boyfriend of the moment. Can't remember his name. She smacks him once, and he drops against his car. She reels back again and he grabs her wrist, but she looks at his hand like she could melt it with her eyes, and he starts apologizing. I can't begin to fathom the dynamics of that relationship.

"Maybe that should be one of the dares? See who can date her and survive."

John laughs at my joke, but it's empty. "Like there'll be another. I think Ricky might be changing his mind." He doesn't seem bothered by this idea. "What are you thinking?"

"The car surfing, it was fun, right?"

John looks up. "Take out me doing a face plant, yeah, I'd say it was fun."

"Kind of like eighth grade. You know?"

John looks back at me and searches my face. "I do, but we both know it can't end like that again. Too much on the line now."

I nod quick. He's right. We pound fists and go our separate ways, while down the street Danielle and her man are kissing, looking like they'll take the action into the backseat.

My house is empty. The way I like it. I grab some cookies from the pantry and head up to my room.

I turn on my computer, pick through the laundry on the floor, and find the dirty blue polo I have to wear to work. I slide it on while holding my breath and pull up our video. Shit, we've got two hundred hits. I check the comments:

Nice ride, bros.

Thought that one kid was going to die. Fucking awesome.

What's next?

They go on, and some suggest what we might do for stunts. I don't want to touch half of them. My stomach draws up and suddenly I don't want the cookie in my mouth. I think John was wrong. I'm pretty sure Ricky's going to want to forge ahead. And if he follows any of these suggestions, we're dead.

CHAPTER 2

Pizza and More is like every little pizza shop around: cute on the front end but dirty as a slaughterhouse on the back side.

I pull my Jeep into the parking lot, and the stench of the Dumpster wafts over me. I get out and dart inside. Chuck stands in the middle of the floor, arms crossed over his barrel, wife-beater-covered chest.

"What time are you supposed to be here?"

Shit, 4:00. Am I late? I glance at the clock over his shoulder. It's ten of. "Four?" I say and crinkle my forehead.

Chuck starts laughing and slaps my shoulder. "I'm messing with you. Of course you're on time. Everyone's on time now that Alexia works here."

I turn red and cringe behind his fat body because Alexia Bellamy's at the counter. He's always doing this, trying to embarrass me through her. He doesn't realize that I'm already embarrassed. Or, knowing Chuck, that's exactly why he does it. Either way, she's on the phone, so I'm in the clear. "Funny, Chuck."

"I know, right?" He puts his hands on his hips and looks genuinely proud. He then slaps my back, and I'm almost thrown to the floor. "How was your first day, Doc? Big senior now."

When I started here I got lost all the time. Chuck started calling me "directionally retarded" which got shortened to "d.r." This got me so jammed up I almost quit. But my dad had me study a map of town day after day, and double-checking my routes on my phone's GPS. I never got lost again. I know all my regular customers by heart and can plan out routes better than anyone, so now "d.r." means Doc.

"Doesn't feel like anything's changed."

"Yeah, welcome to the real world. The calendar only looks different because I buy a new one. You know?"

I do and nod along. "Then I'd better get to those deliveries."

"There we go, but don't get too close to her. You might pass out." He laughs his deep, fat-boy laugh and elbows me. I walk away, shaking my head, wishing for a way to put him in his place. I grab the slips for the outgoing orders.

Alexia hangs up the phone. "Got one more for you. Just an antipasto, so I'll get it." She hands me the slip and smiles with her perfect white teeth and I don't say a word. Can't. I nod, stupidly, and enjoy the sensation of her hand running over my palm. She goes to the refrigerator and I know I must look like a total creeper.

I bag the orders, punch the addresses into the GPS, and sure enough, the navigation system displays the exact order I would have followed.

"Here you go." Alexia dangles the bag before me. She used to do the same when we played as kids, handing a toy over with the same line. I had no clue then how truly fabulous she was.

I take the bag and say thanks.

She lingers. This is new. *I* always linger. Not her.

"I watched the video Ricky mentioned. The car surf?"

My ears are red, I know it. "Uh huh."

"That was awesome! How'd he find it?"

My head is scrambled and it takes a second for me to respond. "I don't know, but I think it was on Jasperg Lane. You know, the one by the farm?" Immediately, I know I've said too much.

Her eyes widen. "Right! Well, if that's where they were, it's a good spot. There's like no one out there."

"Seems like that was the idea." I don't know what else to say, and I know Chuck is watching.

"What do you think's next? There were some crazy ideas posted."

I so want to tell her. It's not like we haven't shared secrets before. But that was then, and like Ricky said, *We can't tell anyone it's us because we'll be arrested. Period. If this is going to work, no one can know.*

"We could bet on it." My stomach wobbles as I speak.

Alexia opens her mouth wide and steps closer to me. "Yeah? Which one are you going to choose?" Her voice is hushed and breathy.

I feel squirmy and way too excited, and so nervous I'll yell out something about her boobs, but manage to say, "There was something on there about the bridge, right?"

Her face pinches. "Really? That's the one you're going with?"

"Uh, yeah, I guess."

"But that's like seventy-five feet."

I hope she's wrong because I assumed it was less, but whatever she thinks is fine by me.

"Hey, Doc, you charging for this consult?"

I straighten at Chuck's words and Alexia jumps and grabs my arm. I look at it and she heads back to the phone, so I shoulder the bags.

"What are you up to, Romeo?" Chuck asks as I walk past.

"You ever check out YouTube?"

"The hell you talking about?"

"Some other time, Chuck. Got to get these out while they're still hot." I pat the bags and head to the Jeep, my head still swimming from Alexia and what I know is coming next.

———

It's a Wednesday so there aren't many deliveries, and by 7:00 Chuck sends us home. I want to walk Alexia to her car, see if I can talk to her some more, but Jesse picks her up and speeds off. The bass of his music vibrates my intestines.

I park in the driveway, and through the front window, my parents are visible at the dining room table. It's an odd scene because we only use that table when we have company, or for the holidays. Or for when they want to talk.

Shit. I bet they found out about the car surfing. Someone saw it and called. I knew the masks and Ricky's editing wouldn't be enough. First they'll rub it in my face about Ricky, especially my dad, and then they'll kill me. At least I was right about one of us dying.

I whip out my phone and pull up our video. We've got one thousand views and over one hundred comments. My legs go heavy. Now I'm sure they've seen this. Seems like the entire town has.

I walk inside and head directly to the dining room. "What's up?"

My parents both smile that fake everything's-fine-why-are-you-asking grin? Mom reaches out and loosely grips my wrist. "Why don't you sit down and tell us about your day?"

She's trying to soften me up before they crack down. Classic move I've seen too many times. Mom's some kind of lab technician and Dad does line work at the local plant, so they tend to do the same things over and over at work, and with Ginny and me. I know the script for this scene, and it's fine. I'll play my part and accept my punishment and go to my room. Later, they'll come up separately and have a little "private" chat about how sorry they are, and how they'll reduce the sentence if I could do this or that for them. I've never been grounded for more than an hour.

I shrug. "Not much to tell. You know, day one nonsense."

"That's too bad. It's your senior year. It should feel different somehow." Mom frowns.

"Give it time. It's bound to feel . . ." Dad doesn't finish. He looks away and coughs into his hand. I turn to my mother, but she's watching him.

"Is everything all right?" I no longer think this has anything to do with the video. Dad doesn't get choked up. Ever.

Mom rubs his back and he nods, coughs again, and turns to me. He looks in my eyes for a moment but then down at the table. "Ben, I'm being relocated. The plant is making cuts and in order not to lose my job, we have to move."

My temples pound. He grips the edge of the table and turns to my mother. A tear runs down her face. "When?" I manage to ask, but it's tough to get the question out. My throat is suddenly tight.

"I don't know yet. Could be a couple of months. Could be longer. I hope it's not shorter." His voice fades with the last sentence. He skims a hand over the tabletop. "I should know next week. Least that's what they're saying now."

"What are you thinking, honey? What's running through that head of yours?" Mom reaches across the table to me, and I barely feel her hand on mine.

I'm numb and don't know what to think except for one question. "Where?"

My father sits back and sighs. "That's also up in the air, but we have sister plants in Michigan, Arizona, and Washington."

It's as if my head is a balloon and someone is inflating it breath by breath. "But that's like across the country. Michigan is halfway."

My parents nod in unison and my mother wipes her tears. "We know this is going to be hard on you. And Ginny. We haven't told her, so no texting or emailing her."

As if I'd do that. What would I write? *Hey, remember that place you call home? Yeah, you can forget about that.* This is unreal. I was expecting to get into trouble, not this. Not ever. All I've ever known is this town. It's my senior year. I can't leave now. Not with the dares. Not if we have one thousand hits.

No, something will work out. It has to. Maybe I'll be in college by the time this ball gets rolling. Or maybe I'll still be a senior. Shit.

"You okay?" Dad's voice pries through my thoughts. His eyes are heavy, and as much as I want to say no, he deserves better. This can't be easy.

"Yeah, I guess. We'll see what's what. Right? Nothing else we can do."

He nods and Mom clasps her hands. "When did we get such a mature young man?" She cries again and I steal a glance at my father. He lifts his chin toward her and I know what to do. I get up and hold her tight and let her cry, when really all I want to do is go up to my room, get on my computer, and focus on other people's lives, their problems. Not mine.

She settles and I release her. My father frowns at me. "We'll keep you posted, bud. Okay?"

"Yeah. That's fine." I choke back my own emotions. "Dad, for what it's worth, I'm sorry."

I get up and leave them to talk or to cry or to figure out whatever they need to. My head has expanded but hasn't yet popped. I hope I can sleep tonight.

I settle in front of my computer but don't get online. I sit and stare at the keyboard and replay the scene from downstairs. Move? I can't move. Sure, I was planning on going away to college, but I'd come back on breaks, keep some part of this life. Should I even bother applying anywhere? Am I going to end up at some shitty community college in the middle of Arizona?

I hop on Twitter and search for Alexia, and her profile pic pops up. She's even cute in thumbnail size. We have no followers in common. No shock there.

I feel like slapping myself. Why am I thinking about following Alexia? I may be gone in a month, so what's the point? If I'm not here I won't be working with her, and she won't be thinking about me. As if she is now. Unless we go viral. Shit.

But even then she won't *know* it's me. I close my eyes and take a deep breath. Ricky's always said, *Stop thinking about the big picture. Enjoy the here and now. It's all we have.* I almost laugh at the hypocrisy. His entire point with these dares is to *Leave them stunned.* Isn't that the big picture?

However, I understand the truth within the contradiction. As much as we know, we can never fully know. We'll just find out. Whatever's around that corner, whether I can see it coming or not, will be there. I'll face it.

I hit the tab and follow Alexia. There's no turning back.

CHAPTER 3

check our stats one more time before leaving for school. We're up to 2,155 views. The comments have doubled as well. And there's an ad before our video, some outdoor adventure brand. What the fuck?

John's waiting for me outside his house, bouncing back and forth on his enormous feet. "Did you see?" He holds out his phone.

"Yeah. Just checked."

"This is unreal. Ricky was right." He watches the video again as we walk. "Man, I wish I didn't look like such an ass."

"You don't," I lie.

"Next dare, I'm on it." John slides his phone into his pocket, and we walk the rest of the way to school. I think about telling him about the move, but I don't want to bust up his good mood. And besides, it might be best to wait until I know for sure. My parents didn't say anything about it this morning. They drank their coffee and read the newspaper like usual.

It feels all slow-mo as we enter the senior hallway. Like in the movies. We're stride for stride, both smiling, nodding our heads. I'm waiting for the fist bumps and high fives. The squealing girls. Ten steps in and we stop. No one's noticed us. Everyone's doing their thing in front of their lockers, sharing iPods, cracking jokes, leaning on each other, and sipping coffee.

Some watch videos and crack up. It could be ours, but it's not like we can walk over and ask. These kids don't know us, and certainly have no idea *we're the ones* from the video. This fact is like a slap in the face. We just risked our lives, but because no one knows this about us, we're as interesting as a poster on the wall for the recycling club.

We head to our lockers. "Hey, guys." Ricky's grin stays hooked on his face as he pulls out his phone. "Someone, somewhere is logging on right now, and they're finding us on YouTube, and they're amped from our video and can't wait for the next installment." His voice has the run to it like some preacher's. I'm afraid he's going to start calling people around like he did in the cafeteria yesterday. "Isn't that amazing?"

John and I look at each other. "Uh, yeah. I guess," John says.

Ricky's eyes widen. "This shit's bigger than us already, and by the time we're through we'll be goddamn weblebrities."

That *weblebrity* is a bit much. "How is that? And how do we have an ad?"

Ricky puts his hand on my shoulder. "Listen, I said we needed to talk, and we do, but now's not the time. We've got some things to consider, some papers to read." He pauses. "And hopefully some signatures to sign."

John and I look at Ricky like we did when he first hatched this plan.

It was some random morning in early August. We'd only been really hanging out again since April, so it was surprising when he showed up with John already in the car and said, "Let's go," dragging me out of my house and driving up to the point—this rock that overlooks the town.

At first, Ricky didn't say a word, only watched the town come to life beneath us. I don't think he'd been to bed. His hair was a mess, and his eyes were bloodshot. When he turned to us, the horizon was behind him, the sun breaking across his shoulders, and he said, "Do you boys want to be famous?"

Ricky's plan for these ten senior-year dares seemed so simple and so awesome, how could I not want to be a part of it?

Maybe it was the early morning, or the way he delivered his speech with the town behind his back like he already owned it. Maybe it was something too painful to admit about ourselves. Regardless of the answer, it's too late because we're in it, and now there's something to do with papers. Something that will make this binding. Something he didn't tell us about.

The bell rings and he peels away. "Lunch. Bring a pen." And with that he disappears into the crowd and the only thing for us to do is wait.

I head to physics and learn about Newton's First Law. Who knew that it took a genius to figure out that objects at rest or in motion stay that way unless acted upon? It seems rather simple: The beginning of something, or the lack of beginning, is up to the individual, unless someone else forces the issue.

English is some last-minute review about a book we all should have read (was it *Ethan Foam*?), and econ is something about how today's economy is nothing like the Great Depression. "Try telling that to the people out of work," some kid says, and I'm reminded of Dad's situation. I guess I'm lucky he hasn't been canned. At least not yet.

And thinking about him reminds me of Ricky. Probably because if Dad finds out that I'm completing these dares because of Ricky, he'll rip my arms off and beat me with them. That's not fair. *I* made the decision. I agreed to set this in motion. And now it is.

I'd better get my head together, because regardless of what happens, I'm going *somewhere.* I just don't know where. But first I have to pass these classes, which hasn't always been my strong suit. What was that First Law again?

—

I enter the cafeteria and immediately spot Alexia. It's like she's surrounded by amber light. That may only be the reflection off the nacho cheese machine behind the counter, but it doesn't matter. She's standing there in all her smiling, glistening beauty, talking to one of her hot friends—Chantel, I think—whose breasts are spilling out of her top. She knows it. She's talking to Alexia but looking around to see who's noticing.

That's not my preference, nothing flashy, but my eyes have a tendency to do their own thing, and she spies me looking, and a little grin touches her lips. She elbows Alexia and says something. My former neighbor, now coworker, whips around. "Hey, Ben." Alexia gives a little wave like a five-year-old. I remember the Twitter follow and flush red.

Ricky and John are at our table. Ricky talking and John staring. Normally, the beanpole eats like a pig at a trough. For him to be staring at his three lunches, not eating, means something's up. Ricky smiles when I approach. "What's up, Ben?"

"Nothing." I look around the table. "Actually, that was my question."

Ricky snorts and pulls out a packet of paper. "Since we're all here, this is it, in black and white." The packet is thick, like some end-of-the-year review compilation, but the font is small and the paragraphs are crammed with words. There are no blanks for answers, but ones for the "undersigned."

"So these dares, as you may have figured out by now, they didn't come from nowhere." Ricky eyes me but looks quickly away. "I, uh, we have a contract offer to complete them. The first was a test." He sits back. "We passed."

John's typically slow on the uptake, so I'm not surprised he stays speechless, but I let my silence speak for me, nudging Ricky on. We both know he needs to add a little more context.

"Back in June I responded to this post on Craigslist for a way to get paid through video stunts. I ended up emailing back and forth with this guy, who owns this adventure gear company, and we set up this idea of the ten stunts."

I remember how polished it felt when Ricky told us. How it seemed like he'd read the lines beforehand. Probably did. Off this guy's email.

Ricky runs a hand through his hair. "We agreed that I'd get

the first one up, and if we got enough hits that he could justify putting up ad space, then we'd have a deal for the other nine." Ricky tacks a laugh onto the end, like this is the goofiest mess he's fallen into. John and I are hunched forward like old men with bad hearing.

But my ears work perfectly well. "So you sold us before you even told us what we were doing?" I ask.

Ricky puts up his hands. "It's not like that. I didn't say anything because what if we pussied out and couldn't do it? What would have been the point of getting your hopes up?"

"But you did. You said we'd have the best year. We'd be legends." John looks downright sad. He stares at the packet. "Now what are we going to be? I don't understand."

"Yeah. I don't either," I say, because it feels like I was tricked into believing in myself, or in us, and it was a joke. Or we were just being used. That hurts more than the way we were before.

Ricky looks around the table. "I meant what I said. These dares will work. The first one already is." He grunts. "I needed to pump you up to get you on the damn car, to get this first one in the bag."

We all look in opposite directions. I don't know what John's thinking, but I have to admit, score one for Ricky. I'm afraid of my own shadow and John can't risk getting injured. Shit, why are we doing this?

Ricky sighs and touches the packet. "It's all here in the contract he sent. We will get *paid* for the other nine stunts."

There's something about the way he said, *paid*. It's familiar and I don't like it. "How much? And why do we need the cash?"

"Depends on the hits we get. It's a percentage thing. The more views, the more money." Ricky's voice is cool again, and he levels his eyes on mine. "I'm sorry that I don't want to deliver pizzas or won't be getting scholarship money. This seems like a much better way of earning cash."

This is the Ricky I can't stand. It's not my damn fault he's too good to work in fast food. Shit, with his grades, he should get ready to do just that for the rest of his life.

"What kind of numbers? What amount of hits equals what amount of cash?" John flips the first page of the contract.

Ricky points to a paragraph. "Here. I think this part explains it."

John pours over the page, and my stomach flops. I don't know how I feel because I was all for these dares. I figured they'd be fun. But I also thought that Ricky was right about the here and now and the big picture. But something about *this*, him selling us on an idea when he had a whole other motive, it sucks.

"I don't understand a word." John throws the contract back to the table, and it lands near Ricky's plate.

"Don't worry, *I* do." Ricky picks it up, and the grooves of his thumbs are embedded in the edge of the pages. "Guys, relax. We were going to do this anyway, so why not get paid?"

"But we don't even know what we're doing. What does the *contract* say about that?" I don't mean for the word to come out like a curse, but it does, and Ricky's jaw tightens.

"We have say over the next one, but then we have to pick from a list of suggestions offered in the comments section."

I go for my phone. "Have you seen some of these?"

Ricky waves his hand. "It's not like we're going to have to play Russian roulette."

I stop digging for my phone, but John already has his out. "Yeah, but there's swimming with eels or sharks, or launching over some canyon—I don't know where. We're going to have to pick from one of these?"

And this is why I love John. He may be a little slow at times, but when he attacks, he brings it.

"No. No. You don't get it. He's not trying to kill us, he wants to make money. He can't do that if we're dead." Ricky grabs his hair with both hands, and after he drags them through, it stands up like Einstein's. "How can't you see that this is a win-win? He makes money, we get paid."

"But you said this was about having an awesome year. Building a legacy. You stood up and spoke to the cafeteria. Was that a lie?" John's voice is soft, like Eeyore's.

Ricky rests his palms on the table and takes a few deep breaths. I look around the cafeteria. Kids everywhere are laughing and throwing food at one another, enjoying themselves. John's got a point. We're sitting around this table like it's a goddamn board meeting. I can't believe I'm thinking this, but isn't the fun of the dares enough? But I may not be here in another month, and I want to enjoy however much time I have left with these guys, not argue over cash.

"You know what?" My voice is louder than I expected. "Who cares? Ricky's right. We were going to do this. This is a still a fantastic idea. Even though Ricky can't take credit for it, so what? This could be the best time any of us ever had. And now we'll get paid. What's the problem?"

"He lied, Ben. And I don't know, this shit is really dangerous." John's eyes are so sad.

John's right. Ricky lied, but he had a reason. He only withheld the source of the dares and the plan to get paid. Is that so bad? And in spite of the danger and the deceit, I want to continue. Riding that car made me feel a little badass. I miss that feeling already. How am I going to feel after three or ten?

Ricky clears his throat. "I'm sorry, guys. I guess I was thinking . . . of other things."

John and I nod and I wonder if John's thinking what I am: *What "other things"?*

Ricky picks up the packet, and three lines sit waiting for our names. "We still cool?"

John and I don't answer.

Ricky sighs, takes a pen out of his pocket, clicks it dramatically, and signs on the first line. He passes the packet to me.

I look at John, his face an explosion of questions that he keeps himself from asking. I sign and pass it to him.

John looks directly at me, as if there's still a chance to ask his questions, but he doesn't ask anything and just signs.

CHAPTER 4

I know I just took another three classes, but I have no idea what the hell they were. Yeah, I zoned out as usual. But in my defense, this development merits some consideration. We didn't even talk about the second dare. Ricky tucked the contract away, and we all tried to eat something before the bell rang. What little of my sandwich I did eat sat like a stone in my gut the rest of the afternoon, and now I have to shit so bad I'm sweating.

John walks up to my locker. "Ready?"

"Yeah. If I can't make it home, I'm dropping a deuce at your house."

"That's fine."

We take off and kids peel out of the parking lot. Jesse Holmes's car leads the pack. Principal McNeil stands on the corner and shakes his head. He's got a clipboard in hand, trying to take down names.

"So how much you think we'll get?" John's sneakers scuff the sidewalk.

"You mean with our deal?"

He nods.

"I doubt that much. We talked about this kind of thing last year in Business and Marketing. Some kids did a presentation. You have to have enormous exposure to really pull it in."

"I figured." John sighs.

"What, were you planning on building some dream home with the money?"

"No, man, but having some cash would be nice. Can't work and play ball at the same time."

"I hear you. Guess we'll wait and see?" I don't say anything about how some cash would be nice with my dad's job on the line. Maybe enough to help pay for a bill or buy groceries or something.

We pull up to John's house. "You blowing it up?" he asks.

I consider it, but would rather be home. "No, I'll make it, but if you hear a rumor that I was running down the street half-naked you'll know why."

He laughs. "Put on a ski mask, and you'll be safe."

As soon as I get home I do some serious damage to my toilet, but I open the window, run the fan, and light a candle. Nerves and my insides do not mix. The rest of this school year is going to be horrible.

I change, grab a quick bite to eat, and am off to work. I take my time driving, windows down, tunes cranked. I wish Pizza and More was farther away.

"Hey, Doc, how many lives you save today?" Chuck's mixing a vat of sauce.

"Just my own."

"Some days you're the windshield and others you're the bug."

"Thanks, Chuck. I'll get that tattooed."

He keeps churning the sauce. "You should, that's some damn good advice. Like this is: Alexia was talking about how you are *following* each other, whatever the hell that stalkery shit means. But she seemed to like it. You should go for her."

Here he goes again. I swear he wishes he could be young again. But his game didn't seem to work out so well the first time around, and he hasn't seemed to learn much since then. He may need to rethink his entire approach. I want to offer this advice, but instead, I pull out my phone and check Twitter. Sure enough, there's the follow back. I've got another follow, from Chantel. Wow! Her big boobs are pretty much all of her profile pic. I tap to follow and wonder where this will lead. Chuck grumbles and I look up.

"You know, I meant by actually talking to her. You kids and those stupid phones. Face-to-face is the only way to get shit done."

Chuck doesn't even own a computer. We only have a website because his cousin built it for him. But you can't order through it, and it hasn't been updated in forever. He's a dinosaur, but I take his advice. "Watch, I'll go talk to her."

"Good, but don't make an ass out of yourself."

I walk to the counter where Alexia is counting the drawer. I wait until she slides the money into the drop envelope before I speak. I can't stand it when people try to speak to me when I'm dealing with numbers, especially cash. "Hey, Alexia."

She jumps and puts a hand to her chest. "You almost gave me a heart attack."

"I know CPR. I would have brought you back to life." As I say it, I feel a little like Chuck.

"Thanks, I guess." She rolls her eyes and swats me with the envelope. "Hey, I saw that link on a bunch of people's pages. Tell Ricky that was a nice catch."

My ears ring but I play it cool. "All right. We still have our bet for the second stunt?"

"You still sticking with the bridge jump?"

My face is hopping, like it wants to smile, but if I do, she'll know something's up. And after signing that contract today— for exactly what, I'm not sure—there's too much on the line for me to lose it around Alexia. It takes a lot of effort to say, "Yeah, I am. You?"

"I think it would be hilarious if they went streaking through some store."

"Is that your thing? Guys running around naked?"

She blushes and I feel bad, but it is also so familiar. I could do this all afternoon.

"No, you know that's not what does it for me." She turns away, and when she speaks, her voice is barely a whisper. "I'd like to stay hidden forever."

Everything freezes for a moment. Did she just say what I think she said? Her eyes scan mine. She doesn't only look at me; she is searching to find out whether I remember. Of course I do. "But if you stay hidden forever. The game never ends."

Her face droops. "Yeah, that's it."

I want to touch her hand or shoulder, something. She was smiling, but her tone was sad. I don't know why reminiscing about hide-and-seek would do that. Alexia shakes her head, as if getting rid of a thought, and looks up.

"If it's a bet, then something has to be at stake."

"Of course. Name it."

She raises an eyebrow. "Hmm. Let me think."

I can't imagine I have much she'd want, but I wait patiently.

"This is totally going to sound stupid."

"No, it'll be fine. What?"

She shields half her face from me. "Talking about when we were kids got me thinking." She pauses. "You remember that one story, the one I loved?"

"The legend of Sherlock's corner?" As if I need to ask.

"Yeah, that's it! I win, you tell it to me."

I'd recite that story right now if she asked. I don't understand why she'd want me to retell it, because I'm sure she knows it by heart, but this is her bet. "And if I win?"

"Fine, *if* you win?"

"You bring me to a party."

Alexia stares. "Just you?" And the way she asks lets me know how to answer.

"By *me* I meant John and Ricky, too."

"You're hanging with Ricky again, aren't you?"

I'm surprised she's noticed. "Yeah. We're older now . . ." I don't finish, because I don't really know if anything's changed.

ERIC DEVINE

"Sure. The three of you, that'd be fun." She extends her hand.

I shake it and force myself not to hold on longer than necessary, but enough to say, "Deal," and feel the delicacy of her wrist as we shake. And because of that fragility I look down. There at the edge of her wrist and palm, beneath the pinkie, are bruises. Not one random. A pattern of four, equidistant, and thick, with a fifth toward her elbow, square in the center. Shit.

I'd ask about this if I could. But if we weren't working together we'd probably never have spoken again. She's got Jesse Holmes, the king of the school. And it's obvious that in her mind I'm still her friend. The one she used to play childhood games with.

We turn away from each other and I don't know if it's because she saw me noticing or simply because our conversation is over. So I say good night to Chuck and drive home. Thank God I'm good with directions because I don't pay attention to a single sign or light.

CHAPTER 5

"The Gorge" is an old quarry that is now filled with water. Ragged rocks line the sides of steep slopes that turn into pools of black, cold water. Some kid supposedly dove into the largest with his scuba gear and said it was over one hundred feet deep.

"You have to jump from right here," Ricky says. "Move left or right and we're filming a suicide." I chew on my lip. John holds his breath. None of us, including Ricky, has ever jumped off the bridge.

There's a silence that follows, which is broken by a passing truck. The driver looks over and stares, probably wondering what we're up to, but he keeps on driving. It's too early on a Saturday for him, I'm sure. Ricky picked us up around 5:30, and the sun's now coming up. He wanted time to set up his new camera and make sure the angle was correct and that we could all work it.

"Where'd you get that," I ask, although I have an idea.

"Our business partner. He wants to make sure we have the most high-def video possible."

Of course he does. And the camera now rests on the tripod in the early sunlight, like some happy rooster calling us to the show.

Our partner has also added another touch—uniforms. Ricky gave us full black outfits, shoes, pants, and long-sleeve tees.

Apparently he didn't like all the blurring either.

But what the fuck? This is . . . holy shit, too much. There's more to worry about here than anywhere else in my life. This *here and now* is ridiculous.

I look over the railing, at the water rolling below, the tight fit of the rock sides, and I can't help it, I think, *This will be amazing.* What is wrong with me?

Maybe it's the fact that I'm *not* moving for at least another month. "They still don't know," is all Dad said. My parents then got drunk celebrating. Possibly I want to see the reaction at school? It was tepid after the surfing because no one knew, but they know now, and will be watching. Or maybe it's because I'll win the bet with Alexia? That's as petty as Ricky can be. Or is it? Shit, I don't know, and I highly doubt I will until after this is over. Maybe not even then?

I walk over to my bag and pull out the black linen napkins that I bought at this store in the mall. I think I was the only person in there under eighty-five. The idea just came to me and I moved on it. Because I guess that's how I roll. Shit, I'm losing it.

"Guys, I'd like to add one last touch to this dare."

Ricky and John come away from the railing. I walk to them and place a napkin in their hands.

"We're going to do this blindfolded."

"The fuck you just say?" Ricky asks.

John shakes his head.

"Think about it. It's one thing to do this jump. It takes balls.

But there are guys in our school who have done this. They'll dis this dare, saying how it's not that dangerous." I swallow, surprised at how dry my throat has gone. "But there's no one I've heard of who has ever had the stones to do this without being able to see."

Another silence. Then Ricky. "Hot damn, motherfucker! This is what's going to make us famous. I love you, Ben!" He gives me a hug.

John stares blankly for a second, then asks, "Under or over the masks?"

"Over. We need to get them off so we can see after the jump, right?"

Ricky cracks out his phone and starts texting.

"Who?" I ask, and point at his phone.

Ricky ignores me, but a moment later yells, "That's what I thought!" He holds up his phone. "Our partner loves the idea. Nice job, Ben."

"Doesn't he have a name?" John asks.

That's a damn good question, and I'm glad John asked, because now I can focus on something else, instead of how scary being blind will be.

Ricky steps toward him. "His name's on the contract. It's O. P. Daniels, the same one from the comment section."

He looks around at us, I think to see if we're surprised. I'm not in the slightest. There's something to the fact that Ricky hasn't said this man's name until now. I don't know what it is, but I'll figure it out soon enough.

John opens his mouth to speak, but Ricky interrupts.

"John, listen. I know you may be scared. I don't blame you with your scholarship and all." His voice is soothing. "But we're doing this jump because it's fucking awesome. We're doing this jump because we're going to make money. And we're doing this jump blindfolded because Ben had a sweet idea. It's about our legacy. Remember."

John looks at me and doesn't answer Ricky.

Ricky grabs him around the neck with one hand and loops the other around mine before walking to the railing. "Trust me."

"You okay?" I ask John, but I keep my eyes on Ricky.

"Not really. You?"

"I may shit myself I'm so nervous." I laugh and John chuckles a little.

Then he asks, "So why the blindfolds? Isn't the bridge enough?"

I feel as if Dad's standing next to me, not John. His tone is the same as when I used to get lectured about Ricky. But it's not Dad, and I'm not in eighth grade. "I want this to work. I don't know why, except . . ." I don't finish.

"Except what? Seriously, Ben, I'd love to know, because this is some crazy shit and we both know I'm not smart enough to figure all this out. Hook me up. Why are we doing this? The contract?"

"I'm not concerned about the contract. That's not why I wanted to do the first dare. I don't want to get to the end of senior year and feel like it all passed me by. You know?"

John grunts.

"Maybe you wouldn't. You have basketball. What do I have?"

"You got me." John shoulders me. "And that brain of yours."

"I guess. But you know what I mean. Stories. Action. A fucking life. I get decent grades, do as I'm told, and it's just so boring."

John claps my shoulder. "This sure as shit won't be boring. Let's get to it."

There's no time to thank John, because Ricky's back to business.

"Here we are, gentlemen. Dare number two. Time to man up. Let's get our masks on." He pauses. "Who's going first?"

Another silence. We look at one another, through the slits of our ski masks, while holding black napkins. We must look like some cult. John steps up. "I want this over with."

"Ben, hit up the camera. I gotta direct." Ricky shows John where to plant his feet and talks about going in like a pencil.

I turn the power on and stare at the screen. It feels, for a moment, like I'm not here with them, like this is someone else's post and I'm at home in front of my computer. I like that idea a little too much, the voyeurism. It feels so *safe*. Then I look over the railing. It's a long way down, and the water's moving at a good clip. We've got to grab a section of rock and pull ourselves out, after. There's no time to panic. I turn back to Ricky and John and none of this feels fake anymore.

"All right. So Ben, you'll get me, then a shot of the Gorge, and then John jumping," Ricky says. "Stay tight on him. I'll grab the camera from you and run across the bridge and narrate as he gets out. Do a little interview and that'll be that. We'll take turns with the camera. Cool?"

"Sure."

"Good. John, you solid?"

"Yeah." His voice is weak, but he's sitting on the railing, both legs over the side. All he has to do is stand. And jump.

"On me, Ben. In three, two, one . . ."

I hit record.

"Here we are today for our second dare. For those of you that missed the first, make sure to search YouTube for 'Brookwood High Senior Year Dare Number One,' now brought to you by Get Out There Adventure."

I cringe when he says this.

"Today we will be jumping off the Wash Kill Bridge, into what is known around here as the Gorge." Ricky motions for me to pan, so I do.

The camera follows a line over the railing and down to the water below. Ricky continues.

"The jump is estimated at seventy-five feet into a moving river, depth unknown. There's only a twenty-foot width of water at this point, so we can't waver in either direction."

I pan up the walls of the far ledge and my heart pounds in my chest. I return to Ricky's smiling face.

"To add a true element of danger, we will be jumping blind-folded." Ricky holds out the napkin and motions to John.

I zoom in on him and he's calming himself, holding his breath and letting it out slow. The napkin is tied around his head and he looks more like some prisoner of war than my friend. I feel awful for what I've made him do.

"Now, let's test to make sure he can't really see." Ricky holds up his phone and has pulled up a pic of some model in a bikini. There's no way John won't react if he sees a little skin. Ricky walks over to the railing.

"How many fingers am I holding up?" Ricky places the phone in front of John's face.

"Funny. I bet one." He doesn't say anything about the model.

Ricky cocks his head and shrugs, then steps back and squares to the camera.

"Without further ado." Ricky steps back to John, saying something to him, and John stands while Ricky holds his elbow. He releases John and my knees wobble. John's stooped, and this looks like it's going to end badly. I want to scream for him to stop but I don't.

Ricky counts. "In five, four, three, two, one . . ."

John straightens, presses his arms to his sides, and jumps into the air like he's on the edge of a pool. I hold the camera on him, and he seems to hover, his mouth working like a fish. In an instant he's gone, and I'm following his splash in the water below.

He surfaces, the napkin blown off his face, and screams, "Yeah, woo hoo! What's up now?"

We cheer and it takes all I have to stay focused on him and not lose my shit screaming my head off. Ricky rushes over, grabs the camera like I'm handing him a football, and sprints across the bridge. He crouches along the rock ledge and shouts questions to John. I hear pieces of what John's saying, mostly, "Awesome," and, "I'd do it again."

John and Ricky cross the street, and John shakes like a dog when he's close to us. "How you like me now? Yeah."

"Nice work," I say and pound fists with him.

Ricky clasps my shoulder. "You're up."

I look over at the bridge and my stomach knots.

"Don't hesitate, Ben. Just go for it," John says. I don't argue, only nod, and in a moment I'm on the railing and Ricky has tied the napkin around my eyes. Everything is black and Ricky asks John, "Ready?"

I'm not.

"All you have to do is stand and hop." Ricky's voice tickles my ear.

Goose bumps rise along my neck as I feel Ricky's hand beneath my elbow. I rise with him and stand.

I can hear the water rushing below. I can feel the gentle whip of breeze. I'm trying to get calm, to find my zone of relaxation. Then something rumbles and my legs wobble.

"Shit. Car. Sit down, Ben." Ricky's at my side again, grabbing my elbow. My stomach lurches, but he pulls me to the railing. I sit and go to rip off my napkin, but his hand is at my wrist. "Hold up."

The bridge rumbles with the car and the brakes squeak. "Hey, what you all doing?" Sounds like a local hick.

"Filming a movie for school. You know, class project about the

Gorge?" Ricky's voice is smooth.

"Is that right? Why you all wearing masks? And dressed the same? And why is that boy sitting on the railing? That's dangerous. Kid got killed 'bout three years back jumping. You ain't doing that now, are you?"

I want to take the napkin off and for this to be over. I want to thank the man for stopping and then force Ricky to stop. I was wrong to push this, to want this. We got lucky with John.

"No, no, no." Ricky sounds offended. "We're not like those hooligans. We're AP students. Going to submit this for a scholarship. The masks are so no one on the committee recognizes us. Same with the outfits."

"Well, I'll be." The man then says something I can't hear. "I'll be off now. Good luck, son."

"Thanks."

The car rumbles away and Ricky says, "John, were you recording?"

"Yeah."

"We'll edit that out later." His footsteps crunch back to me. "Ready?"

I don't have time to respond, because he's at my elbow again and I'm standing and all is as it was before, except I'm more used to the blindfold. In fact, I'm glad I have it on, because I'm numb.

"In five, four, three . . ."

Ricky's voice fades and I hop. For a moment, I feel nothing and wonder if I haven't jumped far enough. But then I'm falling, the wind rushing by and my insides shaking. I remember to tighten up just before I hit.

The impact is like I feared falling off the car while surfing would be. The water is cold and dark. I look up and the surface seems impossibly far away. The current pulls and I know if I don't start swimming, I'm dead.

My head pounds as I kick and pull. My lungs scream and I swim faster, harder. It's getting lighter, but I'm not there yet. I bump into the rocks, skimming my forehead. I panic and charge one last time.

Air.

I breathe and hear the guys yelling above. I don't scream like John, I'm too afraid. Blood is filling my eye and I still need to get a hold of the rocks and get out, but I'm being pulled.

"The tree limb!" Ricky's voice pierces through and I see what he means, a limb about twenty feet downstream.

I grab it and pull myself to the shore. I'm so weak I can barely get out. Ricky crouches at the edge with the camera. "How was it?"

I look up and his face changes. He clicks the camera off and stares at me. "You okay?"

I sit on the tree and rip off the saturated mask, touch the source of the blood. I've got a good-sized gash. It doesn't seem deep but is spilling fast. I rip off my shirt and press it to my forehead.

"Hardcore, Benny!" John yells down.

I give him a thumbs-up because it's all I can manage. I can't look at him or Ricky. I barely want to see myself.

CHAPTER 6

Again, we all lived. My cut was the worst of it. Once he knew I was fine, Ricky made a big spectacle of his jump, taking off his shirt. He'd written GET OUT THERE ADVENTURE on his chest with a Sharpie. He made a speech and then climbed onto the railing and jumped from there. Not that it matters, but now he has bragging rights to say he jumped from the highest spot. Dick.

"I'll text you when I have it up," Ricky yells from the car.

"All right." I wave and turn toward my front door. I don't know what I'm going to tell my parents when they ask about the cut. My parents aren't idiots. I've been gone since the crack of dawn. They'll see through any nonsense.

The house smells like bacon, and my stomach guides me to the kitchen. I check the microwave, and sure enough, there's a plate for me. Mom likes to leave one in there on the weekends when I'm too lazy to get up. Perfect, maybe they'll think I was sleeping. But where the hell are they?

I ignore the question because my hunger is stronger than my interest, pop bread into the toaster, pour a glass of milk, and lean against the counter. The scenes from this morning replay, and I shudder at the memory of hitting my head. I go to the bathroom and get a good look. It's nasty, red, and raw. I should probably put a Band-Aid on it, but that would look ridiculous. May have to, though. I doubt Chuck will want me delivering looking like I came out of a gang fight. I hope the video is posted by then. Maybe Alexia has seen it, and I'll have won our bet.

I devour my breakfast and then see the note on the table:

> Ben,
> Didn't want to wake you.
> We're going out for groceries
> and to run some errands.
> See you later. Hope you found
> the bacon in the microwave.
> Mom

Shit, yes! In the clear. All I have to do is figure out a story, and I've got plenty of time. First, I'm showering and hitting the sheets. Next time we do a dare, it won't be at six in the morning.

I shower, crawl back into bed, and close my eyes, but I can't drift off. All I can see is that view from beneath the water. I try to shake the image away but it doesn't help. I grab my phone and text John: **U okay?**

He texts back a moment later: **Yeah. What about your head?**

No worries, just a cut.

Good. U working tonight?

Yeah. Swing by.

Maybe tonight I'll let him know what's up with Dad's job and all. Least he'll be clued in to another bit of my motivation. But I still need to tell Ricky I might ruin all of this for us by moving. He's going to fly off the handle, like his dad.

I slide my phone onto my nightstand and roll over, burying my head in pillows, and soon enough, am out.

—

"Ben! Ben! Jesus, it's one o'clock. Get up." Mom's voice accompanies the removal of my pillows. She gasps. "What happened?"

Shit, I never came up with an excuse.

"I, uh, hit it during the night. Fell off the bed."

She looks at me like I told her my imaginary friend tried to perform brain surgery.

"Maybe I was sleepwalking?" I turn away because even I'm barely buying this.

"Right. Okay. You can tell me what really happened when you're awake. You've got to be at work at 3:00 so you may want to get moving." She settles my pillows and gives me a concerned look.

I nod and rub my eyes. "How were your errands?"

She doesn't answer. I look up, expecting her to be gone, but she's standing there looking like I asked her about the meaning of life.

"Mom?"

She jumps. "What? Oh, right. Fine. Just fine. Now get out of bed."

She leaves in a huff and I wonder what that was all about, but there's no point in trying to understand. They've been weird all week, and I'm sure the end of the month will only be worse. I lay back and grab my phone.

There's a text from Ricky: **Video's ready.**

I scramble out of bed and turn on my computer. My leg thrums while I wait. I log on and pull down the bookmark and there it is, Dare #2. I watch and it scares the hell out of me all over again. It's worse than watching the surfing, which is ridiculous, because I know none of us got hurt. Not really. But seeing it now, how close we were to the ledge, how high up it was, and how ridiculous the blindfold made it, I cringe.

But we've got hits. We're already over five hundred views. The comments are pouring in, and all are giving us props.

I text Ricky: **Nice job. O. P. happy?** I'm sure he got in touch with him first.

Off the charts. We're making some loot. Says he'll know how much by Monday.

Sweet. I don't ask for more. I'm going to enjoy this for now and see what happens.

—

Mom didn't check on my cut again because she and Dad spent the afternoon having one intense conversation. The last I caught of it was Dad at the kitchen table, hunched over, Mom hovering with her hands at her hips. I heard him say, "I don't know if we can swing it." She sighed, and I told them I was leaving. Neither said a word to me.

I pull into Pizza and More, and Chuck's throwing bags into the Dumpster. I climb out, grab two that are sitting by the back door, and toss them in.

"Thanks, Doc."

"No problem." I turn to head in, but Chuck stops me.

"No, no, no. Explain." He points to his forehead.

"Oh, that? Yeah, craziest thing. I must have fallen out of bed or something. I woke up with this."

Chuck frowns. "Really?"

I should have spent more time on this. I look away. "Yeah. Ridiculous, right?"

"I think ridiculous fits."

I look at him and he hits me with a hard glare, but then smiles. "Come on, I already have orders waiting."

I grab bags and check the slips and punch the addresses into my phone.

"Oh my God! I saw the video!" Alexia bursts in and I almost drop my phone. I have no idea where she came from.

I look around and Chuck raises an eyebrow but goes back to kneading dough. "Yeah, me too. Crazy, wasn't it?"

Her eyes grow huge. "Insane! Do you know those guys?"

I look away. "No, no, remember, Ricky stumbled across their video."

"I know, I just thought maybe you were protecting them or whatever. Wonder who they are? You know? We should try to figure it out."

"Sure. We can bet on that too, but since you already owe me . . ."

I trail off because Alexia isn't smiling like I believed she would.

"What happened to your head?" She reaches out to touch my forehead, but I grab her wrist before she can. She pulls her hand back like she's touched a stove and tucks her arm across her face. I stare and she peeks out, looks around, and blushes. "Sorry. I . . ." Now Alexia doesn't finish.

"I know how nasty it looks. Surprised you didn't faint." I try to lighten it up because she needs me to.

She frowns. "Yeah, it does look pretty nasty."

"Right." This is so awkward. I don't know what to say. I want to ask what that was all about, because that reaction paired with those bruises equals someone in her life who shouldn't be. But who am I to do that? Maybe I should talk to her friend, Chantel?

The phone rings and we look at each other. "Gotta get that."

I laugh like this is hilarious, and when she goes to the phone, I pick up my deliveries.

As I head out the door I notice Chuck, who I know watched that exchange. He doesn't say a word, but I can tell his brain's turning faster than his hands spinning the dough. He nods and watches Alexia like a parent in the stands of something athletic. Maybe he'll have the courage I don't possess.

Funny how I can go from being badass to my regular timid self in a few short hours. Funny, or maybe pathetic?

—

I text John after the last of my first run is delivered: **Want me to pick you up?**

He replies instantly: **I'm already here. Outside.**

Chuck doesn't allow me to have people ride along while I work, but I usually pick up John at his house and he hides out while I'm getting orders. Why is he there now? I rip back to the shop as fast as I can.

His enormous frame is a shadow at one of the two tables we have out front. He's slurping on a soda.

"What's up?" I sit next to him.

"Nothing. Couldn't stay home any longer."

His voice is flat and I don't know how many times he's said these exact words to me. His parents are always at each other. "I hear you. I couldn't wait to get out either. My parents were . . ." I pause, not sure what to say.

John looks up. "Mine are getting divorced."

He's also said these words a few dozen times over the years, so I hate to ask, but have to, "For real?"

He turns back to his soda. "Maybe. Once I'm at school, I bet."

"Big-ass fight today?"

He nods.

There's no way I'm going to drag him into the bullshit of Dad's job and whatever that fight was about today. He's got enough. "Let me grab up these next orders. Meet me down at the park. Okay?"

"Sure." John stands and it seems to take all his strength.

"You okay?"

"Yeah, just sore from the jump. You know?"

"Even my feet hurt." I open the door.

"Hey, Ben?"

I turn to John.

"We're going to be all right? Yeah?"

For a moment I think he's talking about the dares. But then I process. They're nothing in comparison to what he's going through. They're a diversion, at best. The heaviness of his beat-down voice makes me feel old. And because I don't want to lie, I say, "Why wouldn't we be?"

I turn into the shop and instantly think of a dozen reasons.

CHAPTER 7

Thursday morning, and John and I are quiet. It's been crazy at school ever since Ricky posted the video. Which is what we want, but it's exhausting waiting for something to happen, for someone to figure us out. I scratch the skin around the scab over my cut, careful not to get near the middle, which is still a little goopy.

John turns and watches me. "We should get you a helmet for the next dare."

"Funny. Did Ricky tell you what it is?"

"No. Remember, we've got to pick from a list now. But you know him. He'll see how much he can one-up that jump. Helmets might be a good idea for all of us."

"Wonder what it says in the *contract*?"

I meant it as a joke, but John shakes his head. "We should have read it."

"Why? You think something's up?"

John looks over. "With Ricky anything's possible. But don't you think it's weird how we went from surfing for fun to signing a contract and getting paid?"

"We've haven't gotten paid, so let's not hold our breath on that. Yeah, it was fast, but like Ricky said, we had to prove ourselves."

"I understand that. Why *us*? If it was a Craigslist ad, then the guy's local."

I hadn't considered this.

"So why did he choose us? What did Ricky say to him?"

I sigh. "Good question. We should ask."

"Go for it," John says, and we walk into school and the middle of some kids' conversation.

"Did you see that jump?"

"Of course I did. *Everyone* has."

"Right, but did you really watch it? INSANE! Those guys are awesome. We have to figure out who they are." I look at John and he seems as concerned as me, but we don't speak, just cruise to Ricky's locker.

We pass Alexia and Chantel, and they wave. Jesse is with Alexia and he sets his jaw and says something in her ear. She shrugs and he leans in and says something harsh. I can't hear the words, but I watch her face. She's pissed, but scared too. Yeah, I totally need to talk to Chantel.

We pass kids still buzzing over us, talking about the jump. Some are miming what we did, while a group is clustered around a laptop.

This is exactly what I thought would happen. But at the same time, it's surreal. I'm watching others watch me, but they don't know it's me. Unnerving. But beyond that, another idea emerges: *What if we get caught?* Why haven't we had a conversation about that?

We reach Ricky and he's looking around the hallway. "This is what four thousand views does for you, boys. Can you imagine what will happen after our next dare?"

My brain shifts from freaking out to processing the numbers. Four thousand views in sixty hours is impressive. I remember the stats those kids presented on average views for YouTube. I think something like only 11 percent reach that many in the first month. Holy shit.

"Yeah, but they're going to try to figure out who we are. Do you have everything locked up online?" I ask Ricky. "We can't get caught."

"Yeah. What's O. P. doing to keep us safe?" John asks, his voice tight.

Ricky smiles his enormous wolf smile at our questions. "Relax. We're fine. And O. P.'s ecstatic. He's sending the check any day, and he's going to create an ad to promote our third dare."

"That's not what I asked." John leans in.

Ricky's face hardens. "Look at the two of you. Things get a little edgy and you turn into pussies."

John leans in a bit more. "You really want to go there?"

Ricky's eyes bug and then he looks at me. "All I'm saying is that the two of you need to relax. We haven't done anything illegal, and I've got this figured out."

"Heard that before," I say.

John straightens and folds his arms over his chest. Ricky looks at the two of us and then down at the ground and mutters to himself.

The bell rings but I don't want to scatter. I want to know more, to know what Ricky knows. What's the online safety? How much money? When will we get the list for the next dare? But the grace period for being late to class has worn off. Teachers are no longer minding their beginning-of-the-year manners, if they had any to begin with.

We split and I head to calculus, where we discuss the logic of the relationship between differentiability and continuity—things are more likely to be different than continuous. I almost laugh out loud at this, but instead look around at the class. They're spellbound.

In PE we learn how to throw a football. Seriously. At least the kid I'm paired with doesn't make fun of the way I throw. However, he keeps a stream of ideas flowing for what he'd like to see in the next dare. The irony almost kills me, but his visions are worse—all weird, sexual, perverse shit, like stripping down and whipping each other, or covering ourselves in plastic wrap after we're naked and then going grocery shopping. I lob the ball and say, "unh huh," while the kids around us laugh so hard they miss passes and footballs bounce every which way.

I head to study hall and have to do a check on the room number. Chantel's here. She wasn't last time. I'd remember. I take a deep breath and move down the aisle and try to quiet all the panic alarms going off in my head. I need to talk to her. She's close to Alexia, and it's worth fighting my fear to have this conversation. I sit and force myself to be brave. "Chantel, right?"

She crinkles her nose. "Yeah."

"You're Alexia's friend."

She doesn't answer, but looks at me blankly and my heart beats triple time.

"Sorry. I'm Ben, Alexia and I work together. She's pointed you out to me." It's a plausible lie.

She sits up. "That's right. I know you."

I feel a wash of relief. Beautiful girls, in my experience, have a way of filling your fantasies, but in reality, smash the shit out of you. "Did you change your schedule?"

"Yeah. I decided not to take psychology. Mr. Timms is an ass."

I've never had him, but I agree. That's what you're supposed to do when beautiful girls make proclamations.

I turn back to my physics book, because I don't want to seem desperate or pushy. I can't blow this opportunity. I read Newton's Second Law: *The acceleration of an object as produced by a net force is directly proportional to the magnitude of the net force, in the same direction as the net force, and inversely proportional to the mass of the object.*

Right. So, positive things continue in a positive direction, negative, well, negatively; the acceleration matches the force applied, and the larger the mass, the slower the acceleration. Hmm. Was Newton also psychic?

I look over at Chantel, and Newton is wiped away by her lips. She's putting on gloss and I can't stop staring.

"Ben, everything okay?" Chantel frowns.

"Uh, yeah." I close my eyes so I can focus, so I can keep myself from saying the wrong thing. My head's a mess from the conversation with Ricky earlier, but I refuse to let that get in the way. Here goes nothing. "What's up with Alexia?"

Chantel gives me a small smile and looks around to see if anyone is listening. No one is. She leans across the aisle. "Where do you want me to begin?"

—

We're at Ricky's locker and I can't focus on what they're talking about. Something about the check from O. P. Instead, I scratch my forehead and think about what Chantel said: "Alexia's has had a rough go of it. Her dad's responsible for the shit going down at the plant. Money's tight, and her parents, they totally go after each other. Big fights."

I asked what she meant by "go after" but she shook her head and zipped her lips. I understand. It was a bit too much prying, and who knows, maybe Chantel assumed I was trying to get dirt on Alexia. That's what everyone does around here—pretends to be a friend and then stabs you in the back. I don't think this town or school is unique. Or the situation. Because that's how it felt when Alexia moved away and stopped talking to me. I didn't understand, and I had no way of asking her. Regardless, it seems like Alexia and I are living pretty close existences now. Except for the parents beating on each other thing.

"Ben?"

I look up and Ricky's smiling, John has his perpetually confused look, and I have no idea what's what. I start to ask, but am cut off.

"Gentleman."

We turn to Principal McNeil.

"Come with me," he says and walks down the hall.

"Stay cool," Ricky mouths to us.

I don't know how that is possible. We follow McNeil to his office and my heart pounds and I have that terrible watery-leg sensation. This has to be about the videos. I've never been in trouble before, barely have an idea where McNeil's office is after three years of being here. But Ricky does.

We enter McNeil's office, and Ricky and John take the only available seats, which is fine by me because I get to stand near the open window. My face has lost all blood, and if it weren't for the cool breeze and the wall for support, I'd be on the ground. How the hell did I manage those two dares?

"Let's cut to the chase, boys. You know why I've called you in."

Ricky tilts his head. "No, sir, not really." He sounds like some fifth grader, and McNeil looks like he caught a whiff of something foul.

He looks us over, lingering on each. His gaze moves toward mine, and I try to look away. I cannot let this man examine me. He'll read the nerves streaming, firing off messages like texts. But McNeil's bloodshot eyes grab mine and pull.

"Candido, what's this I hear about the three of you informing the school about some dare?"

I stare. It's all I can do. I try to think of an excuse, some answer that will satisfy his question, but keep us safe. He's being purposely vague. *"Some dare"?* As if he doesn't know and hasn't already watched both. All I can do is swallow and say, "I don't know."

Ricky shifts in his seat and I feel like slamming my head against the desk. McNeil's eyes widen. "Right. Tell me more."

I lean against the wall and do not look at him. I have to break his spell.

"Mr. McNeil, you know how things are senior year. Some kids are trying to live it up, have some fun." Ricky's voice is smooth and deep. I'm jealous.

McNeil reluctantly turns from me to Ricky. "Fun is not the same as risking one's life? Hmm?"

"You could debate that," Ricky says, and McNeil's face bulges. "But we won't. I understand your point. Sir."

I'm holding my breath, waiting for McNeil to explode—to let loose and sound like the gates of hell have opened within his lungs. But nothing happens. He stares at Ricky and then looks out the window. "A few years ago we had a senior, Douglas Kipling, you probably don't remember. He died right around Memorial Day." McNeil turns back to us. "Do you know what he did?"

Of course we do. He's the kid that hick from the bridge was talking about. But Kipling was drunk, and a lot of people said he was trying to commit suicide.

McNeil doesn't wait for an answer. "I had to go out to the Gorge that day. I saw his parents, saw his body. It was one of the worst days of my life." McNeil's voice has dropped, as has my head. But not Ricky's. He looks the man square in the face.

"I understand. My cousin was friends with him. It was awful."

I pick my brain but cannot think of any cousin of Ricky's that would have been in school with Doug.

"*Awful* doesn't come close." McNeil inhales and holds it for a moment before letting the air out his nose. It whistles at the end.

"Sir, we don't actually know who it is. I stumbled across the first video and just let the school know. I apologize if somehow that was against our code of conduct." Ricky's good; he sounds very conciliatory.

McNeil looks from him to John and me. We both nod, and it feels like I'm back in middle school.

"You didn't technically break any rules, Puckman. But as you can imagine, you've provided some publicity, and it seems that was the fuel this fire needed."

There's less of an edge to McNeil's voice, but we're not quite in the clear. I lean a little more into the wall and pray Ricky knows how to see this through.

Ricky pats the desk, like so many teachers I've seen and turns back to us. "Guys, can we agree, no more talking about *those* dares?" He nods gently and John and I follow along, chiming in with "yeah" and "no more," "absolutely." I get what we're agreeing to. Well played.

ERIC DEVINE

McNeil sighs. "Thank you, boys, but I have one additional request. An atonement if you will."

Ricky squints and turns so slightly to me, as if I can telepathically give him the definition. McNeil continues.

"Since you stumbled across the video, possibly you can *stumble* across the real individuals? Hmm?" McNeil purses his lips.

"You want us to find out who's completing these dares?" John asks, his first words since we've entered the room.

McNeil offers a flat, like-I'm-dealing-with-the-stupid grin. "Yes, Mr. Forrest, that's exactly what I mean." He looks back at Ricky and me. "So, what do you say?"

Ricky shakes his head slightly. "Absolutely, sir. We'll do what we can, but these guys seem to be laying low, so . . . no guarantees."

McNeil nods. "This is true. I know. But please know my door is open if you hear anything."

We nod and file out into the hall, and lean against the lockers.

"Jesus Christ that was close." John runs a hand through his hair.

Ricky goes to the water fountain. "You have no idea. That was nothing."

He drinks and John shrugs at me. I say, "Guys, I'm sorry, I didn't know what to say. I've never been in there before and . . ."

"No shit." Ricky cuts me off. "Reminds me of another time."

We all know what he means. When we were in eighth grade and got suspended for weeks—almost expelled—after we shot

65

videos of the girls changing and Ricky uploaded it without telling us. The firestorm from the girls and their parents, and then the blame game that went down after, is what forced us apart. That, and the fact that John and I sided with the girls because what Ricky did was really fucked up. He better not go *there*.

Ricky squeezes my shoulder. "But we made it. Now we need to steer McNeil in the wrong direction. If he ever figures out a computer, we're fucked."

"Fucked is right." The voice makes us all jump. We turn, and leaning up against the wall is Trevor Culin, Ricky's enemy. Trevor moves toward us. Under the lights he looks worse than the last time I saw him. He's more gaunt, as if he's anorexic, and decked out in his ultrastylish tight jeans and black T-shirt.

"What do *you* want?" John asks.

Trevor ignores him and keeps staring at Ricky. They go way back. We all do, but it's different between the two of them. There's more history that even I don't know.

"I think it's more a matter of what *you* need." Trevor flicks his head toward us but stares at Ricky.

"And what's that?" Ricky's smooth tone is gone, and the sound that's emerged is ragged.

"Please, you whisper like a drunk chick. 'If he ever figures out a computer . . .'" Trevor smirks. "Nice job, by the way. Seems like your editing skills have come a long way."

Ricky slams Trevor into the lockers across the hall. I look around, but no one's seem to have heard.

"Listen, you piece of shit. I have no idea what the fuck you're talking about, so either say what you mean or I'll shut your mouth for you."

Trevor should be petrified and start begging for forgiveness. Ricky's no joke. I've seen him throw down and win against guys way bigger than him. And Trevor's small, fragile, but he reaches up and pats Ricky's hand. "That'll do, Ricky. That'll do."

I wait for the punch, but Ricky shoves Trevor hard and steps away. Trevor rubs his neck. "Seems like we may need to have you cool down before we can talk. I'll meet you after school."

Trevor turns on his heel and walks down the hall. He's the quintessential computer geek: stooped shoulders, tight face, with an aura of constantly being the only one aware of some inside joke. Little bastard.

"What the hell?" I can't tell if John's question is directed at Ricky, Trevor, or himself.

Ricky waves a hand at him. "I'll deal with it, whatever it is he thinks he knows. I'm not losing this opportunity because of *him*." He watches Trevor disappear down the hall and then moves away from us.

Opportunity. Why that word? What we're doing is fun, and yeah, I guess getting paid makes it like a job. But opportunity?

John bumps me and we follow Ricky and I think I should start helping him with his linguistics.

CHAPTER 8

The rest of the day is a blur. In fact, every class has been a blur since I started this year. I don't know what I'm learning, if I'm learning. Between the dares and my impending move, and now this nonsense with McNeil and Trevor, it's unlikely my head will clear anytime soon.

I pull into the parking lot and check my phone. I've got a text from Ricky: **Took care of shit with Trevor. We have a new cameraman. We'll talk later.**

He's got to be joking. *Trevor?* Our cameraman?

"Doc, you on the phone or are you up to something else?"

I hold up my phone. "Text."

"You're probably ambidextrous. Get out here and help me with this trash."

I slide my phone into my pocket and get out of the Jeep. I'll get the details on this development ASAP, but for now, I grab two bags and haul them to the trash can. Chuck watches me toss them in like a coach critiquing the shot put. I finish and he stands there, mustache twitching. "What?" I finally say.

He grabs his chin, rubs it in his palm, and nods. "No other way to say this. I know about those dares at your school."

"How'd you find out about all that?" Listening to myself, I sound relaxed, but that could be wishful thinking.

"I may sell pizzas, but I'm not stupid. I hear things and I had Bobby, the cook, do some digging for me."

"Sure," I say, not sure where he wants to go with this.

Chuck drops his hand from his chin. "I want ad space."

I don't even know how to answer. "You want to advertise on YouTube?"

"No, nothing fancy like that. I want you to give those boys some of my shirts. People are watching that shit, and if they do that, all the kids from your school will be in here. I could even run some kind of special."

Oh, hell no, he can't do that. I mean, he can, but . . . shit, how do I get out of this one? "But I don't know who they are."

Chuck frowns and crosses his arms over his chest, making his belly protrude even more. "Your school ain't that big. Find out for me, will ya?"

"Yeah, give me a week."

"I can already see the steam coming out your ears, Doc. You'll figure it out in no time."

I say, "Thanks," and stagger inside.

"Ben, hey. I was just thinking about you." Alexia bounds over and throws herself around my neck. This has become a very adorable pattern. She squeezes me and smells like fruit. I go from feeling nauseous to tingly in a fraction of a second. She slides off but grabs my hand. "Those guys. The ones you found, they're like the hottest shit right now."

I blush. I feel it creep up, and it's embarrassing. But the

cooks look over and seem to appreciate what she's saying. "Crazy, huh?"

"Completely. How awesome?" Alexia grabs me around the neck again. I must appear to be like some life-sized doll she can tussle with. I don't resist now, nearly as much as I did back then. "Don't worry, I haven't forgotten I owe you a party. Maybe this weekend?"

She lets go and we straighten. I think, *Perfect opportunity*, but catch myself at the words. What *opportunity*? What the hell do I think I'll find at the cool kids' party? And after what Chantel said about Jesse and Alexia, I'm not sure I want to see.

"Enough, you two. You're making me sick. Alexia, get the Doctor some prescriptions and get him out the door. His mere presence isn't making me any money."

Alexia pouts at Chuck and rolls her eyes at me. She walks to the counter and Chuck comes up behind me. "A party? With her? If you can't find out who's trying to kill themselves, at least you'll have some eye candy."

"Chuck, come on! It's Alexia. We're friends. Besides . . ."

"*Besides* what? Don't tell me I can't look. I'm not dead, yet. Like with those kids. It'll happen, just not today."

I sigh and shake my head. I can't fix Chuck. I can't produce some daredevils for McNeil. I have only a notion of what's up with Alexia, and my home and dad's job are on shaky ground. Which, in turn, makes my college plans and the future quite unstable. That and the fact that I'm terrible at school this year.

So how do I make sense of any of this? What would Newton do? From the pictures I've seen, probably go curl his hair.

—

I'm sitting in my driveway, afraid to walk through the door. Everything that's happened today makes me feel as if our secret's been revealed. Too many people are curious for this to stay underground.

I have this feeling that someone has called my parents, or they bumped into someone while running "errands" or whatever it is they're doing these days, and they know and I'm dead. All I want to do is take a shower and check in with Ricky, because John's been blowing up my phone asking if I've heard from him. Apparently, he didn't bother to tell him about Trevor.

But I know I'll go in and my parents will sit me down at the dining room table, and this time they won't tell me about moving—which I might welcome over the punishment. Instead, they'll tell me how *disappointed* they are. That they've seen the dares and they know it's me and that they *expected* so much more.

I slide out of the Jeep and stare at my feet as I walk to the door. Their voices carry through the air. I stop and listen. They're high-pitched and giddy. I turn the handle and step through.

Laughter. Mom's laughter is echoing off the walls in the dining room, followed by Dad's. The hell? I turn the corner and hear, "So I told my professor, that he should check the one slide because of the typo, but he didn't believe me. I insisted. He got all angry, but then he did, and sure enough, it was *shit your booklet when finished*, not *shut*."

Ginny raises her hand in an I-told-you-so shrug and my parents laugh again. They're all drinking wine, including my sister, who's not twenty-one, and I focus on this for some reason. "You're drinking? With Mom and Dad?"

They all turn to me and have the same frown. I can read the message loud and clear: *Really, Ben?*

"Hi, bro. How are you? Long time, no see. Yes, this year is going well, so nice of you to ask." Ginny's face is almost as flushed as the wine she sips, and I feel like cracking her upside the head. Some things never change.

Dad clears his throat. "Ben, Ginny's home for the weekend. Came home a day early, even. Please, let's not start off this way. We, uh, have a lot to discuss." He looks at Mom.

"Your father's right. We have a lot to talk about, so that's why we asked Ginny to come home. Okay?"

I wish I had a damn glass. I'd down the contents and ask for a refill. If this means we're going to have a "family powwow," as they like to call it, I should be intoxicated. The prospect of moving sucks, but add to it the fact that my annoying sister is going to throw in her opinion on the matter, and I may run myself over with the Jeep to get out of this.

"Okay," I say. "I just need to go shower."

"Take your time. We're getting caught up." Mom and Dad

look back at Ginny. They're already absorbed by her, and I haven't even left the room.

—

I return and it's as if they've decided my therapy session with Ginny should begin. She nods at the chair across from her and I sit.

"Ben, Mom and Dad have explained the situation to me, and there's no reason for you to be afraid."

I turn to my parents, but they nod like she's some amazing guru.

"Why should I be afraid?"

She rolls her eyes, like I'm being cute.

"Benny, it's okay to be honest about your feelings. The more you repress them, the worse you'll feel and that may manifest in some pretty terrible behavior."

Dad says, "Huh?" Exactly what I was thinking.

Ginny runs a hand through her long hair and whips it over her shoulder. "It's basic psychology, Dad. I learned it in class. Ben is very introverted and that could be dangerous."

I want to strangle her with her own hair. She's like all the kids in class with me, who are on every club that exists, work every community service project, play twelve instruments, and train blind horses. I can picture her at college, Miss-know-it-all, asking questions she already knows the answers to.

"To be fair, we haven't told Benjamin everything. We've been waiting for the right moment," Mom says.

"Everything?" I ask.

Mom sighs. "We're selling the house and are looking at apartments or possibly a condo. Your father may not agree to the transfer."

This takes a moment to process. My day has been out of control, and this, shit, I don't know. So I ask the only logical question, "What the fuck are you talking about?"

"Jesus, Ben, watch your mouth!" Dad shouts.

"Sorry, sorry. It's just, what do you want me to say? You all seem to have this figured out."

Dad frowns. "I understand how it must feel to you." He leans forward in his seat. "Here's the situation: we're moving, one way or another. Either to save money or to take advantage of an *appropriate* opportunity. I refuse to get stuck in something that doesn't make sense for us all."

"So we'll be across the country, or across town?"

"It all depends on the plant's next move."

"It's going to be so hard to say good-bye to this house," Ginny says and looks around, as if at someone's deathbed. "The memories."

She and Mom embrace, and I stare at my father. He shrugs and looks out at the night.

I sit for a moment longer and then say good night, pat Dad on the shoulder, and head to my room.

I hop online, hoping for distraction, but there's a Facebook message from Ricky.

Benny. So all I can say is that some shit has changed. We're gonna have Trev as our cameraman. He's nasty with comput- ers, so this is prolly good, but please go along with it, cuz if you do, John will be down. O. P. says the check is on the way and that he'll send the list tonight, too. Cool?

I don't know how to respond—at this point I have no energy for anything more—so I shut down my computer and close my eyes and concentrate on breathing.

When I was eight, Mom had me take a course with her on dealing with anxiety. The only takeaway was the deep breathing. Couple that with a quiet room and I'm usually good to go.

Ten minutes later and I'm calm, almost asleep. I pull myself out of the chair and head to the bathroom. Ginny's standing in it, sniffling. I take another deep breath.

"Sorry, finishing up." She blows her nose and wipes her eyes and I lean against the wall.

My exhaustion takes over, and I may fall asleep right here.

"You okay, Benny?"

I open my eyes and she's hovering, looking not like the semi- adult from downstairs, but the red-eyed, puffy-faced sister I remember. I sigh. "Yeah. It's a lot all at once. You know?"

"That's it. Exactly." She steps into the hall.

I don't know what else to say, so I shrug and mumble, "Good night." I piss and when I come out, she's gone and her door is closed. I shut my own, kill the light, and plow into my bed. I think I'm asleep before I even shut my eyes.

CHAPTER 9

The first thing I do when I wake up is check my phone. Text from Ricky, sent at 3 a.m.: **Check fb. List.** My heart takes a wild gallop as I untangle from my sheets and head to the computer. My brain is fried and I need some serious caffeine. At least my parents will have a pot of coffee brewing since they're probably hung over, along with my sister.

I read Ricky's message. The next options are:

1. Riding bikes off a jump into a nearby pond or lake

2. Playing chicken in traffic

3. Skiing behind a car

4. Rooftop jump

5. Underwater breath-holding (weighted down for 3 minutes)

I want to type "WTF?" because these seem insane. The bridge was extreme enough, do we really have to top that? And logistically, we don't all have bikes and skis, so how in the hell can we do those? And biologically, how can we hold our breath for three minutes? You die after that long. I'd panic before I hit thirty seconds.

I log off and scramble to the shower, hoping it will clear my head. It doesn't, but seeing that Ginny's door is still closed makes me happy. Bet she has a raging headache. I stomp extra loud past her room and head downstairs.

My parents are, indeed, huddled at the kitchen table with a pot of coffee between them. Dad reads the paper while Mom stares at nothing. Both are in their robes, not dressed for work. Neither seems to notice me when I reach between them and fill a travel mug. I look at the calendar to be sure it's Friday and not Saturday. Maybe they're taking the day off? Maybe they both quit their jobs? Maybe they're not really my parents and when I come home tonight they'll have moved on and my real parents will be here? Hopefully they'll take Ginny with them. I grab a cereal bar and head out the door.

John's sitting on his front porch when I roll up. "Man, you look like hell," he says.

I chew on the bar and nod. "I know. Ginny came home last night, so I didn't get to bed until late. Then Ricky was all messaging me."

"What's going on? He hasn't sent me anything." John crouches to be at my face, and I feel bad waving him off.

"Nope. I'm not saying jack until we're all together. I don't know what's up, because he wasn't exactly clear." I know that's a half lie, but I'm too groggy for anything else.

"But what'd he say? Did we get the list? The check? What's the deal with Trevor?"

I pull a hand over my face, and it only makes me feel more tired. "I don't know."

John accepts this like he accepts everything else, with a nod. Maybe Ricky was right? Maybe John needs my guidance on this? But right now he's like a friggin' giraffe next to me, and I feel like a terrible zookeeper.

"Mornin', boys." Ricky's all smiles and doesn't look like he barely slept last night. I feel like punching him so his eyes are as dark as mine. Or maybe for other reasons, too.

We nod, but I refuse to speak. I'm supporting John on this. He wants the list.

"So here it is." Ricky pulls three sheets of paper from his pocket and hands one to each of us. It's a printout of the message. John reads and I watch his face.

He goes white.

"These are crazy. I don't ski, and with the season coming, I really shouldn't do half of these." John looks up.

Ricky asks, "But what's more important?"

I think he means for the question to be rhetorical, but John clears his throat. "That's not fair."

"What's not fair is agreeing to something and then not seeing it through."

John nods. "I know, but these are scary, and really dangerous. Come on. You have to understand where I'm coming from."

Ricky squeezes his shoulder. "I do. But you can't tell me the car surfing and the jump weren't dangerous? You want this."

John chews on his lip and then looks over at me. I stare at the list and ignore him.

"Read those again and number them. You know, which ones you'd most like to do as number one, and so on. We'll decide at lunch. All right?"

John nods, but of course he does. At least he spoke up.

I say, "Yeah, sure," but wish I could articulate more.

The bell rings, and John and I look at Ricky as if we need more time.

"See you at lunch," he says and takes off.

We cram the papers into our pockets and head to class, and I pray the caffeine provides me the ability to concentrate.

—

I bombed quizzes in all of my classes. No multiple choice, all short answer and essay. I know Newton's laws, but when I was staring at the questions asking me to describe each, all I could think of was my messed-up life. The dares or the crap at home may apply, but I certainly wouldn't get credit for writing *losing my house* as an example for the First Law, and *playing chicken in traffic* for the Second.

Math was as ridiculous. This whole "show your work" nonsense is just that—bullshit. I could have maybe guessed the answers, but I have no clue how to actually get there. Kind of like with the bike and the pond scenario, or which is better, a mortgage or rent? I'm sure I could figure it out, but is it worth it?

And English. Jesus Christ, I can't even write fluff today. I'm normally an expert at the fill-in-the-blank essay format, inserting the names of characters and plot points where they belong. But not today. The only stories I had were of my family living in a shack or of how John, Ricky, and I all died jumping from a rooftop and slamming into the alley below, or being pinned underwater by some rock, waiting for the stopwatch to reach three minutes.

I give up. It's already October, so why shouldn't I? By Thanksgiving I'll be on academic probation, but it doesn't matter. I'll either be living in some shitty apartment downtown or out in Arizona with the tumbleweeds. Or dead.

I close my locker and John's face replaces the space where the metal grille was.

"You decide?"

I sigh. "No. You?"

"I tried. But this was hard. It was a hell of a lot easier when Ricky was telling us what to do."

When we arrive at the cafeteria, all is the usual until I look at our table. There, planted at Ricky's elbow, is Trevor. The two of them are talking about something real intensely. Trevor's gesturing and Ricky's nodding and adding comments to whatever Trevor's saying. If I didn't know them, I'd think they were friends. They both look up when John and I sit down, but keep talking. They use words like "bandwidth" and "screen splitter."

We eat and ignore the big question hanging over us. I think it's called the "elephant in the room," but what would I know? My English essay might as well have been written in crayon.

"Guys, hey, sorry about that, Trevor and I needed to get some of this camera work stuff out of the way."

John and I stop eating, but he was almost done anyway, so that doesn't really count. I wait for more, but Ricky moves on like everything is normal.

"So, lists? Let's take a look." Ricky pulls his out of his pocket, and I'm glad to see that Trevor doesn't have his own copy. Neither John nor I move, though.

"No, you explain what's going on here." John points with his fork. "Since eighth grade you've been ready to punch this weasel into the ground. And now? He's in on this?"

Trevor stares ahead as if John's talking about someone else, not him.

Ricky smooths his list on the table. "I told you that I would be talking to Trevor. That we'd sort this out. We did, and then decided that it would be best if he did our camera work and helped us with online security. He's good and it would make things easier. *You* remember our conversation with McNeil, right?"

I know John's not going to answer, so I clear my throat. "Of course we remember, but that's not the issue. It seems like *you* decided something pretty significant for *us*. Aren't you the one who told us not to tell anyone? So it's kind of f'ed that *you* did. And besides that, you hate him. What's the deal?" The fog in my head hasn't lifted and this exertion isn't helping, but Ricky had better have one hell of a good answer. I know when shit is worth worrying about, and this is monumentally concerning.

Ricky clenches his jaw and turns to me. "I sent you that message last night. You could have told John before now."

A pit opens up in my stomach, and I feel John's eyes on me. Well played. "Still, I only would have been telling him what you are now. Which is?"

Ricky backs away from the table, hands up, like a politician. "Hey, of course. I understand. That's what this list is all about. We decide together. I went ahead with Trevor because I thought it would be best for *us*." He leans back in. "And you heard what McNeil said. Trevor is the only one that can keep us off his radar."

Ricky's always been up to no good, so I don't know if I should be surprised, but this is the first time Ricky's sided with an enemy. I don't like it. At all.

"Bullshit. I'm calling bullshit on all of this. We all know that Trevor's dead to us. So forget the damn list for a second and answer that question first."

"Which one?" Ricky offers his fuck-you smile.

I stand. "You tell me what's the deal with him or I walk. Because right now I feel like I'm being played. You got us to get this shit started and kept Trevor in the wing for some reason I don't understand. So you explain or I'm out."

Ricky twitches. "So like you, Ben. You fold when shit gets tough."

"*I'm* not the one who sold us out. The kid sitting next to you did."

John adjusts in his seat and is about to stand with me, but Ricky sticks out his hand. "John, please. Hold on. Give me a second."

I like how his voice quavers a bit. It's good to see him a little nervous. Shocking that I caused it, but good. I sit because all that bravado has left me feeling weak.

Ricky balls up his fists and rubs them against his temples. He speaks to the table. "I was wrong to spring this on you, but please believe me that I'm not pulling any shit. There's no master plan with Trevor. Things collided and then all of a sudden made sense."

"Like with O. P., there was nothing you kept from us, right?" John's voice is cold.

Ricky looks up. "That's fair." He nods. "Shit, I get how this looks. Fuck, I don't really know how to make you believe me, so walk if you want to. I'll still give you your cut of the cash."

"That's it? Nothing more?" I ask.

Ricky looks at me, and he appears genuinely hurt. "Ben, I don't have word skills like you. I don't know what else to say. Trevor and I buried the hatchet. He put two and two together after he heard us talking about McNeil. He offered to help. You know, as a sign that he's sorry." He pauses. "The three of us have been tight since April. I figured we could *all* be that way again."

And I feel like an asshole. Ricky poured his heart out, and it all seemed so genuine and not at all a giant scheme. Shit. I look at him and then Trevor, and more than anything, I want to say, "I'm sorry," but I can't. I guess I still don't trust something here.

But I don't know if that's just me and my messed-up head, or if it's intuition.

"Trevor, what's your plan for all of this?" I ask.

He frowns. "It's really all about anonymity and password protection. We put up the videos and encrypt each of them with a separate password. McNeil may find the videos, but he won't be able to see them. He'd have to bother to find the passwords."

Trevor has a slight lisp that I normally find annoying, but now, because of what he's talking about, it makes him sound intelligent. Weird.

"We'll dispense those passwords via Twitter, not Facebook. Stay off Facebook. Take down any messages you've already posted, and I'll create a Twitter account through an external IP address. That way it can't be traced to us."

John says, "Huh."

I clear my throat. "How are you going to *know*? Can't McNeil, or anyone really, stumble across it?"

Trevor's mouth shifts beneath his beady eyes. "It's unlikely, but don't worry, if that happens, *I've* got the technology covered. Ricky has some other ideas to keep you safe, the answer to the other half of your question. But I don't want to go blabbing about either in the cafeteria where people could hear." He tilts his head, indicating the room.

I look around. No one's paying any attention to us. Still, I'll give it to him, it's a solid point, and overall, none of that sounded like he was pulling it out of his ass. He seems to know what he's talking about. The only question is whether Ricky does.

"So what now?"

John nods and says, "Yeah?"

Ricky sighs. "Back to the list. How did you rank them?"

I go first and read my preferences, and then John does the same, followed by Ricky.

Playing chicken and skiing behind a car tie for last place. Holding our breath underwater is next to last. The rooftop jump comes in second and riding bikes into a pond is the top pick. John mutters an "amen."

"So I'll get back to O. P. and let him know. We'll need some gear for this, right? Who needs a bike?"

We both raise our hands, and John adds, "How does O. P. know we have a pond around here?"

Now there's a damn good question. Probably designed to see if there's more to this Craigslist connection. Nice.

"I don't know. Maybe he went on Google Earth?" Ricky shrugs.

That got us nowhere. Trevor's staring blankly into space, as if none of this concerns him. I envy him a little.

"What about the ramp? Where's that coming from?" I ask.

"O. P." Ricky spits the answer.

"Is he going to come here and build it himself?"

Ricky looks at me now. "I don't know. I'll find out."

"Fine. The checks?"

Ricky shifts. "It should be here this afternoon."

I grip the table. "It?"

Ricky looks me in the eye. "Yes. We only get one. I promise to divide it evenly."

I focus on the point that matters. "Why only one?"

"That's what's in the contract."

Shit. I knew we should have read that more closely. "Get us copies."

"Sure. Why?"

"You want this all to be cool with us, right?"

Ricky nods. "I do, Ben. Seriously."

"Do this, then, and we're cool?"

Ricky reaches across the table and we shake hands. "Thank you," he says.

I don't know what he's thanking me for—there's so much it could be—but there's no point in asking. He deserves a bit of dignity. "You're welcome."

CHAPTER 10

The last period ends and I run from school like it's on fire. I don't even see John next to me until we're a block away.

"That was some craziness at lunch," he says.

"Crazy doesn't touch it."

John frowns. "I get what Ricky meant, but I don't trust Trevor. And there's more to it, I know it. Ricky's pushing these dares like his life depends on it." He pauses. "You think there's something we're missing? Is that why you asked for the contract?"

"Yeah, you nailed it. I don't know what's there, but one thing is for certain." I turn to him. "You and I have to stick together. I'm not getting burned by Ricky again, and you sure as hell can't afford to, either."

Neither of us says anything for a bit, probably because that was pretty messed up. Or maybe it wasn't messed up at all, but smart.

I stop walking. It's time to tell him. "Hey, we're selling our house."

John stops and looks at me as if waiting for the rest of the joke. When it doesn't come, he asks, "What? Why are you doing that?"

I shrug. "My parents, man. Bunch of nonsense with my dad's job. So we're selling."

"Where are you going?"

"I don't know." I almost laugh, but am glad I don't because John grabs my shoulder.

"What do you mean you don't know?" His voice rises and falls.

"If my dad takes a transfer for his job, we're gone, like across the country. If he doesn't, we'll need to save cash, so we're moving into an apartment around here."

John looks up at the sky. "Please tell me you're going to be around for the rest of the year."

I know he's not that stupid and can comprehend the fact that there are two scenarios to what I said, but I say, "Of course."

His shoulders come down from around his ears. "Good, cause you've lived down the street from me my entire life. You can't just up and go."

I slap his back. "Don't worry. One way or another, I'll be around." I don't have a clue if that's even remotely true.

We part ways at his house, and when I head inside mine, Ginny's on the couch with her laptop and a couple of thick textbooks. She's wearing her glasses, not her contacts, and looks like a strung-out secretary. She doesn't do hangovers well.

"How you feeling?" I slam the door behind me.

She scowls. "Don't start with me, Benny. I've got a paper to write."

I go to the kitchen, make a sandwich, and think about today. How can so much be happening at once, when normally my life is so boring it hurts? I don't have answers and know I won't find them sitting here.

I change into my work shirt and delete my conversation from last night with Ricky. It feels strange following Trevor's advice, but who am I to question? I make sure to slam the door again on the way out, and Ginny yells behind me.

I drive to Pizza and More and walk into Chuck at the end of some joke. He and the cooks are laughing. He sees me and turns on his heel.

"Doctor, doctor, doctor. What's the prognosis for my ad?"

Damn it! I blanked on that. "Um, I've got some leads, but I want to make sure before I talk to them."

"Smart. But I've always known that about you." Chuck returns to the cooks and I go and punch in. Alexia's on her cell and her face is intense as she fires off a text. She grunts and mumbles, "Asshole."

I snatch up the order slips, get the pizzas together, and head out the door with the deliveries.

It's a slow evening, so I take my time driving, not concerned about what time I get back. The weather's got the fall crisp to it, but the sun's still strong enough to warm me and I feel peaceful. With all that's going on, a bit of a clear head is exactly what I need.

Back at the shop Alexia is pouting over the counter. I sneak up and stand beside her. She doesn't see me. She keeps staring out the front window at the traffic. "You're not getting any ideas are you?"

Alexia jumps and puts a hand to her chest. "Jesus, Ben! You

scared the shit out of me!" She swats, but there's no real anger behind it.

"I'm sorry. You looked so depressed. Were you thinking about playing in traffic?" I hoped she would laugh, but she sinks lower on the counter.

"I should. Jesse broke up with me."

I do a fist pump in my head. "Really? That's awful. Why?" I sit on the stool next to her.

"No reason. He's being a douche. Like all guys. Can't be tied down or some shit. It's his senior year. This isn't the first time he's pulled this." Her voice wavers at the end, and I'm reminded of my conversation with Chantel. I need to speak with her again. Or if I get the courage, to Alexia.

"When I got my braces off, at first I wasn't happy. My mouth felt weird, like there was way too much space. I kind of wanted the braces put back on," I say. "Crazy, I know. But then after a while, I realized how much easier everything was—eating, talking, smiling. You know what I mean?" I know Alexia's never needed braces, she's a natural beauty, but I hope she understands the analogy.

She turns to me, eyes dancing. "I remember that. You really looked happier without them."

The moment is too intense. That's not new for us, but such a distant emotion. "You said it, not me."

"Truth." She nods. "Thanks, Ben."

"You're welcome. But I think you would have figured that out on your own."

"Yeah. Maybe?"

Damn, I so want her to be more decisive. But that's self-serving so I switch gears. "Remember, you owe me a party?"

"You're right, I do. Um, I think Danielle Thompson is throwing one in a couple of weeks."

"If so, then I'm bringing John."

Alexia looks at me like she's expecting me to say I'm kidding, but just as quickly, seems to realize I'm not and turns away. Seeing that makes me want to smack myself. Very hard.

"Doc! Big order coming out!" Chuck startles us both, and I slap the counter to steady myself. Alexia sits up, but pats the back of my hand.

"Thanks." She slides off her stool and gets the order slip before I can say anything.

I load the pizza, wings, antipasto, bread, and bucket of meatballs. The house is in the rich part of town, so I double check my GPS, hoping that it's updated for those streets. I turn on the Jeep and the lights illuminate the dusk. Standing in front of my Jeep is Chantel.

I roll down my window, but don't get a chance to speak.

"You going for a ride?" She asks.

"One more delivery. You here to see Alexia?"

She smiles. "Yeah, but since I've seen you first, can I come along?"

I know Chuck's rule, but I have a feeling he'd cut me slack this time. "Sure."

Chantel steps around and climbs into the passenger seat. She buckles the seatbelt and it cinches between her boobs, making them pop. "Let's go," she says.

There are two routes we can take, and because I have a feeling Chantel will enjoy it—or maybe only I will—we take the second. I turn at the top of the hill, onto the off-road path.

Her eyes go wide for a moment, displaying every fear I am currently feeling. She doesn't deserve this. But then she grabs the *oh-shit* handle and laughs. "I love off-roading."

I pop into four-wheel and hit the first turn.

We go up and down the inclines, pitch left and right around the bends until the new development looms in the distance and the trail plateaus on a small rise. I park. "Ben, that was so not what I expected."

"Me neither." I look out the window and down the slope, to the pond below and realize where we are and how steep the jump will be.

"Whatcha doing?" Chantel asks.

"Sorry, I was, uh, just thinking." I know I'm blushing. I hope the almost-dark covers it up.

"About what?" She leans toward me.

Right now I should be able to supply some line, something witty like I can manage with Alexia, but I can't. I am overpowered by her appeal. Or my fear of the upcoming dare.

"It's okay, you don't have to tell me." She slides away.

"No, it's . . . complicated."

Chantel turns back. "Here, this isn't." And with that we're kissing. She's unbuckled her seatbelt, and I follow her lead. We're leaning over the seats and my mouth is entwined with hers.

She laughs, and it vibrates against my teeth and we pull away. I don't know why she's laughing and I search her face. She pats the stick shift. "It was jabbing my thigh. Thought it was something else."

I sit back in my seat. The worry floats away.

"You feel better?"

I turn to her. "I do. Thanks."

She smiles and I almost wish she didn't, because my mind turns. What's her interest in me? Where is it coming from? We don't know each other. Have only talked once, and that was about her friend. Is this possibly some by-product of completing the dares? Like what Ricky said?

She scrunches her face and then leans over and kisses me again. It's a quick kiss, but full on the lips and she nibbles at the end. "You're adorable." I blush and she slides away, but my questions do not.

—

The owner doesn't tip me when I finally arrive with his dinner. He yells about how late I am and says he's already called Chuck to complain. I apologize but find it difficult to really care.

After I drop Chantel off in the brand-new, expensive development over, she blows me a kiss and tells me she'll see me later. I float back to work and almost can't look at Alexia when I return. Somehow Chantel and I both forgot that she had come to see Alexia. Chuck storms at me when I come through and sniffs the air around me like he's some drug dog.

"Doc, you, uh, mistake your mom's perfume for your cologne?"

I laugh and play it off for two reasons. One, Chuck would yell at me for the ride-along, but then pull me into his office for details. He is one horny and vicariously living man. No, thank you. Two, I might have to explain myself in front of Alexia. No way. She's always been fragile. Me getting frisky with her friend right after she's broken up with Jesse, there's no way that's going over well.

His eyes dance off his face. "Doc, I'm glad your shift is over. You're starting to lose it. I'm docking your pay for that order."

I don't argue. I punch out, say good night to Alexia, and bolt. When I get in the Jeep I check my phone and have a text from Ricky: **Check's here. We'll take care of it tomorrow.** I am relieved that we got paid, that at least that end of the equation isn't something I have to unscramble, but I am more concerned about what happened with Chantel.

My Jeep reeks of her perfume. Not a bad thing. A first for me, really. But the problem is Alexia. We're rekindling this friendship, and I don't think Chantel is worth the risk of what it might do to that.

I'm an idiot, I know. I'm sacrificing a hot girl who's into me for a girl with some real baggage. But I know that baggage. I feel as if I have the matching set.

I step through my front door, and Ginny's where she was earlier. But now she has her laptop turned toward me, and it's paused on our bridge jump. I freeze. "Care to explain?" she says.

I can hear my parents in the background, arguing. I look between my sister's face and the image of me on the screen, and all the good sensations fall away.

"Don't even try to deny it. I know it's you three idiots."

I sit, because if I don't, I might fall down. "How?" is all I can manage.

Ginny beams with her superior intelligence grin. "This nonsense is what I'm studying. But I've known you your whole life. The distortion doesn't remove what I know."

This is it. I'm done. John and Ricky will go on without me, maybe replacing me with Trevor. Ginny has taken this away. "Why, Ginny? Why do you care?"

"Are you crazy? Ha, stupid question, that's a given. You are going to get hurt Ben, you already have. Right?" She points to her forehead. "You might die. Don't you realize this?" She's slid closer on the couch and her voice sounds more pleading than accusatory.

But still. "Ginny, we play it up to be worse than it is. You know, for the drama. We'll be fine."

"Famous last words right there."

My parents' voices rise and move toward us. At any moment

they'll enter and she'll spill the beans. "Please, Ginny. What will it take for you to keep your mouth shut?"

She tilts her head. "Who said that was even an option?"

"It has to be. There's more to this than the dares." And I don't quite know what to say, because I'm still not completely sure myself. There's the money, but there's more with Ricky.

"Like what?" she asks.

"I need time to figure that out."

Ginny shoves her laptop to the side. "Figure *what* out? Ben, you aren't making any sense."

My parents enter the living room, still arguing, but see us and stop. "Sorry," Dad says.

Mom takes a deep breath and looks at us. "What are you two talking about? You seem worse than we do." She grabs my Dad's hand and tugs on it. He looks down, sees it, and pulls her close. It's a beautiful gesture, a way of saying: *it's not you, it's the world I can't stand.*

I think Ginny must recognize it, too, because she says, "School work and Ben's future." She shoots me a look and I know she's not going any further, but I also know we're not finished.

CHAPTER 11

f I had been paying attention in physics, I could probably calculate how fast I'll be going when I hit the water. But I'm not paying attention in physics or in any other class, so I wouldn't know what to do with the dimensions of the ramp if I had them. Anyway, what good would my computations do me? We're already here.

"Gather round." Ricky straddles his bike. The same BMX we all now own, compliments of O. P.

We roll into a knot and the cold morning air tickles the skin at the back of my neck. So much for completing these dares later in the day.

"We'll draw for order. Grab a slip." Ricky holds his mask, and we each reach in and grab a slip of paper. We're decked out in our uniform and now have helmets, which are wrapped in the company's logo.

"Open 'em," Ricky says, and we all look.

"Yeah, number three, baby!" Ricky shouts.

"Shit, same order as last time." John throws his slip to the ground.

But this won't be anything like last time. Everything's different. Trevor's on camera, we got paid for the bridge jump, and now Ginny knows. And in spite of how much Ricky swears he has this all worked out, he still hasn't brought us copies of the contract. My brain is screaming questions I don't have answers to, ones I should have asked over the past weeks but didn't.

Ricky claps his hands like some coach and says, "Let's do this!" Maybe that's how he sees himself now. These past two weeks have been all about getting the ramp built and creating a quiet buzz for the dare. Trevor's edited pieces of our last stunts into a fifteen-second commercial that pops up here and there, but no one can add its link anywhere or bookmark it. It's unembeddable or something like that. He's a shifty kid, but he meant what he said about knowing computers. It almost makes me wish I was an übernerd like him, rather than average, or possibly above.

Ricky points toward the ramp. Three guys showed up and built the thing after the crates were dropped off. Apparently O. P. paid them. "Start where I've spray-painted, because you need at least that much speed. Pedal until you reach the ramp and then coast. Remember," his voice rises, "do *not* hit your brakes at any time! All you need to do is ride it out, and once you're in the air, push the bike away from you. All right?"

I have a dozen questions. No, more. But it's too late for the answers.

The only one that does is this: we're doing this because we all believe in the premise of becoming legends. At least that's what I'm telling myself.

"Good. John, get in position. I'll check with Trev, and then give you the signal."

John pulls his mask on and buckles his helmet strap.

"Trev." That's what Ricky calls him, now. Trev. Like he's some pet. In a way, he is. He hangs on Ricky's side like one of those handbag dogs. I know they made up and all, but John and I didn't exactly forgive and forget, so I'm not really sure what they are to each other besides former enemies.

Newton would find out the answer. He was too smart not to. But would he complete this dare?

"John, I'm going to do the intro and then it's all you buddy. You good?"

John gives a thumbs-up but does not look at us. He stares down the hill, at the ramp. Ball starts in two weeks. I can only imagine what he's thinking.

"In five, four, three . . ." Trevor gives the countdown and Ricky coughs once to clear his throat.

"Welcome to Dare Number Three, brought to you by Get Out There Adventure. Check out the website for all your outdoor adventure needs."

Ricky rambles on talking about the ramp and the distance and the height and speed we'll be traveling, but I tune him out. I can't listen or I know I'll balk. It's like going on a roller coaster. I can't watch the thing go round and round. I need to climb onboard and let it ride.

Ricky turns and extends a hand to John. "And now for the first ride. Ready?"

John gives no sign that he's heard.

Ricky asks again.

Elting Memorial Library
93 Main Street
New Paltz, New York 12561-1593

John shakes his head.

Ricky coughs. "Let's count it down." He looks at me, and in his eyes I see a familiar and unwelcome sheen. "Ten, nine, eight . . ."

I join him and John's head snaps up when he hit seven. He grips the handles at five, looks over at us at three, and never looks back after one. His long-ass legs pump so fast he churns up patches of grass. He skids once, and my stomach drops. John hits the ramp and looks like a kid who just came off training wheels. He tilts to the left, then right, and I bite my hand.

He corrects himself about halfway up the ramp, and begins to look steady. He gains speed, comes to the slope of the vert and . . . what the fuck? John squeezes the brakes and the bike comes to a dead stop. He flips over the handle bars and into the edge of the ramp. There's a loud *crack*, followed by his scream, and then suddenly he's gone, creating a loud wet slap.

We run and I almost fall charging the pond. Out of the corner of my eye, I see the end of the ramp. There's a piece of wood missing. I get to the edge of the water, and John's treading and gnashing his teeth.

"It's broken. I broke my arm."

My head is screaming unintelligible thoughts, but one point is clear. I jump in and paddle out to John. He's crying.

"Benny. What am I gonna do?"

I don't answer. Can't. All that matters is that we get him out of this water. When I get a close look, though, I almost puke. From the middle of his forearm to his wrist, his arm is bent away from his body at a forty-five-degree angle. "Let me pull you in." I swim around to his good arm and grab him under the elbow. It's tough enough swimming in my clothes, but with his weight it feels like I'm moving through cement.

"Benny, I got you. Reach." Ricky's voice is right behind me and I turn. He's anchored off the ramp, so I drag John to him and help pull John on shore and up onto the grass. I, like him, fall into a heap.

"We have to take him to the hospital, Ricky. It's bad."

"I know."

I sit up and we both look over at John, who's on his back. Ricky's gotten his helmet and mask off and has put them under John's feet. I look over my shoulder, up to Trevor. He's still, watching, and I remember how creepy he is.

"Come on. Let's go." I stand.

"We have to finish." Ricky says, still trying to make John comfortable, which seems impossible by the way he's panting.

"The fuck's wrong with you? We're done. John's going to the hospital. That's it!"

Ricky pulls on his mask and straps his helmet.

"I'm not riding, Rick. We're leaving, *now*!" I step toward John, furious at everything all at once.

"Ben, no!" Ricky pulls me back. I struggle, but he shoves me to the ground. "If we don't ride, we don't get paid. Understand?"

I feel like kicking him in the nuts. "I don't give a shit about the money. John's hurt, you asshole!"

"And what good is it going to do him to be hurt and without cash? Adding insult to injury? Least he had the balls to do it. Now his scholarship's fucked. You know that."

Ricky says the last part low, I think so John doesn't hear. But it's too late for that. It's too late for anything.

I stand and look over at John. He's writhing and punching the ground with his good hand. What have we done?

I look at Ricky and again at Trevor, and know somewhere we've taken a turn. We put this thing in motion with good intentions—I think—but we've slipped toward some negative trajectory. Plain and simple, this sucks. And again, I feel like I've been played. Question is, how much longer am I going to let that happen?

—

The ER's pretty dead when John's parents walk in. Seeing them, I remember that they're getting divorced. Sometime. And when I watch them move to the desk and ask about their son, it's all I can think about. The nurse says something and then disappears. John's parents wait by the desk but do not speak to each other. His mom looks over at us and our eyes meet for a moment, but she turns away and the nurse returns with a doctor. He speaks and goes through the motion of what looks like some kind of operation. There's a lot of twisting and pulling. John's dad looks up and closes his eyes. I manage to read the one word that comes from his lips: *Basketball?*

I look away but hear him cursing and John's mom crying.

I'm all alone here. Ricky and Trevor took off to edit. I didn't try to stop them, was actually glad they went. I hit the ramp and was out of the water in seconds, leaving the bike to sink, but Ricky vaulted like a showman, like he had something to prove. Then we hopped into Ricky's car and took off like we'd robbed a bank.

John didn't speak. He stared out the window with his eyes glazed over. Trevor rewound and played the footage and conferred with Ricky over the driver's seat. Least the little shit had the courtesy to give John shotgun.

"What were you doing?" John's dad's voice is low and raspy. He's standing in front of me.

"We were riding our bikes."

He reels back. "John's bike's too small for him."

"He borrowed one of mine." I know this sounds ridiculous considering John's almost seven feet tall and I'm not even six-foot.

"Jesus! But you don't fuck up your arm like that by falling off a bike, not at his age."

I turn away because John's father is downright scary—as tall as John, but thicker, with a personality 180 degrees from his son's. "We were on the trails. Off-roading. It was pretty steep. I think he might have hit a rock."

John's father stops the pacing he had begun. "What were you thinking? Why did you let him? You know about his scholarship, right? So how could you let him?"

All good questions. And I don't know how to answer any.

Fortunately, John's mom wisps over and says, "Tom, enough!" She glares at her soon-to-be ex-husband. "We can go see him now."

John's father rips down the hall, muttering about his stupid wife and his son's stupid friend. His mother touches my shoulder. "Ben, forget about whatever he said. That's how I stay sane." She tries on a smile, but it doesn't fit. "Don't beat yourself up. It's not your fault. John's a big boy and makes his own decisions. *I* know that. And I know you wouldn't do anything to intentionally get him hurt."

She moves away before I can answer. As if I could say anything that would be close to the truth. Because it is my fault. John's following my lead, not making his own decisions. And I did intentionally risk his safety.

Yet at the same time, I'm also pissed at John. Why did he hit the brakes? If he hadn't, none of this would have happened. We all would have gone home and waited for a message from Ricky and kept the positive, positive.

I stand and think to call my parents. But they may or may not be home, and I don't really want to lie my way through some explanation if I do make contact. Getting picked up at a hospital soaking wet in my all-black "uniform" isn't something that can be easily ignored. Unless the person driving doesn't care.

I call Pizza and More. Alexia answers, and I ask for Chuck.

"What's going on?" she asks. "Weren't you meeting up with Chantel?"

It may be my exhaustion, or my eagerness to talk to Chuck,

but it sounds like there's a bit of happiness in Alexia's voice over the fact that I'm not with Chantel. "I was, but something came up, which is why I need to talk to Chuck. Is he there?"

"Yeah, he's here. But what came up?"

I hear Chuck in the background and then the phone rumbles and Chuck's voice scruffs through, "Doc?"

"Hey, Chuck. Listen. I'm kind of in a bind, could you give me a lift?"

Chuck doesn't respond and I almost repeat myself, but he cuts in and says, "Where are you?"

"Saint Hilary's."

Chuck takes a sharp breath. "Jesus, Doc, ain't that priceless. Are you hurt?"

"No, my friend."

The phone crackles and Chuck says something I can't hear, but then is back on. "If I do this, you'll get me in with those kids. Pronto. Deal?"

I want to scream at him for using this moment as leverage, but I also can't help thinking, *if there is a next time?* "Deal."

———

The entire ride Chuck's said one thing, "You owe me." As if I could have forgotten. But now we pull up to my house and stuck in the ground is a FOR SALE sign. "What's the deal, Doc?"

Chuck's voice startles me. "Um, well, we're moving," I say.

"Moving? Where to?"

I don't really want to get into this, but he drove me home and he is my boss. "It's complicated, but hopefully around here."

"*Hopefully?* Doc, what's up?"

I sigh. No point in trying to hide. I give him the summary and avoid making eye contact.

"You're in it up to your eyeballs, huh?"

I nod. That's a pretty fair assessment.

"Let me know if I can help. *Capeesh?*"

"Thanks, Chuck."

"I'd say *anytime*, but you'd know that's complete bullshit." He pulls away.

I walk in and slip off my soaked sneakers. If I can get to my room and change, I'm set. I climb the stairs, listening for my parents, but don't hear them. I rip off my wet gear and change quick, and head back out into the hall. Still nothing. I peek in their room and the office, and then head downstairs to the kitchen, where there is a note on the table.

> Ben,
> Sorry, no bacon this time. We're in a rush. Had to go look at some apartments ASAP. We're already getting bids on the house.
> We'll talk later.
> Mom

"Bids?" I say to the empty kitchen. "How?" I look around at my worn-out house and wonder who in their right mind would want this place. And isn't the economy supposed to blow right now? People not buying homes? Or is it not selling them? My head spins, and I grab the chair in front of me. I should eat. It's after 3:00 and I haven't had anything since breakfast. But my insides are too twisted for food. I need to lie down.

I head back to my room, and climbing the stairs feels like I'm scaling a damn mountain. My legs are shot. Thank God I don't have to work until tomorrow or I'd be throwing pizzas onto people's lawns from the Jeep like some newspaper carrier.

I crash onto my bed and check my phone before putting it on my nightstand. Nothing from Ricky, but I do have a text from Ginny: **Did you go through with the dare?**

I grind my jaw and close my eyes. The other night floods back, the part after my parents left us to go finish their own conversation.

Ginny said she found the video while doing research for her paper. I didn't believe her at first. "Why are you doing this?" she asked.

I couldn't answer because the truth was too painful. Ginny was like Alexia in school: popular and attractive, lots of friends. She wouldn't have understood.

"You better have something better for Mom and Dad. They won't take the silent treatment." Her face turned ugly then. "How could you do this to them, anyway? Now? When they've got so much they have to deal with? Important things. You're so immature."

I kept my mouth shut because she was right on all counts. I

am immature and this is the kind of shit my parents will kill me for and they deserve better. But I felt like I needed the fun the dares provided. Or used to. It sucks trying to live up to her Goody-Two-shoes nature and I wanted something for myself, something she would never do. Couldn't say that, though.

Then an idea crawled across her face and spread like a rash. "I could go show them this video right now, and you'd be screwed from here to eternity. But . . ." She paused and looked back at the screen and then at me. "But if you agree to let me interview you and your friends, I won't say a word."

"Why would you want to do that?"

"The research I'm doing. I need a project for my adolescent psych course, and this is perfect. I can use the YouTube videos and the interview, and piece together research about the effects of peer pressure on males in our culture. . . ." And she rambled on, and I spaced out because it was all way over my head.

I agreed so she would stay silent. But now? She wants the passwords and updates and wants to come home next weekend to interview us. After John's accident, I don't know if that's possible.

The dare will be up in a few hours, and I'll text her the password if she didn't get it on Twitter already. The question will answer itself; my parents will come home and tell me we're moving to some shit hole; John's parents will come looking for answers, and Chantel won't want anything to do with me. Why I ever agreed to all of this in the first place is beyond me. Then again, I really didn't agree to *this*. It's all morphed and I don't like it.

—

My phone wakes me and I scramble for it. Ricky: **Video's up.** I stare at the screen and wait until it fades away. I get out of bed and go to my computer. It's after 5:00 and I still don't think my parents are home. I don't remember them checking on me. Although, I feel like I was more dead than sleeping.

I pull up our channel and type in the password: PONDSCUM. Apparently O. P. and Trevor are using keywords from O. P.'s site. That way if anyone types pondscum right now, in say, Google, they should hit on his site and some product to get pond scum off your water skis. Whatever.

On my screen is a shot of the ramp. I hit PLAY and watch this morning unfold.

I have to admit, Trevor does nice work. He zooms in at all the right times, like when John was shaking his head and staring down the ramp, and then he pans back for the perspective of the jump. We look like toys on a play set. I'm watching and holding my breath without realizing it. Then John's at the lip. He pedals and wobbles and then . . . he's in the water, looking fine, as if nothing happened.

I watch the video again, in case for some reason I missed it. But it's not there.

"Benny? We're home." Mom's voice carries up the stairs and then down the hall. She stands in my doorway.

"Are you okay? You look exhausted." She moves into my

room, and I quickly close out the screen before she gets close enough.

"Tired. Finishing some school work." I run a hand through my hair.

She furrows her brow. "You're not coming down with something, are you?" She crosses to me, grabs the back of my neck, and kisses my forehead. "No fever. That's good," she murmurs close to my face. I feel awful. John's lying in the hospital, all sorts of messed-up and dealing with asshole parents, while I'm here lying my ass off to my sweetheart mother.

"Yeah. Kind of beat, but I'm feeling good now." I add some perk onto the end, because she's obviously bouncing on something, and if that diverts her attention from me, I'm all for it.

"Good. So did you see the sign?"

I almost forgot. "Yeah, and I got your note. Bids?"

She sits on the edge of my bed and her eyes are wide. "I know. Already. Benny, you don't know how worried we've been, thinking financially we might have to take the transfer. . . . But now . . ." She tears up, and I let her go. "Now we can afford to stay here if your father's company decides to relocate him."

I am genuinely relieved, but then think to ask, "So where are we going?"

She laughs a sound that has nothing to do with humor. More like dread. "Still haven't figured that out. There are some nice condos over by that new development, but that wouldn't be much of a savings. We may need to focus more on downtown."

The "new development" is where Trevor lives, and the condos are between him and Chantel. I don't know anyone who lives downtown, and I want nothing to do with that gross area, ever.

She grabs my hand. "I know it's not what you want, but we'll make it work. I promise."

She sounds like she's talking about my life to a T. I didn't want what I had before, and now I'm not sure I want what I have or what's coming. But that's how things work, right? Damn Newton. "I know, Mom. Thanks."

She squeezes me tight and then leaves. "I've got pizza if you're hungry," she says as she's leaving my room.

"From where?" I ask, but I know.

"Please. The only place in town to order from, your lovely establishment." She walks away.

I pick up my phone to text Ricky and find out what the hell's up, but I have a text from Alexia: **Party tonight. I owe you.**

I scramble online and sure enough, Danielle Thompson is throwing a rager. I stare at my phone and the options to send a text or to call. I look back at the screen and pull up our severely edited video. My life no longer resembles anything it used to. I don't know if this is good or bad, or something that just happens senior year. But I do know one thing, I want more. And the only part that feels right at the moment is Alexia. Which, in itself, is ridiculous. But these dares may be gone, and maybe what Ricky and John and I had, so I might as well salvage what I can.

I close out the screen and text Alexia.

CHAPTER 12

The beer is buzzing in my head and the party is rocking. Someone screams, "One more time!" and the chant ensues. Danielle screams and flips her giant plasma TV to display the Internet. Our latest video is waiting for the replay. She clicks the TAB and the event unfolds again.

It's surreal, standing in a room of kids, drunk and smiling, watching us on the screen when none of them know who the hell we really are. The footage rolls and the room reacts the same way as it did earlier, laughing at John's blunder, cheering for me, and then losing their shit over Ricky's acrobatics. When it's over, they applaud and scream and "cheers" one another and drink.

I turn away and take a big swallow of my beer. Ricky and Trevor do the same. It sucks without John, and having them here instead doesn't feel right. I didn't even want to bring them, but Alexia brought it up when we texted, and since she was calling the shots, I didn't want to seem rude. And I know I'm only pissed at how Ricky behaved. It was John, and he was hurt, and Ricky wasn't there for him, wasn't concerned.

Most of the room was watching our bridge jump when Alexia ushered us into Danielle's. Heads turned, but only briefly.

"I gotta go check on things," she said after we all got beers. "Have fun." Then she disappeared, and I haven't seen her since. So now I'm stuck with these two, and I need a stiffer drink.

"We need to talk." Ricky leans closer to me, not drunk, but not steady either. Trevor bites on his cup, as if he's nervous for what Ricky's going to say.

"About what?"

"O. P."

I take a deep, calming breath, not caring what either thinks. I don't give a shit about our business partner at the moment.

"He's not happy."

"Why's that?" I ask.

"The dare. It didn't exactly go off as planned."

"That's an understatement. But what does he care about that?"

Ricky looks at Trevor, only for a moment, but it's enough for me to suspect what I figured was right.

"We're not getting paid," Ricky says.

"What? How is that? We completed the dare."

Ricky turns to the side, directing our conversation away from the crowd and into the wall. "Not technically."

I skip the deep breath. "What do you mean? We just watched it."

Ricky sighs. "Not all of us."

I think I understand but play dumb. "Huh?"

"In the contract, it states that all three of us have to complete the dare or none of us gets paid." I don't remember seeing this, but I didn't read it thoroughly and Ricky hasn't given me my copy, so I can't argue the point. "That's bullshit. It's not John's fault." Even as I say this I know it is. "This asshole's going to withhold three grand because he hit the brakes?"

"It's not three grand. Did you see the amount of hits?"

"Something like six thousand."

"Right, but what matters is the amount we get in the first twenty-four hours. We get paid a dollar for every hit. We had fifty-five, twenty-five, then."

Another point I don't remember. I finish my beer and calculate in my head. "So, each of us lost eighteen hundred?"

Ricky, again, looks at Trevor.

The beer opens my mouth. "Fucking say it. You keep looking at him like you want to."

"Easy, Ben. Take it easy." Ricky talks to me like I'm a child, and that only makes it worse. I lower my head and step closer to him.

"Tell me."

Ricky clears his throat. "From here on out, we're giving Trev an equal cut."

My head surges. I don't know if the money is the hot button or not. It might be the fact that Ricky decided without us. It might be the fact that I don't know if he can because I haven't read the contract. It might be that I'm pissed at Ricky for being Ricky? This is how he rolls.

"Do what you want. You were going to anyway. It's not as if you give a shit about John or me."

Ricky's face twists. "The fuck is that supposed to mean?"

The words build, and I clench my jaw and feel tears stinging my eyes. It's either let it out or lose it. "Think for a minute. John's arm is busted. Ball starts in two weeks. If he loses his scholarship because of this . . ." I take a breath because I'm too far gone not to. "And my dad's out of work. I could use that money we're not getting, and now you're kicking it to Trevor. And why exactly you're doing that, I don't know. So right now I'd like to punch you in the nuts and walk away from all of this. You asshole."

Ricky lets out a short laugh. "I'm not surprised, Ben. You walk when things get tough. Like in eighth grade. You couldn't sell the lie, had to throw me under the bus."

"Really? Did you really just say that? The kid who told Principal McGee that we'd snaked that spy cam into the girls' bathroom is standing right next to you."

Trevor's eyes bulge, but he only nods, doesn't speak.

Ricky leans into me again. "But as soon as he spilled, you piled on. You and John. It was our word against his, until you cracked."

It's true, which makes me feel like a dick, but also adds to this ridiculous layer of *friendship* we have. Why is Ricky back? Why are John and I?

"That's besides the point. *You* uploaded that shit. *You* thought it was funny as hell. Not *us.* So, now, this time, *if* we move forward, you explain to John what's up."

"If?" Ricky says.

"Yeah. Because either you stay on the level and I get a copy of the contract—which you somehow keep *forgetting* to give me—and we arrange a meeting with O. P., or I walk."

"Didn't you say you needed the cash? Dad out of work? And that you're worried about John?" His voice isn't remotely sympathetic.

"I did and I am, but, again, that's not the point. Or did you forget your own lie? The one where you sold us on being legends?"

"That's still the truth!"

People turn and look now, and we wait until they go back to their conversations before Ricky speaks again.

"I haven't lied to you yet."

"Yet." I hope that word has the impact I want it to.

"Think whatever you want, Ben, but if you walk away, the loss is on you. Don't go blaming me."

That stings. Because he's right. I can't prove he's lied, just that he hasn't been forthcoming. However, Ricky's pretty poor, and John and I are close, so there's leverage there. Trevor's loaded, so him earning anything is a shitty deal. But there's nothing I can do about that. I'll focus on what I can.

"I want a copy of the contract, and I want a meeting with O. P."

"The contract is a no-brainer. I'm sorry I forgot to get it to you. The meeting with O. P. . . . I don't know where he lives."

"You said you found him through Craigslist."

"Yeah, but there's no guarantee he's local. That shit gets posted all over."

I could argue this point but Trevor steps in.

"We could do a conference call, Skype or FaceTime?"

Ricky looks at me. "Will that work?"

"I'd rather face-to-face, but it'll work."

"All right. Glad we got that out of the way." Ricky looks at his empty cup. "Refills?"

"Yeah. But one more thing." I was going to wait until later, but there's no reason to now. "Chuck wants to advertise with us."

"You didn't tell him, did you?"

"No, he thinks because we go to school with *these kids* I should be able to make contact."

"So we need to make it seem as if we know these guys, that's all?" Ricky asks.

"I guess. I don't know what Chuck wants, but I need to get him off my back."

"That's fine. Tell him you saw them here." Ricky waves his hand around the room. "Which, by the way, we should be enjoying. Thanks to Alexia. What's up there?"

I don't even know how to answer, so I don't. "Shit, sorry, one last thing."

"You're killing me, Benny. Like seriously, I have no pulse." But Ricky smiles when he says this.

"Ginny wants to do this interview with us. Some shit for a school project. Of course our identities will be hidden."

Ricky stares, open-mouthed. "Why the fuck did you tell her?"

I put up my hands. "I didn't, I swear. *She* found out. There was nothing I could do. She would have thrown me under . . ." I don't finish.

Ricky nods. "At least you know the feeling. We'll do the interview. Have Trev record it. Who knows, maybe we could use it later?"

I don't see how that's remotely possible. It's more likely he wants to feel like he's got some control or shit. Whatever, so long as he isn't freaking out. Goddamn I need a drink.

"Thanks."

We head toward the kitchen, and Ricky puts his hand on my shoulder. "Hey, I'm sorry about your dad. I know what that's like. All that plant shit?"

"Yeah. Sucks."

"I hear you. And about John, too. We'll do what we can, but let's hold out for that scholarship."

I'm about to ask about Trevor, but don't get the chance.

"There you are!" Alexia's voice sends a jolt through me, and I turn around. Jesse's behind her. His pack of friends linger in the distance, eyeballing us, but I turn my attention to Alexia as she stumbles over and gives me a hug. "Are you having a good time?" I stay stiff in her arms. She grabs my forearm. "What's wrong?"

"I thought you two were, you know . . ." I look at Jesse and watch him watch his girlfriend hang on me. I look back at her and am astounded by how enormous and beautiful her eyes are. They're like cartoonish orbs taking me in.

"Some things you can't resist. You know?" She pouts and grows even more adorable, more like she used to be.

"I do." This voice is deeper, husky, and, I know, belongs to Chantel.

I turn, and Chantel breaks through the crowd and Alexia's hold on me. She plants a rough wet kiss on my mouth. I grab her and kiss back. Chantel releases me and someone whistles, and my head feels as if it's floating.

"You need a drink?" Chantel grabs my cup and turns to Ricky and Trevor and grabs theirs as well. She heads toward the keg in the kitchen, and Ricky is eating his grin.

"So, you two are an item?" Alexia's voice is quiet.

She's hurt. I know the look all too well. And I'm pissed because she's curled back into Jesse, who is giving me a new appraisal. "I guess," I say to answer her question, and it pains me to do so. I want to say more, but can't. Not with *him* around. "You on tomorrow?"

She either doesn't hear me or doesn't care to respond or isn't working, because she melts into the crowd without answering. I watch Jesse mouth something to his friends. They nod and each plant a foot against the wall, giving the three of us another slow and hateful look.

Chantel returns with our beers. We cheers and I keep my eyes on those watching us and wish I could somehow see through them, to Alexia.

—

I think it's like 3 a.m., but the clock is wobbly, the red numbers looking more like felt than digits. I don't know whose room this is, but Chantel locked the door and is now making her way back to me. She straddles my waist and leans over and kisses my neck. Her hair brushes against my face and every part of me tingles.

I run my hands up her back, and she kisses my mouth. It's like being back in my Jeep, except now I'm drunk and we're alone and I'm not sure where this is going.

My hands work on their own, independent of me, and fumble with her bra. I've taken off only one other, and that was because Alexia dared me. Too many ideas are running through my head.

"Benjamin, you dirty little boy," Chantel says.

I stop and plant my hands firmly on the mattress. "Sorry," I mumble against her teeth.

Chantel kisses me again and sits up. "Here, let me help you." She unclasps the bra, pulls it out of the sleeve of one arm, and tosses it to the floor. "Nice trick, huh?"

It is nice and I'm so thoroughly aroused I'm afraid I might embarrass myself.

Chantel sighs and stares at me a minute. "Don't get any ideas, Ben. I don't usually move this fast. There's just something about you." She pulls her shirt over her head.

Something about me? This is Ricky's line, about how people would sense we were somehow different. They wouldn't know why, but we would seem more meaningful. I'll give him credit, because there's no way Chantel ever found me meaningful prior to all this.

"Damn," I say, looking at her half-naked body, and my voice doesn't sound like my own. It's full and thick.

She squeals and falls on me, and we kiss some more and I caress her. I don't know if I'm doing what I should, but she seems happy enough to let me continue. So far, so good.

Chantel pulls my shirt off in a flash, and is immediately back to kissing me. It's harder than before, like she's trying to gnaw at something within me.

"You got protection?" Her breath sends goose bumps along my neck as she leans in to ask.

I shake my head and cannot believe what she asked. Why would I have a condom? I didn't expect this.

"No prob, I have some." She slides off me and goes to her bag, which she must have left here at some point.

Did she plan this? And is it a good thing or kind of a slutty thing that she has condoms with her? God, I have no experience and no clue, and the room is spinning and I can't focus on anything beyond this girl slowly walking back to the bed, now wearing nothing but her panties. I take a very deep breath and let it out very slowly.

Chantel undoes my pants and pulls them off. She gently sits on top of me, warm against my boxer briefs and I'm losing the ability to focus beyond the one possibility that is inches away.

"Ben . . . I don't know, something's different about you, and whatever it is . . . it does it for me." She bows her head, and her hair tickles my belly. I think I might explode. She looks up and I hate to admit it, but her eyes remind me of Alexia's.

"Then I'm glad I'm someone different." I stroke her thigh.

She bites her lower lip and looks as if she might cry, but presses the condom into my hand. I curl it into my palm and roll on top of her. We kiss, and then she's pulling down my underwear and I do the same for her.

I sit on my heels and hope I don't screw this up, because before me is an unbelievably hot girl, naked, willing, and into me.

There are actually directions inside the condom, and I might normally crack a joke about this, but in my state, I'm glad for the reminder and follow the basic steps. Much like the dares, it's go time, and I admit, I'm scared as hell, but equally excited.

I move toward Chantel and she grabs my shoulders and looks up at me while I slide in. She moans and this feels softer and more sensational than I ever imagined. I let my weight fall onto her and feel her beautiful body against mine. She says my name and everything fades away except for the singular sensation of me losing my virginity.

CHAPTER 13

"**D**oc, you look like a mix of shit and sunshine." Chuck's belly bobs as he laughs. "The hell happened?"

My head is pounding and my mouth is so dry that I'm afraid to speak. I woke up alone in the bed at Danielle's house and thought for a moment that I had imagined the entire event with Chantel. But she'd texted a picture of the two of us lying together before she left.

I know I shouldn't, because it will only add fuel to the fire, but I show Chuck the picture.

He grabs the phone from my hands, and if I had any strength, I'd fight for it back. "Are you fucking kidding me? My God, Doc. That is . . . she is . . . way out of your league." He hands the phone back. "You pay her or something?"

I pocket the evidence and feel a deep shame. Why did I do that? But I also have to admit he's right. "No, she's a friend of Alexia's."

"So you're picking up second best?"

"No, no, it's not like that." I want to scream at him that he doesn't understand, that Chantel is into me and that I only showed him to get him off my back. But I can't. I'm too hung over for much beyond sitting down.

"You going to be able to work?" Chuck squints at me.

"Yeah. I just need some Gatorade."

Chuck walks to the cooler and then sets one before me. "Here, Doc. Take your medicine. You've got an hour before your shift starts, so let's hope it works. And hey, any luck with connections?"

"I think so," I say. Then last night comes back in pieces and I stare at the wall and try to fit them together. In spite of the awesomeness that was Chantel, the negative floods back as well. I cradle my head and dial John.

"What's up, Ben?" John sounds like I woke him up.

"Hey, how are you? I've been trying to get through."

"I know. I saw. My parents turned off my phone, but they're at church now."

He's more talkative than usual. It's either the meds or the isolation. "You okay?"

He sighs a long, dramatic sound. "No. Not even close. I've got a rod and three screws in my arm."

"Shit."

There's a pause, and I know what's coming before he says it.

"Which means I won't be at tryouts."

I can't respond. What am I supposed to say? Alexia walks in and I mutter, "Sorry."

"Yeah. But it's not your fault," John says.

Alexia shoots me a look but keeps on going and punches in.

"Hey, I gotta work, but I wanted to let you know that we're going to meet with O. P."

"Why?" John's voices drops.

How do I say this? "I think we should. You know, we need to look out for ourselves after your injury." I'll tell him about our lack of pay later.

"Right." John clears his throat. "How'd you get Ricky to agree to that?"

"More like Trevor did."

John sighs again, and I can feel his pain through the vibration of the phone. "At least he's good for something." He pauses. "I gotta go. Thanks, Ben."

He hangs up and I stare at my phone, imagining him crying.

I watch Alexia out of the corner of my eye. Her hair's falling in front of her face, and she's moving super slow. Maybe she's as bad off as me? She turns and we lock eyes. The left side of her face is bruised. My phone slips from my hand to the floor. She turns away. My head swims and I grip the table.

I get steady, scoop up my phone, and cross the room to Alexia. She's counting the drawer. "What happened?"

Her mouth moves over the numbers and she turns away from me. I remember the bruises on her wrist, the conversation with Chantel about how Jesse can be a "little rough." But this?

I look over my shoulder. The cooks are chopping vegetables and shredding cheese, seemingly more hung over than I am. Chuck is in the fridge, pulling out dough. "Alexia, come on, what happened?"

She slams down the money and a shudder takes over her back.

I hear the sob and close in next to her.

"It's nothing. Just an accident." A tear falls onto the counter.

"Okay." I don't believe her. "So what did you run into?"

Alexia looks at me and her face is lost, like I'm speaking another language. Then her eyes dart and she gets it. "Right. Yeah. A door at Jesse's. I didn't see it. I was sooo hammered."

Even though my head is still pounding and I'd like nothing more than to lie down on the cold tile, I grit my teeth and ask, "At Jesse's, huh?"

She nods and the tears start up again.

I don't think, but react, and grab her up in my arms. "Alexia, please. You deserve better. You can't let this . . . I mean, shit, he can't do this."

She nods, but says, "He's all I know."

This isn't true. She knows me. Not in the way she knows Jesse, but possibly it's enough. "Chantel told me a little. Shit at home. Jesse. Trust me, I understand. Please believe that you deserve better than this."

She smiles a broken smile and leans against my chest. I hold her. And that's all I want to do. It's not like it was with Chantel. I see Alexia for more than the hottie she is. I watched her grow up, a little tomboy who, of all people, hung out with me. I want better for her. For John, too. And Ricky, as tough as that is to admit.

"Jesus Christ. The two of you. Enough." Chuck whips past, and I let go of Alexia.

She wipes her tears and whispers, "I'm sorry."

"Don't be." I squeeze her elbow. "But why did you get back together with him?"

She gives me a piercing look that I don't fully understand and then shakes her head. "I don't know, Benny. I don't know."

I wish I had an answer for her, maybe something logical, like from Newton. But Newton's useless when it comes to relationships.

I stare out the window at the gray fall afternoon and wonder what's next.

—

The deliveries were painful. I confused orders, tripped over stairs, and went to the wrong house, twice. I figured Chuck would be waiting in the parking lot, ready to fire me or kick my ass. Or both. Nothing happened. I punched out and left. Alexia managed to slip away before me, so any hope of getting more of the story is gone. Not that it would have made a difference. Tomorrow she'll have everything covered up. That's the thing about identity: once you have it, it's more you than even you are. Unless, of course, you create an alternate digital self, like us.

Chantel's blown up my phone all shift, but when I call her back, she doesn't answer. I can only hope she's with Alexia. Someone needs to be.

So I don't want to do what I'm about to, but going home doesn't feel like an option right now, and I've got nothing else I should be doing. I park the Jeep in Ricky's driveway.

His house is the same setup as mine. It was weird when we were younger and I first started hanging out with him, because I'd go over and expect to find the same stuff from my house in his. But Ricky's home isn't like mine in more ways than the furniture.

I ring the doorbell and wait. The door flies open, and Ricky's dad glares at me. He's an ox, works in the metal factory, a welder or something. Hands like sausages and the rest of his body as thick. "Ben? Thought you were that other faggot."

I open my mouth but don't know what to say. Is he calling me gay? Or is there a gay kid who looks like me showing up on their doorstep?

"I'll get Rick." He shuts the door and leaves me out in the cold, which is fine because I'm sure inside is as dreary as it is out here. Rick's mom left when he was five. Hooked up with some guy from work and moved to Florida. His dad drank more and worked more, and Ricky spent a lot of time alone.

The door opens again and Ricky steps out. "Shit, Ben, what's up?" His eyes are bloodshot.

"Nothing. I finished work and wanted to stop over." I say this like it's something I do all the time, but the fact is I don't think I've hung out at Ricky's since like seventh grade. Before everything hit the fan between us.

"Yeah? Okay." He shuffles his feet and hugs himself.

I look over his shoulder, at the moldy siding and grimy window, and feel the anger I had for him lift. "I talked to John. He's got pins and shit."

"Kind of figured that. How is he?"

"Sounded pretty shitty."

Ricky shrugs.

Shit, if that's all I'm going to get, I'm just going to say it. "I want to know about Trevor."

"What do you mean?" His eyes draw down to slits.

Now it's my turn to shrug.

Ricky looks away. "Shit changed is all."

"Like overnight. What happened?"

He turns back to me. "I told you. He's good with a camera, and we needed someone with what O. P. is looking for."

"Yeah, but it's Trevor. You *hate* Trevor."

He turns away again. "Not anymore."

"No shit? So what changed? Because we all hated Trevor because of what he did, and then we stopped hanging out and now we're *all* together again, and . . ." I run out of steam.

"Jesus, Benny! You okay?"

I believed I was. I thought I could come over and ask about Trevor. Have an honest conversation about what I've been thinking. Instead, I ask the first question that comes to mind. "Trevor been coming here a lot?"

Ricky scowls. "Yeah. Before we go to his house to work on the footage. Why?"

"That all?"

"Yeah, that's all!" Ricky moves closer to me, and as he does, I see him differently. I don't know why, but what rolls inside my brain are the rumors about Trevor. But they surround Ricky now.

"Everything cool? You good?"

Ricky nods. "Why wouldn't I be good? All is as planned."

"Yeah, but is it? I mean, not exactly, right? What about John?"

Ricky looks at me for a long moment and then away. "Benny, you know shit never works out exactly from paper to the real deal."

Do I ever.

"It's going good enough, right?"

"How? John might lose his scholarship and we're not getting paid for the dare that caused the injury. You haven't explained what's what with Trevor or what's going on with you. Don't act as if everything's fine. I know that game too well."

Ricky's face pulls back. "Jesus, Benny, unleash much?"

"Fuck you! If you can't even talk to me, forget it. I won't bother to help with John. And you know he's going to need some serious coaxing."

"Benny, come on." Ricky comes all the way down the steps. "Lighten up."

I stare. I don't in any way go along with his shit. I've done enough.

"Fine. This is like therapy." He pauses. "First, John will go along if he needs the money. He'll understand how the contract works now, and we'll be fine."

I interrupt. "Which he and I both need copies of."

Ricky frowns. "They're inside. I swear. But I'm not going in to get them. Not with Dad."

"All right."

"Speaking of which, he keeps saying to 'get ready for being eighteen.' Whatever the fuck that means. I swear, he'd throw me out right now if he could." He rubs his face. "And I agreed last night to set something up with O. P. Remember? Or were you too busy with Chantel?"

I blush and Ricky jabs my side. "Keep going, I was starting to like you again."

He shakes his head. "We'll get paid, don't worry. We had one mishap. We'll be more careful. I don't know if it will be enough to cover John's scholarship if he can't play. But one, we don't know if that's the case, and two, that wasn't really the plan from the start. He didn't have to do anything he didn't want to."

I could argue this but don't. "And Trevor?"

Ricky looks back at his house and then at me. "You ever wish you lived somewhere else?"

I laugh at the irony.

"What?"

I explain and Ricky shakes his head. "Ben, I'm sorry."

"I know, but come on and finish your point about Trevor. I'm freezing my ass off."

He nods. "Right now I need to get away from here. And he's got no one. It works. You know?"

I don't. He admitted to using the kid, but I'm not going to

argue because it's not as if I woke up with Chantel and took her to breakfast. "It works because you have a home away from home? Or because you have that and certain company?"

Ricky glares at me like he wants to punch me more than he does his father.

"I'm only asking, not judging."

He turns from me. "Honestly, it's both. I don't know what it means. I'm in a strange place in my life, and the kid I hated for so long is helping me through. I don't know what else to say."

"You don't need to say anything. That was fine." I clasp his shoulder. "Thanks, Rick. Be you. I really don't care."

He frowns.

"I'm still down with what we're doing."

Ricky shifts. "Yeah? Why is that?"

Now I turn away and the memories flood back. "You remember all the pranks we used to pull? On substitutes? Teachers? Camp counselors? And then . . ."

"I don't think any of us forgets that last one."

"You know what I mean, everything before the shit hit the fan."

"Of course I do? Why?"

"Even after the prank with the camera in the bathroom, I still wanted to do stupid shit like that. I would have kept up with you, but my dad squashed that."

"So what's your point? You trying to get back at your dad?"

I dig deeper into my pockets, wanting to get this point across before my teeth start chattering. "No, not that. I wanted to reclaim that feeling. That rush. I missed it. I didn't know I did until after we surfed. Later, watching that video, thinking about it, shit, I felt so goddamn alive."

Ricky reaches out, and we embrace. He claps my back. "Knowing that, I guarantee we're going to be fine, Benny."

I hug him back and hope like hell I did the right thing.

CHAPTER 14

My parents have narrowed down their selection of apartments to three, and I have to go see the last one this afternoon. It better have more to offer than crack-dealing neighbors and a backyard surrounded by broken fences and piles of garbage. "We need to cut costs, my dear," Mom said, after the last visit to the ghetto.

She has a point, but still, it's more than dollars and cents. Right?

But that's the same question I had after I read the contract. So maybe I'm wrong.

I step into physics, and it seems as if we're continuing a theme here. On the board is written: *Newton's Third Law: For every action there is an equal and opposite reaction.* The words are more like something out of a fortune cookie than a scientific law. Still, maybe I should pay more attention in here.

In English we continue reading *The Count of Monte Cristo.* The unabridged version. So the movie won't even help.

In econ we define a series of terms that sound as exciting as white paint: *diminishing marginal utility, marginal costs, price elasticity of supply.* I might try out some of these with Chuck, see if he needs to know any of this shit to actually run a business. Although, he may not be the best example to ask.

In calculus I realize that I could figure out an answer to all of my problems by using all that I haven't learned. I can graph what I'm supposed to know along with what I actually do, and make a best guess for how this will end up.

I can't wait for my interim report. I may actually be that kid who waits for the mail the day it goes home, so I can keep the damn thing from my parents.

John and I are heading out when a group of basketball players pass. They're all tall, like John, and now with swagger, as the season is getting underway. One of them taps John's cast as he passes and says, "Thanks, man." He laughs, and the rest of the team cracks up.

John watches them go and looks as if they've stolen his spine.

"You okay?"

"Not with my scholarship on hold until after I get this off." He holds up the cast like it's a diseased limb. "My dad's ready to kill me. Like seriously, with a gun. Says he doesn't know how I could do this, or how he'll pay for college. Not like my grades are good."

"Let's hope there's enough cash from these dares so you can tell him where to stick it."

"Yeah, I hear you. But it'll take a lot of money for that. He's an enormous asshole."

We crack up, and Ricky and Trevor round the corner.

"Ben, John, it's time," Ricky says, like some pregnant wife might to her husband.

"Great, I'll get the hot water," I say, but no one else gets the joke. Or they do and realize it's lame.

"Benny, you ready for this?" Ricky's tone is stern, and I understand he's scared. He wasn't thrilled with this idea when I pitched it to him. But when I connected it to keeping us safe so the money could keep coming in, he backed off.

I wave. "Yeah. I'll be fine."

"I think you may be underestimating him," Trevor says.

"Thanks, Trev." I stalk down the hall to McNeil's, the guys behind me. His secretary whisks us in, and we sit like before.

"So, gentlemen, we meet again." McNeil's eyes hover over each of us. They linger on Trevor. "Were you here last time, Mr. Culin?"

"Of course, sir. I'm sorry if I don't stick out."

McNeil's expression speaks volumes about how much Trevor sticks out, but he lets it pass. "Mr. Forrest, how's the wing? What's the prognosis?"

John touches his cast. "Six weeks and then they'll re-evaluate."

"That's most of the season. What about your scholarship to State?"

John looks down and shrugs.

"I am so sorry to hear that, John. It will work out. Just watch." McNeil adjusts his seat. "So what's the news?"

Ricky turns to me. "Ben?"

I clear my throat. "Mr. McNeil, we believe that Jesse Holmes and his friends are the group completing the stunts."

McNeil's face tightens and his eyes go cold. "On what basis do you make this claim?"

"We've talked to kids, at your request, and their names kept coming up. Then we reviewed the footage over and over. If you look, the three guys in the videos look a lot like Jesse Holmes, Chris Carsdale, and Danny Blackman." There, I've said it, I've spun the lie that should, at minimum, produce the shadow of suspicion we can operate under.

McNeil sits back in his chair and presses his hands to his face, as if in prayer. I swallow and feel lightheaded.

"If this theory of yours is true, wouldn't a whole host of students have something to gain by turning them in? Any of our baseball players, or track stars in Danny's case? Really, anyone with a vendetta or an inclination to see them suffer." McNeil stares at us.

"I hadn't considered that," I say, "but maybe?"

McNeil opens his mouth, but Trevor cuts him off. "Even though all of what you said may be true, that doesn't mean it's not occurring."

McNeil looks at Trevor, and his disdain is visible. "Logic would dictate, yes."

Deep breaths, lots of deep breaths. *It's going to be fine.*

McNeil sits up. "Thank you, boys. You've at least given me an avenue to consider. If you hear any more, you know where to find me."

We all nod and say thanks, and then file into the hall.

Ricky looks at me. "So what do you think? What's going to happen?"

I completely ignore Newton's Third law, and focus on the first two. "We set that ball in motion. The best thing we can do is stay out of its way and let it run its course."

—

"There's my little brother." Ginny looks up from her laptop. Mom asked her to come home to see this last apartment. And like the dutiful child she is, she obliged.

"Hey, Ginny." I wave and move toward the stairs to head up to my room, but my mother bounds in.

"I thought I heard you. Great, let's head to the showing."

I feel like sitting down on the floor and not moving, making them pick me up and carry me to the car. Instead I say, "Oh, right," dump my bag, and head back out the door.

Ginny catches up to me and puts an arm around my shoulder. "We're set for the interview, right?"

I nod and do not look at her. "Yeah. Tomorrow night."

She squeezes me. It's an odd sensation.

"Awesome. There's a bunch of us following you now."

My insides go cold, and I turn around to check for Mom. She's back at the house locking up. "Keep it down, will you? Shit."

"Chill, Benny boy. I won't blow your cover." Ginny says, and I feel worse than before. I only mentioned the interview once, to Ricky and Trevor, while we were all drunk.

We pile in, Ginny taking shotgun, which is fine by me. Mom and Ginny chat it up and I start texting: **Interview with Ginny. Tomorrow @ 10 p.m.**

Ricky replies: **Is this what you wanted Trevor to record?**

"He remembered?" I say out loud, and my mother and Ginny turn and look at me. "Nothing. Talking to myself." Mom frowns and Ginny shakes her head, but they pick up the conversation again. I text back: **Yeah. What about our meeting with O. P.?**

You're not working tonight, right?

Right.

Tonight @ Trev's. Bring John.

Shit, he actually did it. **K.**

I tuck my phone away and look up. I look again. I know this street. There are nice houses with lawns that have gardeners tend to them. What are we doing here? As I'm about to ask, Mom turns the bend and the spread of condos emerges.

"Here we are," Mom declares in that singsong voice.

"Aren't these out of our price range?" I slump through the front seats to get a better look.

"They were, but one just came on the market at a reasonable price. I think someone may have died in it."

"Eww, gross." Ginny recoils.

"What? It's not like you'll be here much." Mom looks at Ginny. Then at me. "Either of you. Soon it will be only summers. And then, not even." She starts crying, and Ginny has to grab the wheel so we don't crash. Ginny guides Mom into a parking spot and she collects herself. "Follow me."

If someone didn't die in here, they should have killed themselves. It's heinous. Wallpaper everywhere. And all floral print, big pink and purple. The carpet is raspberry and the air feels like it's being pumped in from some meth lab.

Mom twirls. "It's bigger than the pictures make it seem." She goes up to the second floor. "Ooo, there's a fireplace up here, too."

"Probably burned the corpse in it." My sister looks at me all wide-eyed.

"What a nightmare."

"Yeah, you may need to come visit me more often," Ginny says.

More like *ever*. Ginny has never had me come stay with her. "Right. Because we do that."

She frowns. "Ben, don't be a shit. You weren't old enough before. You're going to college next year." She tilts her head. "Where are you going, by the way?"

I have no idea. Haven't signed up for my second round with the SATs, and I think my GPA is at an all-time low. "Still narrowing it down."

"Let me know if I can help."

I don't understand why she's being so nice. No, shit, yes I do. The interview. She's using me. "Right, like with the interview?"

She narrows her eyes. "Ben, it's not like that."

"Really? How?"

"It's mutually beneficial. I get my data, and if you use the recording correctly, it could help you get exposure. Word will spread."

"Did you see how many hits we got for our last stunt?"

She doesn't answer.

"Exactly. More than the kids who go to your school."

"Is that really the entire point, Ben? How many hits? How many follows?" Ginny steps closer, uncomfortably close.

Part of me feels like a kid again and wants to yank her hair and run away. Another part is frightened by how old she seems. How smart.

"Benny, Ginny, get up here and see this view."

We stare at each other for a second and then take the stairs up to Mom. She's before a wall of windows that overlook the rest of the development. "Look," she says.

Ginny and I join her and take in the scene. The condo is on the back side of the property, which is against a hill that slopes down to the valley. From here, the view of trees is impressive. I can imagine the dashes of yellow and orange and red of fall, which are now scattered on the ground. But what catches my attention are the properties between the condo and the far off hills. I can see both Chantel's and Trevor's homes from here.

"Breathtaking, isn't it?"

I nod and Ginny mutters something.

My mother pulls us to her. "Welcome home, kids. Welcome home."

—

John and I get out of the Jeep and stare at Trevor's mansion.

"It's weird, huh?" John says,

"His house? I kind of like it."

"No, not that. His house is awesome. But the fact that we're here, going inside, not egging it?"

He's got a point. We've been dropping eggs on this house for years at Ricky's request. And now Ricky's inside with Trevor. I don't think *weird* quite covers this situation.

We walk up and ring the bell. Trevor answers. "Hey, we're all set. Come on in."

After we hang our coats on the rack and kick our shoes onto the mat, we follow Trevor through his open-floor plan, marble, hardwood, stainless steel masterpiece of a home to his bedroom tucked into the far wing. Ricky's sitting at one of three desks covered in computers and editing equipment, looking very comfortable.

"Hey, guys. We're all set with FaceTime, just need to call O. P."

Trevor has his iPad connected to three other monitors so we all have our own view. I sit. "You have his number?"

"Yeah, the one-eight-hundred one."

There goes tracing his location, unless any of the technology in here can make it happen.

"Call him," John says with a nice authority to his voice.

It's good to hear that after everything he's been through. Shit! We haven't told him about the payment. One really deep breath.

"Right." Trevor sits and makes the call. In a moment, all of our screens display Ricky in large profile, and in the upper corner, a guy in his midthirties wearing a baseball hat.

"O. P., is that you?" Ricky sounds like a little kid talking to a mall Santa.

"And you are Ricky, I presume?" His voice is light, almost jolly.

"Yup, it's me." Ricky continues like nothing about this is off. "Thanks for talking to us. We wanted a face-to-face because of how crazy things are going."

"Things look very good on my end. Lots of new hits from this marketing campaign."

"Right, right. Sure that makes sense. But as you know, John broke his arm and that's going to give him some problems playing basketball in the future." Ricky pauses and sneaks a glance at John. "And of course, because of that, we didn't get paid."

"What?" John's voice is cutting. "What did he just say?"

He's asking me, but I don't know what to say. I give him the universal "in a minute" sign and he grinds his teeth.

"There are lots of other games to play," O. P. says.

John coughs and kicks Ricky's chair. This is not going to end well.

"Of course, but you see, he's got a scholarship, and now, maybe not."

O. P. moves around onscreen, adjusting his position. He blurs but then becomes clear again. "What's your point?"

If I knew O. P. in the real world I'd want to kick his ass. He's very obviously a dick. Ricky takes a deep breath, and I wait for him to tear into this piece of shit.

"My point is that we'd like to be able to make enough money to take care of John's education in case he loses that scholarship."

O. P. stills for a moment and then laughs and laughs, the sound echoing throughout Trevor's bedroom. John, Trevor, and I all look at one another, but Ricky keeps his eyes on the screen and waits. He should have hung up already.

"I can't make that promise. You get what the contract stipulates, not a cent more. Remember, this is business. If you don't like the terms, too bad, you signed. If you renege on your obligation, you owe me all the money you've earned."

John looks at me again and I shrug. I didn't read that, but apparently Ricky and Trevor did because Ricky isn't raising holy hell and Trev's staring ahead. But Trev does that, regardless.

Ricky swallows. "I understand that. I guess we need to know if the next dare will be something that John will be able to complete with his injury."

O. P. sighs, like an exasperated parent. "Again, not my problem. The other half of the deal—since you seem to need the reminder—is that you *all* complete the dare that I send to you. Can't have any of you ditching because you're scared and then squealing about all this."

"We wouldn't think of that."

"Good. Anything else I can help you with?"

Ricky shakes his head. "Not unless you have the next dare ready?"

"I do, but check your email tomorrow." O. P. hangs up.

I stare at my screen, now blank except for Ricky's face, still staring ahead. I have no doubt that he would love for us all to leave and not dissect what we heard. Normally, I might give him his space, but shit just got real and we need to talk.

"Fuck this, I'm out." John stands.

"What?" I ask. "No, sit down, hold up a minute."

John growls. "When were you planning on telling me we didn't get paid? Huh?" He looks at me and then around the room. "You still want to do *business* with that asshole after he pulls shit like that?"

"John, you heard what he said. It's all of us or nothing. It's in the contract," I say, aware that I don't know where to find the clause, even if I had the thing in front of me.

"Yeah, I heard every word from that creepy ass. No wonder you found him on Craigslist."

Ricky speaks. "We'll get you that money. I promise." He looks at me and Trevor. "All of us will get paid what we deserve. Please don't bail on us, John. Because hanging in there sends him a giant 'Fuck you'! You feel me?"

John takes a long moment, but he nods. It's curt, but it's there. He's still with us.

CHAPTER 15

Work sucked tonight. Everyone was frenzied because of all the orders. I barely saw Alexia, much less had any opportunity to speak with her. Not that I'd know what to say, but I feel like I have to. What's happening between her and Jesse isn't all right. No, it's awful. But maybe throwing him under the bus will do some good, not that McNeil dragged him into his office or anything. At least not that I've heard.

And now . . .

"Jesus, Ben!" Ginny meets me at the door as I walk in. John, Ricky, and Trevor are on the couch.

"What?"

"We've been waiting for an hour."

I hang up my coat. "Hey, you asked to interview us, not the other way around."

Ginny glares at me but says nothing.

I head over. "What's up, guys?"

"Nuthin', just waiting on you," Ricky says, and he's relaxed. In fact, they all are, chilling on my couch together. I think something about seeing what a tool O. P. is changed something here. Or, I could just have a very comfortable couch.

"I'll be right back."

Dad's in the kitchen, cracking a beer. He smiles when he sees me. "Hey, it's nice that you're helping out your sister."

I grab a soda and take a swig. "No problem." I have no idea what Ginny told him we're doing, but he seems fine with it. "Everything cool at work?" It's a lame question, but I have to ask.

He sips his beer and shakes his head. "No. Not even close. But that's my problem, Benny. Don't you worry."

I nod and silence fills around us. "I gotta go before Ricky tries to put moves on Ginny."

"Remind that idiot that I'm upstairs."

"Will do."

Back in the living room, Trevor has mounted the camera and Ginny has a notebook on her lap. I sit in the recliner next to the guys. "As soon as Trevor is ready, we'll get down to the questions." Ginny sighs. "But first, I want to thank you. What you guys are doing is insane, but also a perfect example of what we're studying."

The guys mumble "no problem," but Ricky looks less comfortable than before.

"So, I've got questions, but feel free to talk about whatever comes to mind. I'm going to take notes and record the audio, but Trevor, you'll give me a copy of the video, right?"

"Sure." Trevor's voice has no emotion.

Ginny looks around. "You ready?"

Trevor answers by pointing to the red bulb, indicating that he's recording.

Ginny turns on the digital recorder and clears her throat.

"Tonight, October, 23rd, I am interviewing the Get Out There Daredevil Crew."

The guys smile at this, even Ricky, and I feel a wave of something unnamable pass over me. It's not nausea or déjà vu, but some weird sense of importance at her giving us a name.

"Could one of you tell me how this all began?"

Ricky sits up. "It was my idea. I wanted to have fun during my senior year, and this seemed like a great way."

Ginny looks down at her notes, but it doesn't seem like she's reading them.

"Okay, so how did you get the rest of these guys on board? What you're doing is kind of dangerous."

John rubs his cast and Ricky nods. "Right. It is. But we've been friends forever, and the guys were happy to go along. And then after the first dare was a success, it snowballed."

I feel sweat behind my knees.

"Interesting, you said it was a dare. Who dared you, and can you explain what you mean by *snowballed*?"

John sits up. "We're making money now. We did the one to see if we could make a splash. Which we did. Because of that, Ricky got some deal worked out, and now we're making cash because we complete one of the dares from the list this guy gives us."

Ricky scowls. Sweat breaks out across my back, and I take a few deep breaths.

"Really? Now *that's* interesting. So someone is paying you to do this. Please explain."

John beams. He, too, always liked my sister. "You see, it's like this, Ricky got this contract and we all signed it, so . . ."

"It's not something we can discuss." Ricky's face has resumed its natural color.

We all turn to him.

"It's confidential. I'm sure you understand," he says to Ginny.

Ginny nods and looks back at her notes. "Do you have any input on these dares, then?"

Ricky nods. "Sure. Like John said, we pick them from a list."

"Is this list something you created before you started?"

"No." The way Ricky says the word, we all shift. I want to take off my shirt I'm so damned hot. This is not going well. I'm not sure if John or Trevor can tell, but Ricky can, and that's all that matters.

"So the list comes from your sponsor. The guy behind Get Out There Adventure? Who is he?"

"That's also confidential."

Ginny shoots me a quick look. Her eyes seem to search my face, but I'm not sure what she's looking for.

"Okay. So you complete these dares from a list provided to you from an unnamed sponsor, and you are contractually obligated to complete them? Is that correct?" This time Ginny looks right at Ricky and doesn't bother to include us.

Ricky smiles his big-toothed grin. "Yes."

"Is it safe then to say then that you all feel compelled to complete the dares, even if you don't want to?" Now she turns to John.

He doesn't answer, but stares at the floor.

"No one has to do anything they don't want to." Ricky leans toward Ginny.

"How is that true if you all signed a contract?"

Ricky's eyes swim in his head and a tiny laugh emerges from behind the camera. We all look over, but Trevor stays tucked away behind the tripod.

Ricky's face is red now, and he stares at me like he'd like to rip my throat out. I feel an I-told-you-so moment coming, but with the tension that's building, that may not be the best idea.

Ginny repeats the question and is pressing her notebook so hard she's dented the spine.

John continues to stare at the ground. I'm drenched, trying not to hyperventilate, and I think my phone just vibrated with a text.

Ricky looks away.

"How about this one? Why are you willing to risk your life for this?" Ginny's voice is calm, but her hands shake.

Watching her, I understand why she wanted this interview. *This* is the question she wants answered. Her interview is for her psychology class. *Why are we willing to take it this far?* Shit, it's a good question. Is it the legacy? The money? Because we have to? But do we? What *would* happen if we didn't? We wouldn't get paid. That's it. But then our story would go away, the one we're creating behind the scenes. Who would we be then? I close my eyes and feel the bathroom calling.

Ricky stands up. "No one's died, or come even close."

Ginny stands, too. "So what's next? Is it less risky than the other dares? Are you playing it safe?"

Ricky steps closer to her. "We'll have an ambulance on standby. Stay tuned." He turns and walks out the door without even closing it.

The cold night air whips in like the morning dissolving a dream. We all blink and look around. Trevor powers off the camera. "Well done." He quickly packs up his equipment and follows Ricky's path, but at least has the courtesy to close the door.

In the silence that follows, we all look our separate ways. I reach into my pocket as Ginny turns to me.

"What have you gotten yourself into, Benny?"

I look down at my phone. It's a text from Chantel: **Alexia. Again.**

I look up and answer with more honesty than Ginny can probably comprehend. "I have no idea."

CHAPTER 16

There's a witch and a vampire on my doorstep, and they yell and I fill their bags. I used to love Halloween. Especially in my neighborhood. John, Ricky, and I would get together and hit every house. In middle school we started egging and using shaving cream. It was fun, but not as much as that rush of all that candy and how cool it was to be somebody else. I shut the door and Dad's standing in the hall.

"Everything okay, Benny?" He steps closer.

"Yeah, yeah, I was lost in my head. You know?" I force a little laugh and that brings a smile to his face.

"Do I ever. These days? It's all I do."

Dad lost his job because he refused the transfer; we move in a few days; yesterday my interim came home; today is Halloween and our next dare. I've had to begin packing up my childhood; my grades are in the toilet; and the dare we're about to complete, Ricky says it's going to get us arrested or killed. For real.

And there's Alexia. It's so sad, I don't know if I'm more angry or frustrated or ashamed. She called Chantel crying, and when Chantel went to her house, Alexia had the same kind of bruises I saw around her wrist up around her bicep. Jesse was angry, said he was being set up over the dares, took it out on her. When Chantel told me that, I almost choked. It's my fault this happened. It was my idea to pin it on Jesse. Sometimes I think I have good ideas, and then I do shit like this, and I realize how much I don't understand.

I feel like going up to my room, climbing into one of the boxes and sealing myself off from my life. But I say, "It's okay, Dad. We'll get through this."

"Yeah, I guess," he says, "but I wanted to retire here. In this house." His eyes are filled and I have to look away. "Days like this, the kids. Reminds me of you and Ginny growing up. God, it was so much fun."

I feel like I've been kicked in the ribs, but the doorbell rings again, and I look at Dad.

He runs a hand over his head. "I'll be okay, I promise."

"I know." But I don't. I'm heading out to potentially bring him more headache.

I open the door, take care of the kids, and then say good-bye to Dad, who's leaning against the wall, half-dazed. He waves, and I take the steps and notice the pumpkin. It's fake, plugged into the socket, dimly burning in the fading daylight.

—

I watch the street, notice the parents who are out, and wonder how we're going to get behind the gym without being seen. Between them and the security cameras on each corner, we need to skirt along the edge and haul ass. John's quiet and seems to be thinking the same as me. I point to a house next to the building.

The lights are off. John nods and I move like I know what the hell I'm doing.

I open the metal gate and it creaks. John shuts it behind us and I walk onto the porch, digging in my pocket as if looking for my key. The storm door bumps behind us and my heart pounds in my ears.

"Ben, what are we doing?"

"Turn around and tell me if you see any of those parents watching us."

The floorboards creak under John's feet and I cringe. But there's no light or noise from inside, and a second later John whispers, "We're good."

I take a deep breath. "Count to five and then head to the backyard. We'll hop the fence."

"'K. One, two, three . . ."

While John counts, I take two more steadying breaths. I should have stayed home with my parents and enjoyed our last Halloween in the house.

"Five."

We move together, down the steps and to the back. The front door pops loudly, but we're already halfway to the back. John keeps moving and heads to the far corner, and even with a cast, easily vaults over the low fence and disappears in the shadows. I follow and land next to him. We scramble to a tree twenty yards away, and it feels like we're crossing enemy lines in some war.

We sit and listen. I wait for someone to come out of the house yelling at us, or for the cops to roll up. Nothing happens. The night grows darker. John flicks the wrist on his broken arm as if looking for a watch.

"Shit. I can't wait for this to get cut off. What time is it?"

"I don't know."

John looks at me for a long moment, to the point that it's uncomfortable.

"What? I don't wear a watch."

He looks away. "That's not it." He pauses, looks around. "What are we doing? And don't tell me the next dare, I know that. I mean, big picture. Yeah, I need the money and all, but there's no way we're pulling that off. And I'm starting to think this whole legacy bullshit is just that. What does it matter what kids at school think of us when we're gone? They sure as shit don't think much of us now."

I shake my head and stare into the dark. That was a lot. But it was also exactly what I've been thinking for a while. "But don't you like the dares? Just them, by themselves."

"I guess. It's like it was before with Ricky. But you know how that ended, so it's hard to say they make all of that go away? Is that how it is for you?"

This is so much like the conversation I had with Ricky, I give the same answer. "The rush, like when we were kids. I love it. I'm not gonna lie. But I hope it's different this time. What else can I do?"

John nods. "I get it. I'm not there with you. But I am here."

"Good, you're here." Ricky's voice comes out of the trees, and I sink into John before I realize who's spoken. Ricky emerges with Trevor, who's got his laptop out and is intently working on what he sees on his screen.

"Shit, you scared me!" I sit up and act calm, but my heart is thudding.

Ricky ignores me and turns to Trevor. "How long?"

Trevor scrunches his face. "Two minutes, give or take."

Ricky's eyes play over the screen, and it's difficult to tell if he likes what he sees. He turns to us. "In about two minutes, the school alarm is going to go off. Before that happens, we need to haul ass over to the cemetery. This will buy us a half hour, tops, and we'll need all that time."

"What? Why?" My voice sounds like a small child's.

"Without this distraction, we'll get caught in the cemetery. Trevor's hacked into the system."

"That's insane. You said this could be illegal, but are you trying to get caught?" John's voice is much stronger than mine.

Ricky's jaw tightens. "He's under McNeil's account. It will look like the ass accidentally scheduled a fire drill when they go and investigate."

My brain scrambles with all that's going on. What we're doing *is* illegal. And if whatever we're about to do requires a distraction large enough to pull police and fire crews away from would-be vandals prowling town, there's no way it can be good.

The alarm sounds. Trevor snaps his laptop closed and slides it into the bag around his shoulder. "We should run."

And we do. We fly over the back trails that the cross-country kids use and make our way to the cemetery in no time. Red and blue lights flash out of the entrance and sirens wail, all heading away from where we came. We move down the hill and into the back clearing of the cemetery, where they haven't buried anyone. Yet.

My heart is pounding and my legs are wobbly and my mouth is dry.

"Over here." Ricky motions us over to a wall of overgrown ivy. He pulls back a section, like a curtain, and behind it is a catapult.

Every year the physics class builds these as a project for extra credit. I didn't bother to take the opportunity. They're for tomorrow when kids bring in pumpkins for the annual pumpkin launch. The catapult that throws the pumpkin the farthest wins.

"We have to wheel it out." Ricky points to the dolly beneath it.

He and I take hold and haul the sucker. John shakes his head, and Trevor keeps at his computer.

"Right here," Ricky says, and two orange spray-painted X's are visible.

We set the back edge of the catapult on them and stand aside. I stare at the contraption and consider its function. This is a good one, possibly the best. It's downright medieval looking and the counterweight is enormous.

I peer into the dark and think I see something light-colored in the distance. Then lights flood on.

John and I hunker down.

"I rigged these." Ricky points up to the trees where ten workshop lamps shine down. Four on the catapult. Two on the space just beyond, and four on the light-colored space I saw: hay bales. "They run off a lead cord from the house over there. Let's hope they don't blow a fuse." He laughs, and is the only one doing so. "I had the same guys who built the ramps drag in all this. What do you think?"

It's impressive. The work is intricate and the plan beautifully orchestrated. The sirens are audible in the distance and the entire scene has a sense of urgency that will certainly translate to the film. I refuse to say any of this. "What the fuck are we doing?"

"Really, Benny? You haven't figured this out?" He bends over and unzips a black bag that must have been sitting here. He pulls out a helmet, and affixed to the top is a camera. He hands it to me. "We're going for a ride. And you are first."

I take the helmet, not because I want to, but because I have no choice. Or do I? "Ricky, seriously?"

He nods. "What?"

I wave my arms around. "All this. How much did you tell O. P.? Because there's no way he would come up with this on his own. He is either from this town or this is your idea."

John lets out a low groan at my side. Trevor keeps checking the laptop.

"Got me. I helped with this." Ricky puts up his hands. "Hear me out."

I set down the helmet and cross my arms over my chest. "Go ahead."

"The dare he sent was nothing really ballsy. And because we're trying to make up for lost ground, I decided I'd give my two cents for something that will draw the views." He looks back at the catapult. "I think this should do it."

He's right, this would get me to watch. But still. "Even after realizing how much of a douche O. P. is, you helped him."

"Ben, this is business, you should understand that." He looks at John. "I promised you that I'd make this right. Here's how. What's wrong?"

I know what John's thinking because we talked about it, so I speak up. "It isn't about the dare, the fun, or the legacy anymore, is it? It's only about the cash for you."

Ricky looks like I've spit in his face. He stoops down and picks up the helmet. "Ben, you know me well enough. I dig this shit more than anyone. So for me, it's always about the thrill. I still believe in the legacy. I believe that we can walk away from this shithole as gods." He puts the helmet back in my hands. The weight is significant. "But, yeah, it's *also* about the money. And considering things for all of us, that's not a bad place to be."

I hold his gaze for a moment and take a deep breath. "Help me clip this thing."

"But first, shirts. Guys, put 'em on. And then these." Ricky moves to the bag and holds up black latex gloves. "We have to cover John's cast, so we all need to wear them."

John looks at his cast and shakes his head. We exchange a quick look, collect our gear, and put it all on. When I pick the helmet back up, my hands are shaking. Ricky is directing to Trev, who has the camera on his shoulder. I turn and John helps buckle his helmet. Ricky begins.

"Since it is Halloween, we have a special treat for you, our dear audience. You will get split screen footage of each launch. The helmet cam and our full screen." Trevor's camera light falls on me. I feel like a deer standing in the middle of the road.

"Of course, tonight's dare is brought to you by Get Out There Adventure, but also, by Pizza and More." Ricky twirls his hand and I oblige by slowly spinning for the camera. Chuck's logo is on the front and Ginny's DAREDEVIL CREW is on the back. "So sit back and enjoy, all you ghouls. Here we go."

Ricky steps quickly to me and my fear takes over. I say, "This is insane. If I don't hit the target . . ."

"No more talking. We've had our time for that." He gets close to my face. "You can hear those sirens, right? As soon as they go off, we'd better kill these lights, or they'll be headed our way. Got it?"

I breathe and nod.

"Besides, this should earn you twenty-five hundred. You cool with that?"

I do the math. *Really? 10,000 hits?*

Ricky guides me to the bucket, and I hesitate for a second but then lay inside. It's wooden and sticks into my back and ribs, but

I don't say a word. "And now the helmet cam." Ricky flips a switch and there's an audible hum above my forehead. "Good luck." He pats my shoulder and returns to his narration.

I have no idea what he's saying, but can hear the murmur of his voice. My heart is pounding in my head so severely, I might hurl. I can see the target from here and I can guess that it's about 200 feet. I weigh 150 pounds. How much force is needed to get me from here to there? Fuck, I really should give Newton the credit he deserves. Every law applies right now.

"In three, two . . ."

I cross my arms over my chest and pray.

"One!"

There's a creak and a groan that sounds like an ancient vault being opened and my stomach drops into my spine. But then there's a sudden *whip*, followed by a *whoosh* and I'm airborne. I can see the ground and the trees and the lights, and in the distance, the shining cop cars. Ahead lies the hay, and it seems so far away. And my body is sinking and I'm not going to make it.

I scream.

I don't know what I'm saying. I may be crying, because I've only ever gone this fast in a car, and now I've got nothing to stop me but the ground. I'm not going to land on the hay. I'm going to hit the ground and break every bone in my body.

I'm steadily dropping, and I've stopped screaming and have accepted my punishment. It's almost peaceful to think this is over. I close my eyes and . . . I sink. Into the hay and then bounce. I roll onto my back and stare up at the lights in the trees. The guys are screaming louder than the sirens, and this feels better than sex with Chantel.

As the sensation washes over me, I also know we're all completely fucked, because if we've gone this far, there's no way out now.

—

The day after Halloween is All Saints' Day. I learned this last night while I was online, too wired to sleep. I think it's appropriate because someone must have saved our sorry asses. We managed to pull it off, again. And because it was bigger and more badass than the last it can only mean our trajectory is vaulting in a terrifying direction. Because of Ricky? Or because of O. P.?

Regardless of who's responsible, today we're all anyone is talking about. Ricky and Trevor managed to get the video edited and online before midnight, and the views have been rolling in nonstop. Ricky may be right about the money we're making. I hope so for John's sake. And he's right that I could use the money now. Dad not working is going to hurt.

But this buzz also sucks because I made a promise to myself to pay more attention after my interim came home. I kept it from my parents in the hope that it wouldn't matter, that I could turn things around. So now here I am, trying my ass off, but I don't really care that "mass in motion equals momentum." I pretty much learned that last night.

The dude in *Monte Cristo* is going to get out, eventually. "It's a foregone conclusion." At least that's what some smart girl in class said. It's too painful to read about him trying and failing and trying and failing. Really, great story line.

Econ means nothing to me and I've found a kid in calculus who I can cheat off. So, I'm done. It's kind of frightening how easy it is to give up right after swearing to myself that I'd do better.

—

"**You** didn't break anything, did you?" Ginny asks, and I frown at my phone.

"No, we all are fine, even John. The hay was softer than you'd think." I sit on my bed.

Ginny sighs. "That really isn't much of a comfort, Benny. I'm worried. What's next?"

Even if I knew I wouldn't tell her. "Don't know. But I'm sure you'll get some good details for your research."

"That's not the point and you know it. Can't you see that what you're doing is insane? Most of the stories I read, the interviews with teens who've done shit like you—played chicken in traffic, skied off rooftops, whatever—a lot of them don't make it. They end up dead."

I close my eyes and try not to envision what she's said, but of course I see my body in a heap on the pavement. "Shit, Ginny, thanks for the call. Anything else about my life you want to thrash?"

"I would if there was anything else to your life." She pauses. "How bad are your grades?"

"They're fine," I say through gritted teeth. I'm close to hanging up on her.

"Fine as in you could get into a state school, or fine as in you'll have fun with all the slackers at community college?"

"Jesus, Ginny, what's up your ass?"

"I don't know, Ben, what do you think? Dad lost his job, they essentially lost the house, and now you're trying to kill yourself." She chokes up, but I don't know which part does it to her.

"Ginny, it's not like that. What I'm doing has nothing to do with the other shit."

"Of course it does. You're too blind to see it. Have you checked how many followers you have on your website?"

"Huh?" My head rushes.

"Really, Benny, you don't know how to check on your followers?"

I didn't even know we had a site.

"Get online." The tear-choked voice is gone. Ginny has something to prove, so she's fine again.

I go to my computer and type in the address. It's a real basic page, the background all black. The only content is links to our YouTube videos and Twitter. None for Get Out There Adventure. That's weird. The most important feature is the countdown clock. It reads: TIME UNTIL THE NEXT DARE and displays 30 days, 20 hours, and 15 minutes.

"Look in the right corner, at the bottom," Ginny says.

The number is astounding. "More than eight thousand?"

The phone rumbles as Ginny adjusts it. "Ben, listen to me. This is becoming too big. You're going to get caught, probably arrested, maybe even kicked out of school."

"Not if I'm dead." I try to laugh, but my body seems to realize how inappropriate that was and won't.

Ginny stays silent.

"Sorry," I say.

"Yeah, you are. I wish you were a couple years older, you'd understand."

I could argue that she has no idea what she's talking about because she's never done anything as remotely cool as this. She's always read and studied and completed her projects ahead of time and received endless praise and awards. Not me. I tried that, and couldn't measure up. Besides, if I'm honest, I can admit that being a Goody Two-shoes blows. So these dares are my award.

When we're done and our names are synonymous with "badass," I can look back and say, "I did that." But for now, I've got nothing except some money, so arguing would be futile.

"Well, I'm not, so we'll see what happens in twenty-nine days."

"No, Benny. You've got to stop now."

"Answer me honestly. Do you want to stop your research now?"

"Benny, that's not fair, I know what you're trying to pull."

"Just answer. Come on."

It takes her a second, but she says, "No, I don't, but . . ."

"That's enough." I cut her off. "So don't ask me to stop what I have, what I'm enjoying."

She growls a frustrated sound. "But why? How can *this* be what you're into? You're Ben. Benny Bear."

"But I'm not. And you know it."

She sighs. "Promise me you'll be safe."

"I will."

We hang up and I stare at the countdown clock. That time will move regardless of what I do or what Ginny says. As it does, we'll march closer and closer to whatever's next. A chill runs up my spine at the thought. I'm less afraid of the unknown than I've ever been before. I spy my interim peeking out from beneath my books. I don't know if this is a positive or negative development.

CHAPTER 17

I sit in class and enjoy a little time zoning out. The school is still buzzing today, which is equally cool and unnerving. Ricky was right about the hits. We actually exceeded the ten thousand mark.

McNeil spent yesterday with the technology people and the fire department, probably checking on how the alarm went off. Today he's been with the cops.

And I'm moving tomorrow, which sucks. I've been too busy to think about it, or have avoided doing so. Either way, it's happening, and nothing I could learn in this moment is going to change that. It's all too much, so deep breathing won't settle me, but powering down and living inside my head should do the trick.

At the bell, I snap back and head into the hall and a surge of gossip. Something's up. People are looking at their phones and talking with animated gestures. It looks like something big went down. I haul ass to Ricky's locker. He's with Trevor, and they don't look relieved to see me.

"You heard?" Ricky says.

"No. But I can tell." I motion to the kids in the hall.

"No shit? Here." He thrusts Trev's phone at me, and I press PLAY on the video. Jesse Holmes, Chris Carsdale, and Danny Blackman are being led out of the school in handcuffs, each with a police officer guiding them. McNeil appears in the background, arms crossed, looking like he'd choke them out if he could.

"What the . . . ?" I don't finish. Don't need to.

"Guess McNeil took us seriously," Ricky says. "Rumor is they're charged with setting off the alarm. That and they found the catapult. Put two and two together, I guess."

"Plus our accusation." I whisper this, as if anyone is listening. But no one is paying attention to anything besides their own retelling of the story. This is going to go one of two ways. We're either going to get caught because whatever evidence they have is going to be scrutinized, and if we messed up at all, it's over. Or we're safe. They've got scapegoats.

But I also know what Jesse is capable of. We may prefer the police to him if he manages to think this through.

—

"What is up, Doc?" Chuck's voice knocks me back as I enter the shop.

He barrels over and I wince. He's way too happy for this to be good. "Do you have any idea how many customers I've had in here today looking for you?"

I'm confused. "What? Why would they want *me*?"

"Not *you*. They want to see the guy from the video. They think because I was mentioned as a sponsor the kid from the dare works here. My lunch crowd hasn't been that good in over a year."

I look over at the prep cooks and they nod, both their faces fatigued. "So you haven't heard?"

"Heard what?"

"Those guys were arrested. Guess they pulled the school's fire alarm as a distraction and stole that catapult."

Chuck squints and puts a hand to his forehead. "Shit, Doc. I thought these guys were on the up and up."

"I'm sorry, Chuck." There's no way for me to convey how much I truly mean those words without blowing my cover.

"Not your problem. You only did what I asked." He looks around. "Leave me alone. I need to figure out an alibi." He trudges to his office. I stare at the closed door for a second, but then look over at Alexia and dread my next move.

Of course I heard how she reacted. Horribly. Broke down in tears. Called McNeil a liar. Chantel calmed her down and I think they left school early, so I'm surprised she's here.

"Hey, Alexia," I say as I punch in. "How's it goin'?"

She shakes her head. Her face is puffy and her chin looks fragile, as if she might start crying any second.

"I'm sure Chuck won't care if you take off. We can pick up the slack."

Alexia shakes her head. "I'd rather be here than at home. My parents know and my dad's beyond pissed that I could 'date someone like that.'" She drops her voice to sound like her father and it's pretty spot on. She turns to me, her face a red-streaked mess. "Am I that much of an idiot, Ben?"

I start to answer but she continues.

"Because I just don't see it. Why would Jesse bother with any of that? It makes no sense."

I nod. "Yeah, you're right."

"And why would Chuck sponsor whoever those idiots are?" She throws down the stack of money she was sorting. "You don't know who they are, do you? You said Ricky just saw their first video, right?"

That's the lie we're going with, right? Shit. I didn't think I could feel worse. Wrong about that, and apparently, so much else. I grab the money. "Yeah. Weird, huh? Let me help."

Alexia sits on the stool and stares out the window while I organize the bills into separate piles and calculate the total.

She sighs when I finish and hand over the drop bag. "Thanks, Ben. This has been rough. This whole year."

"I know," I say.

She tilts her head. "Yeah, you would, I guess."

My throat clamps.

"You've been with Chantel a lot. She talks about me?"

Even though I thought she was going to say something else, this question brings no relief. "Little bit," I say.

She smiles like she's stoned, and I'm afraid for her well-being. "Yeah, friends are like that."

If I could be honest with her, we'd have one hell of an interesting conversation about friends. Me included. But I can't. I'm not even sure what she and Chantel are to each other. Same goes for Chantel and me. There was that one night at Danielle's and then really not much else.

More important is my question about *us*. Are we friends? I feel like I did what I did to help her. That's what friends do. But looking at Alexia now, that notion of saving her from him feels pretty stupid. But those bruises . . . and he's such an asshole. But if she doesn't see any of this, what good have I done?

—

Chuck wasn't bullshitting me. All night it was, "Hey, are you the kid from YouTube?"

Every time I shook my head and said, "No, he doesn't work there."

They all laughed and asked me if I was sure. I told them I was positive, but no one believed me. *Nervous* doesn't touch how I feel, and I could probably sell my own video on calming through breathing. My lungs are amazing.

Alexia did leave early, which I was glad to see; she needed the rest. But Chuck left early, too, so I have no idea what's what. Which is pretty much the rule of my life at the moment.

I pull into the driveway and my house is lit up, every light on. I can see my parents through the window, packing our stuff into giant cardboard boxes. I step in and the bright lights are worse.

"Hey, Benny," Dad says with no enthusiasm.

"Hey," I match his tone.

My mother walks in the room with an armful of newspapers and hugs me with her free arm. "We're going to get through this.

You only need to take care of your room." She looks me over. "How about you stay home from school tomorrow and finish up? The movers won't be here until the afternoon anyway." She kisses my cheek.

A day away from the madness sounds wonderful, except for the fact it comes with a hell of a price tag: my home. "Sounds good. I'll go get started."

"Okay," Mom says. I watch the two of them for a moment and head to my room.

I stand in the doorway and look around. I've got a lot of work ahead of me, but I plow into my bed and lie facedown. In spite of how much my mind is spinning, I start drifting off, but my cell vibrates stirring me back. I pull it from my pocket. Ricky: **We hit 15,000!!!** I don't know how to respond. It's awesome because the money is going to be fantastic, but after everything today it scares the shit out of me at the same time.

I roll off my bed and onto my desk chair, pull up our website. We've got over nine thousand followers now. I pull up my calendar and check November to see what I'm supposed to be paying attention to. Damn. The SAT is this Saturday. I haven't studied. At all. I rest my forehead against the desk lip and stare at my sneakers. I'm going to have to cram nonstop. But how? We're moving tomorrow, I'll be exhausted, and I don't even own a review book. There must be websites.

I look back at the screen and stare at the clock ticking. I've signed on for an entire year of this. My senior year is going to be nothing but eluding death and possibly the authorities. There's no evidence of us doing anything illegal. But is it only a matter of time? Has to be with what we did to Holmes and his crew. They'll be scouring for answers. Shit.

I look at our site again and am confused. I know you can make coin off YouTube, and we're certainly doing that or O. P. wouldn't be paying us. So where are the ads? Isn't that how it works?

I type in the web address for Get Out There and wait to be assaulted by ads linking to our videos, but the page looks exactly the same as the last time I saw it. Everything needed for outdoor adventure is a mouse click away.

But why no links to us? And honestly, what business pays a bunch of kids to thwart death? I need to talk with someone who could answer that question, but it's either Trevor or Ginny. Trevor's out, because I don't trust him not to go back to Ricky. Things are settled now, and I'd like to keep it that way. And I'm not calling Ginny. She'll tell me to stop. And at this point, even with the fear of Jesse Holmes or McNeil or the police, what would be the point of stopping?

Yup, we're sticking with Laws One and Two. We'll worry about Three later.

CHAPTER 18

I pull up outside John's and he ambles out, waves to me with his formerly busted hand, and the movement is off. I've been picking him up for the past two weeks, and ever since he got the cast off he's been trying to use his arm more. It's not pretty, and he hasn't said anything, but I'd put money on him losing that scholarship.

"Morning, Benny. Shit, it's cold."

"See, aren't you glad I moved so now you don't have to walk?"

He waves away the ridiculousness of my statement and I drive on.

"Hey, I think we can get our SAT scores next week."

My stomach drops. "What do you mean?"

"They're supposed to be posted in like two to three weeks, so, you know."

Right before Thanksgiving. Right before our next dare. Figures. The Writing and Critical Reading sections were easy except for the grammar. I don't remember learning any of that. The math shit on me. Truly. It felt like problem after problem was dropped right on my head. I should have known how to do everything, but because I never brushed up, it was all out of reach. I went home that afternoon and napped until I had to go to work. Mom thought I was sick.

"Great. Can't wait." I pull into the lot and park.

"Yeah, like you're concerned. I'm mildly retarded, and without ball . . ."

John stops short and I kill the engine. "Without ball you have more free time to mess up your life with me." I smile wide and fake.

"I think you're losing it, Benny."

"Of course I am."

"At least Jesse hasn't come after us. Or anyone else. Guess McNeil is staying tight-lipped and whatever Trev's doing must be working."

It's true. So far, so good. Even Chuck came out fine. Cops showed up, but all he had to say was, "I don't know why they mentioned me or where they got those shirts." They talked to each of us, too. Spent a lot of time with the cooks and Alexia. She said it was because she dates Jesse. Wanted to know who his enemies are. They only asked me how school was going.

We head inside and pass Alexia's locker. Chantel's with her. Jesse's there, too. He's flirting with Alexia, but Chantel's watching his every move. I call to Chantel, but she doesn't turn. Jesse shoots us a look like he's trying to read our minds.

"Cold. Benny, that's ice."

I shake my head. "It's not like that," I say with more force than is necessary. Probably because I'm trying to convince myself more than I'm answering John. Chantel was into me, but then she started protecting Alexia. At least I haven't seen her with any other guys. So there's that.

Ricky's at his locker with Trevor, who has his laptop out. We approach and he says, "Look."

The YouTube video begins and some guy steps back from the camera. He's with two other guys, dressed exactly like us, down to the masks and T-shirts. It's disorienting and feels like I'm watching some twin or that German word—doppelgänger? Why couldn't I remember a word like that for the SAT?

The guy in the video doesn't speak. He just points to his crew, and they all lift baseball bats and smack them into their palms. The camera pans to a mailbox and back to the twin for Ricky. He nods and the setup is clear.

The next scenes are of the car driving down Jasperg Lane, where we did our first dare, to the McMansion development over, where each of them is taking turns smashing every mailbox in it. My mouth goes dry. The video ends with a shot of the car racing away, baseball bats sticking out the windows.

The screen prompts to replay and we all stare.

"Copycats!" Ricky stamps his foot. "These assholes are going to ruin it for us."

"But we don't do stuff like that. It doesn't make any sense." John's voice is high and nasally.

"That's the point. They're trying to get us caught," Trevor says. "Holmes has been denying the charges up and down. Whoever did this wants to keep the cops busy and make us look bad."

I remember how Jesse stared at us as we walked by. Would he? Would he be smart enough to have this figured out? Would he be dumb enough to risk everything after being arrested?

The bell rings and Ricky sighs. "We'll figure this out. Somehow."

We all nod and head to class, not that much will get absorbed today.

—

In physics my teacher rambles on about the importance of equilibrium and stability. He talks about how in spite of the importance of balance, little changes to a system do not necessarily affect the equilibrium and sometimes are good because they cause the system to adjust and learn to help balance.

Econ and English are both filled with quizzes that I fail, and calculus is all about the rate of change.

Balance. Change. The story of events. Are these classes representing my life, or is my life somehow shot through them?

John and I enter the cafeteria into a chorus of angry talk. People are pissed. We slip through to our table. Trevor's got his laptop out and is mumbling. Ricky looks at his food but doesn't eat.

"They've killed our plan. When they find out it's us at the end of the year, it won't matter. Because of this they won't care about all the cool dares we performed," I say.

"No shit," Ricky says, adding, "so we need to figure out who they are and get them back."

John shifts in his seat and clears his throat but doesn't say anything.

"There might be a way." Trevor's voice is calm and clear. He turns the laptop toward us and taps the screen. "Check the comments."

We read the slew of anger.

"So what, Trev?" I say.

Trevor frowns and shakes his head. He's beyond our mental capacity. I wonder two things: what he scored on the SAT and how the hell he deals with Ricky? I love Rick, but he's got street smarts, period.

"It's not *what* they're writing, but *who isn't*." Trevor lets his words hang and for one of us to respond. We don't. He continues after a frustrated growl. "Think about it. All the kids on here are popular. Those mailboxes were all in front of homes with lots of money. These kids are pissed that someone—us—would do that to them. So the question is, who of the popular kids isn't chiming in?"

I get what he's saying, and think maybe Holmes isn't as put together as he seems. "Think about it. Whoever did this isn't that bright. They just took a huge risk. Do you think they'd be smart enough to hop on the comments and act as if they were victims or were pissed that their friends were?"

Trevor says, "Thank you, Ben."

Ricky leans back. "So you're saying somebody who's onto us did this?"

I go to say, "Possibly," but am cut off by John.

"The only people in this school messed up enough to do this

are Jesse and his friends. Trust me, I've seen plenty. We're nuts, but they belong in some home."

I forget at times that John is an athlete, or *was*, and so he knows that world more than any of us. And I remember all that has happened to Alexia and could not agree any more with him.

"Trust me. I know, too." Trevor's voice is more harsh than I've ever heard it. He and John share a glance, and then Trevor looks at Ricky and back at his computer. "We need to fix this."

Ricky sighs. "Let me think. But first I need to get in touch with O. P. and let him know what's what. Benny, you may need some damage control on your end, too."

It takes me a second but then I remember: Chuck.

And just as I'm in my throes of despair, Holmes and company strut past. They settle into their seats and do their thing, but they keep looking our way. Shit, we lit this match out of our desire to be popular. And now it seems the popular kids have caught wind.

Newton, do the popular kids win? Is that how the world always works? Or am I being my usual paranoid self? Or worse, is this evidence for your Third Law?

—

All I want to do is talk to Alexia, but here comes Chuck, his face pizza-sauce red.

"What's going on, Doc? Those kids smashed mailboxes?" Chuck advances on me as he speaks, his large belly pushing me into a corner. "Was it that Jesse kid? Alexia's boyfriend? 'Cause this gives me all the more reason to take his punk ass out."

So he's noticed? I put up my hands. "I don't know." It would be so much easier to throw him under the bus, but if I'm wrong and I squeal twice, I'm dead.

Chuck's eyes dart. "I've had customers in here all day and even more phone calls. They think I'm still connected to those idiots. Do you have any idea how much business I've lost?"

"I'm sorry, Chuck."

He leans in, looks over at Alexia quickly, and then his eyes are on me. "Be straight with me, Doc. Between the two of us, was it that kid? I won't go to the cops. I'll handle it myself."

I have never considered whether Chuck is capable of violence. He's nuts, but harmless. But this, what's before me, isn't someone to tangle with. And I'm responsible, even if not this time. "I honestly don't know. I'd love for you to take him out, but on good conscience, I can't."

He squeezes my shoulder. "You're a good shit, Doc." He releases me and stalks back into his office. I breathe and prepare for Alexia.

The phone rings. She picks it up and sets it right back down without answering.

I slide up. "Everything okay?"

"No. They've been calling since I got here, wanting to know when the mailboxes will be fixed."

"Still, you should probably answer the phone, don't you think? In case it's an order?"

Her face sharpens. "Everyone's saying it's Jesse. That he did this to get back at whoever told the cops he was doing those stupid dares." She stills for a second, and this is the Alexia of my past, the smart neighbor who played with me. "If he really did that, I don't know how I can stay with him. It's bad enough that he's . . . grabbed me a few times. But if he's this stupid, willing to risk so much, then I don't know what he's capable of." She pauses. "And I don't want to find out."

My heart flutters. And not in some hell-yeah moment. Sure, I want Alexia to be as far away from Jesse Holmes as possible, but now for her safety. This doesn't open some door for me. She's hurt and scared and too smart to be blind anymore. It's only a matter of time before this blows up and she realizes I'm behind what happened to Jesse. I will be dead to her then.

—

On my third order a guy grabs my elbow and pulls me inside his house. "You gotta see this."

I stand in his living room while he rewinds the local news on his DVR. When the broadcaster comes on, she begins the top of the news with a breaking story about "Mailbox Baseball Viral Video." She plays the YouTube clip of Jesse and his boys and then our latest adventure. My stomach drops, and I sit on the guy's couch.

The reporter goes on to explain how an anonymous email came into the authorities, alerting them that this baseball was a copycat and who the real suspects were. Jesse Holmes and his friends have been arrested again, the bats they'd used still in the trunk.

The reporter says, "And so this only deepens the confusion. Are these boys the daredevils gone wrong? Or copycats with a vengeance, with our would-be stuntmen still hiding in cyberspace?"

I almost pass out. The guy even looks at me funny.

But the story doesn't end there. The coverage goes out to a crew of workers busy setting new mailboxes along the street. They won't say who is paying them, but all are wearing GET OUT THERE ADVENTURE shirts. The reporter ends with, "This development seems to add credence to the copycat story. It seems our local, unknown celebrities aren't just death-defying daredevils, they also have hearts. Now, if only we could see who they are and thank them."

I scramble out of the house so fast I forget to collect the guy's money. I rip my phone out of my pocket and text Ricky: **Explain.**

Chuck loses his shit on me, gathering me into an enormous bear hug and flinging me around the shop. Alexia goes home early, saying she's sick. Fortunately, my shift is over and Chuck is more than happy to let me go.

My phone chimes. Ricky. **We're good. O. P. likes what we've done. Thinks we should be fine.**

I respond, **What did we do? You just called us out on TV? You said there was another crew.**

Don't worry, I've got it covered.

I'm pretty sure I should be shitting myself. I set my phone down and my parents appear at my door.

"Ben, did you see the news?"

I nod. They look at each other in awe.

"So who is it? Who's the guy you work with doing those dares?" Mom's voice comes out in a rush.

I almost laugh, the sensation spilling across my tongue, but I hold it in. "He doesn't. It's a long story, but no one at the shop is involved in this."

"Really?" Mom says. Dad shakes his head.

"Idiots. Him and his friends. Whoever they are. Gonna get themselves killed. And what for?"

I nod. "I know."

My phone rings and I look at the number. It's Chantel. "Can I take this in private?"

Dad shoots me a thumbs-up before closing the door.

"Hey, Chantel, what's up?"

"Have you talked to Alexia?"

I can't tell if she's pissed or excited. Her voice is this noise, loud and aggressive. "Yeah, at work. Why?"

"I've been trying to reach her, and she hasn't been answering. So I finally called her house. Her dad said he thought she was with me."

The hair on my neck stands on end. "What?" The question barely comes out.

"Exactly. I don't know what's going on or where she is. So if you hear from her, call, text, whatever."

Clamps close around my chest and throat. All I can think about is what she said earlier. "Of course."

Chantel sighs and there sounds like a sob might be attached. "Shit, Ben, I'm sorry I'm taking this out on you. I'm just worried about her."

"It's okay, I am, too."

"I know. You're such a good friend to her. She's told me, you know, about you two growing up. It's sweet."

I cringe at the image, and honestly it's not a topic I want to discuss when at the very moment the girl we're discussing could very well be in some serious trouble. "Thanks."

"I promise, once this is all straightened out, the two of us can get that sweet. Things just got in the way."

I don't know what to say.

"Ben, you haven't given up on me have you?"

I offer a dry "heh" sound. My body is too overcome with hormones and fear for anything more.

"Good. Now, keep your phone with you. 'K?"

"Sure."

She kisses the air and hangs up.

I grip my hair and stare at the floor. This is spiraling out of control.

My insides roil one last time, and I charge to the bathroom. I make it, just in time, and soil our new toilet with my nerves.

John and I head into school and look for any signs of Holmes—
Alexia crying, kids with broken necks. He's not around that I
can tell.

"Mr. Candido, come with me." McNeil's voice makes us jump.

I leave John, looking very concerned and follow our principal
to his office. The bell rings. "Don't worry, I'll write you a pass."

Being late to class ranks pretty low on my lists of concerns.

I sit and focus on breathing and not passing out.

"I'm sure you saw the news last night." McNeil folds his hands
over his belly.

"Yes, sir."

"Tell me what you know."

The room buzzes and I feel a mile away from his desk, but his
eyes are on me and I know I have to speak. "Only what I've heard
from the news and around here. Probably the same as you. Why?"

McNeil leans on his elbows. "Yet you work at Pizza and More.
I find your answer difficult to swallow."

I shake my head and steady myself. I try to think like Ricky.
"I'm sorry you feel that way, sir. If you want to check with the
owner, I'm sure he'll let you know he's as confused about the whole
thing as everyone else."

McNeil stares at me. "I already have." He pauses. Air whistles
through his nose. "And he did. Claims not to know how all this is
connected to him in the first place . . . and that you're an excellent
employee."

Thank God for Chuck. "I'm sorry, Sir, but I don't understand what I can offer you that you don't already know."

McNeil nods into his tented fingers, frustrated. "Let me make this very clear. I'm not saying it's you. You have only a smudge on your record from eighth grade. And considering the company you were with, I doubt it was your fault."

That's tough. I can only imagine what he would say to Ricky. His record isn't smudged, it's downright filthy.

McNeil continues. "But the only lead the authorities have shared with me is the one to Pizza and More." He stares at me for a moment. "So if you hear anything, one of the employees talking about these stunts, whatever, would you pass it along?"

There's only one acceptable answer. "Sure. Absolutely."

McNeil says, "Thank you, Ben. I knew I could count on you."

Out in the hall, pass in hand, I stand frozen in place. I could go back in and tell McNeil all of it and this would be over. We'll never be able to reveal ourselves, anyway. Not without consequences. Big ones. We didn't think this through, or went too far or never should have sold out Holmes. Or all three.

But I can't. This isn't only about me. It's about Ricky and John and Trevor, and now Alexia and Chantel. And there's the money. Who am I to shoot that down? Dad's out of work. John needs a backup, and Ricky seems to need enough for a new beginning. This is larger than us, and we're already in motion and gaining speed. The natural course is to let this run take us where it's going. There are no brakes in freefall.

CHAPTER 19

"**R**icky, this is beyond stupid!** One of us is really going to get killed this time. There are fucking hunters out there. With guns."

Ricky laughs at John's plea. "Are they fucking each other with the guns? Now *that's* sick."

We're standing at the edge of the woods, near an open field where we've seen at least a dozen wild turkeys. Four trucks were parked on the shoulder a few miles away. At our feet are boxes, and in them, as Ricky just explained, are decoy turkeys. But not just any decoys. They're like spyware for hunters. They have cameras in the eyes, and the idea is to put one in the field and then watch the monitor that comes with it. Instead, O. P.'s fitted them with straps so they wrap around our backs. They'll catch every moment of our dare from an insider's perspective.

I threw up a minute ago.

John kicks a box. "You know what I mean. This is plain stupid."

Ricky's shrugs. "You'll have Kevlar body armor and a bullet-proof helmet. All courtesy of O. P."

John moves away and appears to be trying to blend into the trees. Maybe I should pretend I'm a shrub? Because everything John said is so valid. This dare is fucking ridiculous. Not like car-surfing nuts, or bridge-jumping crazy, but seriously-you-may-end-up-dead institutionalized insane.

Trevor raises a hand to the field. "Let's review one more time."

Ricky runs through it again, which I'm grateful for, because I want to hear it all, in case it's not as crazy as it seemed.

Nope. This is stupid.

"Think about the money, boys. Everyone's home today, looking for something to do instead of hanging out with their families. We're going to get a ton of views." He opens the first box and starts handing out the armor.

I know he doesn't like his dad, but I would still like to have dinner with mine, even in our tiny apartment.

"Ricky, I have to ask." I feel wobbly, but manage to continue. "Whose idea was this? Yours or O. P.'s?"

He tightens his jaw. "Why does that matter?"

John stands next to me. "Because if I live through this I'll know whose ass to kick."

Ricky shakes his head. "It's a mix. Obviously I had some say like last time, with the location and such. But the decoys were all him."

"So you're the one who figured out an absurd way to use them?" I ask.

Ricky nods.

"I call bullshit on this!" John yells.

Ricky waves his hands for him to lower the volume.

"What, you don't want me to scare away the turkeys?"

"Yes. Exactly." Ricky's eyes bulge.

John moves closer to him so he can whisper, loudly. "I still have a fighting chance to play ball." He pauses, the words seeming to hurt. "But there's no way that's going to happen if I get shot and am laid up again."

Ricky looks at me, as if for permission. I don't know what he wants so I shrug.

"John, if you don't go through with this, then we don't get paid. Remember?"

John doesn't dignify the question with a response.

"So if basketball doesn't work out *and* you don't have the money from this dare, or the next, how far is the five grand you've earned going to get you?"

John's struggling with the points of the argument, but I'm not. "Hold up. Rewind to that third point. The one about no money from the next dare."

Ricky scowls at me. "You read the contract, right?"

Shit. "Kind of?"

"Jesus, Ben, what the hell's happened to you?"

"*This!* This is what's happened to me." I spread my arms to indicate the field and the gear at our feet.

Ricky runs his hands through his hair. "I have the option of writing either of you out of the contract if you refuse to complete the dares."

"What?" I barely get the word out.

"It's a fail-safe from shit like this. O. P. doesn't earn if we don't produce. Vice versa, obviously. So if one of the wheels is dragging us down, I can let it go."

John steps a little closer. "What if you're that wheel?"

"Never going to happen."

I see the clenched fists, the gritted teeth, and think to put on the gear in preparation for the fight. Trevor has come to my side, and I'm amazed he's not filming.

"Why's that, Ricky? Because it's all about the money?"

"I told *you* that I'd make right on what happened, so I don't think you have a leg to stand on with that argument." Ricky pauses. "And the hand you're sticking out was already broken. Or did you forget that? "

John stares at Ricky, who matches John's glare and looks so much like his father.

"Come on, John. Stop being a bitch about the contract and the money. You need it. Ben needs it. I need—"

I don't know what Ricky was going to say because John punches him square in the jaw with his good arm and Ricky falls straight to the ground.

John turns away and walks back into the bushes. Trevor sets down the camera and rushes to Ricky, who's rolling on the ground, surprisingly not passed out.

I look up at the sky and wish it held answers. Then I walk over to John and try to help him find some.

"Hey, you all right?" I ask.

"Kinda." He's rubbing his fist. "That felt good, but it doesn't really help." He looks at me, and he's back to his regular self, no longer pissed. "You think that's true, what he said about the contract?"

"Yeah. I'll read it to be sure, but he's smart enough not to lie about something we could go back and read." I shake my head. "Which we should have read."

"Yeah," John says. "I guess there's no way out of it now. I do need the money."

"So do we all. Except Trevor."

John looks over my shoulder and nods. "He's on his feet." He looks back at me. "So much for our legacy."

"Something tells me when this year is over, we'll be remembered."

"But how?" John asks as we head back to Ricky and Trevor.

"Only time will tell. Until then?"

Ricky squares his shoulders. "We good or are we done?"

John puts out his hand for Ricky to shake. "We're good. I'm sorry."

Ricky takes it. "No big deal. I may have had it coming."

Trevor grabs the camera and we move to the gear, no less confused.

I put the armor on and am surprised at how light it is. How is this going to stop turkey shot? The helmet's much heavier, but I have no idea how I'm going to be able to hold up my head to see where I'm going. Ricky straps on the decoys as the sun sprinkles through the trees.

It's go time.

Trevor helps Ricky with his decoy and slaps him on the helmet, whispers something. He steadies the camera and Ricky says, "Ready?"

John and I look at each other but we don't speak. Instead, we fan out and make our way to our potential graves.

The grass is tall and wet and I'm saturated in minutes. All I can see are a few inches in front of me, a foot at best. My back is an inch or so below the field, which means the decoy is riding perfectly. Shit.

I can hear real turkeys around us clucking away. Some even sound like they're purring. It's like I'm a friggin' field researcher. But in no way am I excited about this.

Ricky told us to move in slow, straight lines, but to stop every so often. I slide along and stop. Slide some more and stop. Does this look even remotely like the real thing? So what if it doesn't? Maybe that way I won't get killed? But then what if the hunters can tell what's up? Is there a plan B? What could that possibly be? Attack the hunters while dressed like Native Americans?

Shit, something's near me. The turkey clucks and darts its head forward. It seems to be looking at my decoy, twisting its body to understand. Its claws trample the ground inches from my head, and they are vicious-looking. I do not want to piss it off. I lie still and feel him pluck at the decoy. Fine. Let him. Or her? If a hunter sees a turkey eating one of its own they might run away. If any are out there.

Crack!

A flutter of wings and air rush over me.

Crack!

The turkey hops and cries out. It's almost human sounding.

Crack!

Holy fucking shit, that's gunshot!

I fight the urge to get up and run, and instead slink away. The turkey continues to flap and squawk. I hear distant voices, and the field sounds like a shooting range. The crack of gunfire is everywhere and I pick up the pace, charging, hopefully, back to the woods, so I can save my goddamn life.

Spray zips past me, the sound like insects flying at Mach 10. I freeze and feel like a fish on a line, being tugged toward the surface. I'm rolled to the side by the force, and then I understand. Someone shot the turkey. Shit. I get upright, only so I can continue crawling, but it happens again. A high-pitched hoot comes from the distance.

Again, I get upright and try to move away, but am struck for a third time. The voice who hooted now curses. I have to play dead or I'll actually be dead. I have a feeling this guy will charge across the field and unload on this decoy and I'll be turned to Swiss cheese beneath it. Fuck Kevlar.

Gunshot continues around me, so the rest of the guys must be getting the same treatment. How long am I supposed to wait?

The bullhorn sounds and Trevor's voice booms around us. "Cease fire! I repeat, cease fire!" He sounds like he's straight out of some police standoff and his voice scares me almost as much as the bullets.

The voices rise in the distance, their tone confused, but also angry.

"You are involved in a prank. There are three guys out in that field wearing decoys."

A wave of voices rises up.

"Guys, stand."

I'm afraid to. If they don't believe us . . . shit, even if they do, that doesn't mean they're going to be happy about what we did—ruined their Thanksgiving tradition. I bet they come out here every year and do this.

The voices gasp and so someone must have stood. Shit. I pull my knees under me and stand as well.

It's disorienting after the crawling, but I adjust and look around. Ricky and John are wavering like me, but don't seem injured.

"What the fuck is this?" One of the hunters asks, who I can now clearly see in his orange vest at the opposite end of the woods.

Trevor responds through the bullhorn. "Just a prank."

The hunter turns to his group and their arms fling wildly. I turn and yell, "Let's go."

We all turn and start hightailing it back from where we came. A single shot splits the air and I almost fall to my knees.

"Don't you go anywhere!" The hunter's voice is loud and full of authority.

I freeze. John and Ricky do, too.

"Put your weapon down!" Trevor continues to sound like a cop.

The rifle cracks again, and I feel like I might shit my pants.

"Listen, you stupid hick! I am recording you right now. I can see every inch of your bearded, douche-bag face through this lens. I've got video of every single one of you shooting at my friends and now firing a threatening shot into the air. If you attack us, I'm going to the police. You want to be charged with attempted murder?"

Holy. Fucking. Shit.

No one moves. Trevor doesn't even look to us for support. He keeps both the bullhorn and the camera trained on the hunters. The spokesperson rests his rifle on his shoulder.

"We should come haul *your* asses to the authorities. You can't do this." He's grasping, but still, they've got firearms and could easily bust up the camera.

"Neither can you. Did you read the *No Hunting* signs everywhere, or was that beyond your literacy level?"

The hunter says something inaudible but is clearly pissed off.

"Exactly. I've got that on film, too. So sit tight. We'll be out of your hair in five minutes, and then you can kill all the turkeys you want."

Trevor pauses a moment and says, "Happy Thanksgiving."

CHAPTER 20

My hands are still shaking and it's been two hours since I
was shot.

I was shot.

I let that fact roll over me like the water streaming out of the
shower head. It's all I could think about on the ride home—a
hot shower and my bed. I didn't even care that it would be in the
yellowed and nasty stall in the condo. I just wanted to get warm
and be safe.

We barely spoke after we inspected our decoys. Each was rid-
dled with holes. Our vests and helmets were also puckered and
ripped. I felt so disconnected then, couldn't quite believe that
the gear I was looking at had kept me from getting shot, hurt, or
possibly killed.

I was so out of touch I barely heard Trevor's explanation of
how the turkeys were hooked up for wireless transmission and that
the video would already be on his computer. How he'd begin editing immediately. It didn't sound as if he was going to spend any
time with his family, but that didn't strike me as odd.

What did hit me was that he had called us his friends. Sure, it
could have been something he said in the moment, trying to get
the hunters' attention. But still, what if it wasn't? What if he feels
that way? Because if he does . . . I guess the feeling's mutual. He

saved our asses today. But it's more than that. He's helping Ricky and seems to hate Jesse Holmes almost as much as I do. Friendships have been built on less.

I towel off and dress in pajama pants and a long-sleeve T. Mom appears at my door.

"Where were you so early?"

"John wanted to go running. He's trying to get back in shape. You know, with missing the beginning of the season and all."

"That's so nice of you. I wish you would have left a note, but that's okay."

"Sorry." I sniff the air. "It smells fantastic in here."

She turns toward the kitchen. "It won't be like usual. You know in the big old dining room. But we'll make it work."

"I'm sure of it, Mom."

She leaves and I hop online. I've put this off long enough. I figured if I died I wouldn't have to know my score, but since I'm here.

A knock bumps at my door and before I can say, "Hold up," Ginny's pushing her way through.

I minimize the screen and try to act casual. "What's up?"

"Really, you're asking me that question?" She sits on the edge of my bed. "You tell me. What have *you* been up to?"

I sigh and look back at the screen. She got home yesterday for Thanksgiving break, and I know what she wants to talk about. Guess this is a great way to stall that conversation. "My SAT score is ready."

She sits upright. "What are you waiting for?"

Ginny got a 2200 on her SAT. I'll be lucky to get 1500. I shrug.

"Get out of the way. I'll do it."

She shoves me out of my chair, maximizes my email, and clicks the link. "Give me the details."

"Benny5 and Bigpimpin. Capital Bs on both."

"Seriously?"

"Yeah, no *g* at the end, either."

"That doesn't make it any better."

I turn away and listen to her reaction. "Eww." It's like she's removed a Band-Aid and does not like the look of the wound beneath.

"That bad?" Her comment made me slump so far forward I feel like someone's pulled out my spine.

"Um, yeah. You did awful."

"I knew it." I turn and look at the score: 1400.

"What happened, Benny?" Ginny reads through the analysis of the test. "You didn't even do well on the math."

Now I flop onto my back. "I know. I wasn't prepared. I've been so busy with the dares and this girl I'm kind of seeing and the move and . . ."

"Jesus, Benny, shut up. Enough with the excuses." Ginny cuts me off and turns toward the bed. "You have time to take it again. I'll help you study if you need it."

I nod, but only because I'm supposed to.

"Just don't tell Mom and Dad about *this* score. What'd you get last time?"

"Fifteen hundred."

"So, retake it and beef up the math and you should be fine." She pats my knee but it brings me no comfort. "So what's the next dare?"

"Happy Thanksgiving to you, too." I turn away.

"Yeah, yeah. Let's celebrate how we exploited the Native Americans' generosity by giving them blankets with smallpox."

"What?" I have no clue what she's talking about.

"Never mind. Tell me what you're doing." She shoves my shoulder.

I sit up and look at her. "You'll get to see the video soon enough."

"You've already done it?"

I nod. "This morning?"

"What? What did you do?"

I shake my head and can see this morning, as if it were someone else than me. Maybe I'm suffering from post-traumatic stress disorder. "We dressed up as turkeys and got shot."

"Shut up. No, you didn't."

"Yeah, we did. I got lit up, must have been hit five, six times."

"Jesus Christ, Benny, are you okay?" Ginny's eyes search me as if I might be bleeding from a gunshot wound.

"I'm fine. We had Kevlar gear and helmets."

She's quiet, looking at me as if she doesn't know who I am.

Ginny leans forward and closes the door. "Ben, this is beyond insane. The amount of ways that this could have gone wrong. I don't even want to consider the probability." She stops and whispers, "This is too much. How do you top that?"

That's one question I've been thinking about ever since we survived. Along with whether Ricky will write me out of the contract if I don't agree to it. "I don't know?"

"What about those guys you had arrested?"

My scalp tightens. I don't really feel like going into this right now. "It was an anonymous tip."

"Right. The only one it's anonymous to is the police."

She's right. My gut tells me that Jesse knows. "It's been quiet. Really. The kid Jesse, who's like their leader, hasn't said a word."

"Didn't he try to get you guys arrested?"

"Yeah, but that backfired."

"So you're screwed."

"Maybe. Maybe not. There's no guarantee he knows, and he might be a little concerned about getting caught again, since the three-strike rule is pretty universal." I skim my hands across my knees convincing myself this is true.

Ginny leans closer to me. "What's your deal with him, anyway?"

I look at Ginny for a moment, to see what kind of angle she's working, but she seems 100 percent genuine, concerned. "Long story, but he's put his hands on his girlfriend. You remember Alexia from down the street?"

Ginny nods, but doesn't say anything until after she sighs out her nose. "She was cute. Smart, too. But more to the point, he hasn't said anything, hasn't done anything to you guys in retribution?"

She says it like a lawyer peeling back the facts of evidence and I'm anxious. "No. Why?"

"That's not a good sign, Benny. Teen guys are reactive, strike immediately. It's rare that they calculate their next move, especially with an audience watching. Girls do that. And when they strike, it's a hundred times worse."

Like always, she's spot on. The few girl fights I've seen have been all-out brawls with clawing, hair pulling, blood. Still, her arrogance eats at me. "So what's your point, *Doctor*?"

"You'd better be watching your back." She's not offended.

"We're on top of it."

She stares up at the ceiling, inhales a chestful of air and lets it out so slowly, I find it oddly comforting. She levels her judgmental glare on me. "Ben, what do you want after high school? Because, seriously, if, *if* you manage to pull off these dares without getting caught, hurt, or killed, what are you going to do? You've wasted all your time with this shit. No sports or extracurricular activities, no volunteering. Based on your SAT scores, you're not that impressive. And your GPA has never been that exciting, either."

Her words hurt a deep sort of pain, as if someone's exposed a dark secret. I'm angry and ashamed at the truth. Because that's what this is. My neck heats up with anger, but the rest of me is limp with regret. "I don't know, Gin. Wish I was perfect like you."

"Don't make this about me. I'm trying to help you see your way through, since no one else is."

"How could they?" I look up now, snapping.

"You're right." Her voice is softer. "But that fact should scare you. The idea that you can't share this enormous part of who you are. Because like it or not, Benny Bear, this *is* you now. There's no getting back to who you were before."

Not that I'd want to. But Ginny's right. I should be scared. And I am. But that's part of the thrill. Should I be ashamed of that, of who I am?

"I don't know. Obviously I need to think."

"Obviously," she says sarcastically, but then touches my knee. "Sorry, it's just that I'm worried. At first it was a great coincidence, but now, I don't like what I know."

I sigh. "Yeah. I get what you mean, except I wish I knew more than I did."

—

"**Dinner in five**," Mom yells from the kitchen. She's a flurry of pots and pans and dishes that need to be put on the table. Ginny is trying to help, but the kitchen's so small there's barely any room. Dad's on his laptop looking for jobs and drinking beer. His face hasn't moved from a scowl since he started.

My cell vibrates with a text. Ricky: **The video's up. Happy Thanksgiving.**

I reply: **Same to you**, and consider going up to my room. But it's too risky. If either of my parents come up to haul me to dinner and find me watching the video, I'll have to explain. It can wait. I can allow myself not to be wrapped up in these dares for at least an hour.

My cell goes off again. Probably John. No, it's Chantel. **Happy turkey day, sweetie.**

Same to you, I reply, whatever that means.

"Come to the table, you two." Mom spreads her hands across the meal steaming before her. I stare at the turkey and can't help but think of this morning. So weird.

I stand and wave to my dad. His face is animated by whatever he's reading. "Need some help?"

He doesn't look up. "Benny, did those guys who don't work with you do another prank today?"

My veins run cold and I sit back down. "Uh, I don't know," is very constricted coming out of my throat.

"Look at this." He turns the computer toward me and our standard intro rolls, followed by a multi-split screen, one for each of the turkey's perspective, and one for Trevor's lens on the hunters. "This is crazy," Dad says, and I can barely nod.

I watch as the footage alternates to full shots of the field and us slithering across it, to split screens of us and the hunters, and finally, individual frames of us getting pegged off. Because of our masks and all of the gear, I honestly can't tell which one is me, and it's unsettling.

Each of us is rolled and then the editing shifts to us standing and waving to the hunters, who, because of their blurred faces, look more dumbfounded than angry. I don't remember Ricky coming on and narrating at the end, wishing everyone a "Happy Turkey Day" and asking them to share the video with everyone they know. Shit, isn't Trevor setting the controls to keep just that from happening? What is going on?

The video ends, and I watch as my sister and mother come to us. It feels like slow motion, or like I'm underwater. Dad turns the laptop to them and they watch, Ginny looking at me only once. But she, like my mother, clasps her hands to her mouth.

"Like I told you, these idiots go to Ben's school."

I don't even bother to speak because all I'm thinking about is how he found the video. First he would need to know where to look and then he'd need the password. How can Dad, sitting here looking for a job, find this? It makes no sense.

"I am thankful that my boy wasn't out there." Mom's voice is dry. "Benny, don't you ever join them if they ask."

"Okay," I say.

She nods. "I need a drink. Come and sit."

I look over at Ginny and she shakes her head at me. I nod and turn back to Dad. "Come on, or Mom will drink the whole bottle without you." I give him a hand up, and when he's standing, he claps my shoulder.

"You're a good son, Ben. Thanks."

My insides shrivel and I feel like a complete asshole.

We sit, and Dad carves the turkey and Mom passes around the mashed potatoes, stuffing, cranberries, et cetera. I take some of it all, but seeing the video has messed me up. My cell vibrates with another text, and I don't bother to read it.

"This is nice, just the four of us." Mom smiles over her wine glass and pretends to clink it in the air with us. She downs a significant gulp. "Like I said, I'm thankful for Benny not being with those boys, but I'm also thankful for having Ginny home with us, and for this condo becoming more like home." She looks at Ginny and lifts her eyebrows.

Ginny squirms in her chair but then sits upright. "I'm grateful that school is going well and that I'm learning so much about a topic I like and think needs greater study."

So Ginny. So layered with her double meaning. I get it.

"And I'm so thankful that Mom and Dad are making this difficult time work."

Dad snorts and takes a pull on his beer. Ginny's face turns red, and Mom gives Dad a dirty look but then turns to me. "Ben?"

It's like she's speaking from across the room and not two feet away. "Right. I'm grateful for this family and for my future." I can't think of anything more original. My brain is as shot through as my vest was.

"So long as it isn't with some company that says they'll give you a pension and keep you on forever." Dad's words run together and he grabs his beer. "You get settled on which school you're going to, and then be like Ginny, going places."

I don't know what's worse, watching him or knowing that I'm headed in the exact opposite direction from Ginny. I stare at my plate and have no idea how I'm going to get through this meal.

"Did you get your SAT score?" Mom asks. "Someone at work was saying they'd be online this week."

"Nope, not yet." I stab my turkey and hope we can end this conversation.

"Check after dinner," Dad says and dives into his meal.

I open my mouth to respond but am kicked in the leg. I look at Ginny, and she is very subtly shaking her head. I acknowledge her by eating a forkful of turkey. It goes down like tree bark.

—

Chantel's text: **Party at danielle's tomorrow!**

I want to throw my phone, go to bed, and wake up and have it be September. I want to start this year over and say no to Ricky and settle into my schoolwork and not care about how I'm remembered at our stupid high school.

My door opens and Ginny comes in holding an envelope. She sits on my bed. "Some Thanksgiving, huh?"

"One of the best."

"Jesus, Benny." She passes me the envelope.

I know before I even read the return address: BROOKWOOD HIGH SCHOOL. "When did this come?"

"Yesterday. Like it always does."

It figures that she would know this and that I wouldn't. And it figures that I'm wishing I could go back in time instead of owning up to the fact that I'm stuck with the here and the now and whatever the hell comes up on the spinning wheel of death.

I open my report card. I've got C's in everything but PE and English. Somehow I managed an A and a B, respectively. "Shit."

Ginny glances at the paper and her eyes widen. "What are you going to do?"

I know she means in terms of the big picture, like how am I going to turn this around. But I'm not. I'm not even going to try.

It's too much work, and I don't really want it to be September again. I just don't like the bad that comes with the good.

"I'm going to a party." I crumble up my report card and toss it into the garbage.

CHAPTER 21

'm standing with John when Ricky and Trevor walk in.

"How fucking gay are they?" someone says, and I look to see who it is. Some kid I don't know.

His friend rocks back with laughter. "You had the same thought?"

I drink my beer and tuck away the comment. In spite of my conversation with Ricky, I'm not 100 percent sure where he and Trev stand in their relationship. Regardless, if this kid continues, I'm throwing a punch.

"What's up guys, feeling good?" Ricky clinks beers with us. Trevor stands at his side.

"Not bad, we got eighteen thousand hits," John says. This is the first time he's mentioned our hits. We all notice. "What? I'm keeping track. I'd like to make some money before Ricky writes me out of the contract." He drinks his beer before he says any more.

Danielle's TV flashes with our latest dare and drunken kids scream at it. "Light 'em up!"

I don't bother looking for a segue. "Trev, why wasn't there a password this time?"

Ricky's face darkens and Trevor looks at me with fish eyes, but he doesn't answer. I have trouble connecting him to the kid who yelled at those hunters. "Seriously, Trev, my dad found the thing, like right after it was posted. It kicked off my Thanksgiving dinner."

Ricky looks at the ceiling. "I told him to."

John and I say, "What?" at the same time.

Ricky looks over our heads. "O. P. asked me to, so I gave Trev the green light."

"Why did O. P. want that?" John asks.

Ricky keeps looking up, like there's a mural painted up there. "Simple. Like you, he wants more hits."

"But doesn't that hang us out there?" I lean in to speak in case anyone's listening. "We could get caught, especially after Jesse's video."

"One, we were in the middle of a field. Nowhere near anything identifying. Those hunters could say it was them, but what proof do they have? Two, it kind of makes sense to throw off the safeguards. Confuses the police, since that's what Jesse did." Ricky's words are rehearsed. He might be able to make the first point on his own, but not the second. Shit, how much is O. P. feeding him?

Beyond that, why isn't he linking us to his website? I bite my tongue.

"There's my party people!" Danielle yells to the room and we all holler back. She glances at us, but that's all. She holds her gaze on John for a moment, but then is gone. We're still on the fringe. If it weren't for Alexia and Chantel, we wouldn't be here at all.

I look for Chantel, who got a text from Alexia and figured she'd better call her. Alexia keeps doing this, disappearing and reappearing as if nothing has happened. Last time, she and Chantel didn't speak to each other for a week, so I got to see more of Chantel. But now? Who knows?

I turn back to Ricky, angry over what he's done, irritated that Chantel's not around again, tired and sore from yesterday, and no longer in the mood to party. "It's not right that you did that without telling us. Some warning, at least, would have been good. And that contract shit, you going to hang that over our heads?"

"I hear you, but what would you have done differently if you'd known?"

"That's not the point." John says my exact thought.

"What is?" Ricky asks and drinks his beer.

Something about that move, like we're shooting the shit about nothing instead of something so vital it could ruin us, pushes me over the edge. "Really, Rick? Are you that stupid that you can't put this together?"

"The fuck you just say?" Ricky puffs his chest.

I ignore it. "You heard me. If you don't realize that fucking with the two of us," I point at John, "makes us want to walk and ruin the money-making scheme, *and* that what you did with the latest video makes no sense, then you're an idiot."

"You should have read the contract. That's not *my* problem. And what's wrong with making money? You all but begged for us to amp it up for John. And last I checked you were living in a piece of shit condo. Can't imagine that's fun."

I look around, again to see if anyone cares about us. I'm not surprised that they don't. I am shocked, however, by how much I want to punch Ricky in his face. "That's not fair and *you* know it." I hope he gets my inflection because I'm not into playing his game. "What I'm saying is what good is any of this money if we're in jail because you stupidly led the cops to us?"

"So you're still in?" Ricky asks, ignoring the question.

I look at John, but I know the answer. "For now."

"I would never do that." Trevor's voice is quiet as usual, but defensive. "I hate the authorities."

"Trev, I have no problem with you. It was Ricky's decision, and you went along, same as us."

"But you make it seem as if it's even a remote possibility, which it's not, and so I find that offensive," Trevor says.

I look at John and his expression is the same as mine, thoroughly lost. He shrugs. "Nothing's impossible, little man. I believed I was getting a full ride to school. . . ."

We all wait for John to finish, to tell us what is painfully obvious, but he drinks his beer instead.

"Regardless of what is or is not possible, I did this to help us, so don't go shitting on me." Ricky's deflated some, but not much.

This is going nowhere and I'm not waiting for Chantel any longer. "Be careful with the decisions you make for *us*. Keep this shit up and you won't find me risking my life with you."

I turn and walk out into the cold. I'm behind the wheel before I realize John's sitting shotgun.

—

The cold wakes me up. My teeth are chattering, and I struggle to pull the blanket tight enough. I give up and head downstairs.

My parents are sitting in front of the fire, drinking coffee and reading the newspaper. It's easily ten degrees warmer down here.

"There he is. How was your party?" Dad sits up.

"You want some breakfast? I'll make you eggs?" Mom folds her paper and I shake my head.

"I'm good," I say and head to the coffee pot and fill up. "Why didn't you put a fire on upstairs?"

Dad frowns. "Didn't think we'd need it. Cold?"

Why else would I be asking? "Yeah. Is the heat on?"

"Your father wants to see how much we can get out of the fireplaces, instead of using the furnace."

"Got a buddy from the plant who hooked me up with a few cords of wood for free. Why not?"

They stare at each other for a moment and then each returns to their section of the paper. I sip my coffee and Ricky's comments tumble back to me and burn. I wish we were back at our home. I don't know who lives there now, but I envy them. That house was always toasty.

I take my mug and head back upstairs, shower, and change, and feel a little warmer. A half hour later I'm out the door and looking at Chuck's sour face.

"Hey, we're backed up since Alexia called in."

My insides spasm. "What?"

"She says she's sick, but I'd guess hungover is more like it." Chuck walks into the freezer.

I get my orders together. Once I'm in my Jeep, I go to text Chantel, but change my mind. She never bothered to reach out last night after I left, and I'm starting to think I was just a one-night stand.

I open up Twitter and search for Alexia. She hasn't tweeted in two days. Her last reads: **Happy Thanksgiving**. Maybe she's away? But she could tweet from her phone. And she was using it last night. I check Facebook. No activity. She hasn't posted, hasn't liked a thing.

I'm going to pay Alexia a visit.

That may be easier said than done. Every house I go to, it's: "Hey, are *you* the guy?" I have to shake it off and say, "Nope, not me. He *doesn't* work for us." Finally, I deliver my last order, a twelve-cut pepperoni, to a guy who looks like he hasn't slept in a week. He smokes a cigarette, peels off bills, and says, "Next time, you guys gotta dress like Santa and elves or some shit. Get some reindeer." Before I can protest, he's shut the door and I'm wondering if I should take myself up on my own dare and not participate in the next.

I pull onto Alexia's street and slow down. Her parents definitely moved into a better section of town, but this street really isn't that nice compared to the new development. I bet her dad's pissed he didn't get in there when they were first building.

I crawl up and hit the brakes. Holmes's car is parked out front. Immediately, my mouth goes dry and my legs tingle. The text and phone call last night, the lack of online activity, her calling in— they all congeal into one sick image now that I've seen his ride. I pull over and step out. Her neighborhood is quiet, not a person out. I walk to his car and touch the hood. It's cold. He's been here for some time. The opening in my stomach grows deeper.

The doorbell chime echoes through the house. Alexia lives in a sprawling ranch, so I wait, in case her room is way in the back. No one shows. I ring again. Still no one. I step off the front walk-way and look around the side of the house. A light's on in a room. Someone moves past the window. I bolt back to the door and ring again.

Alexia pokes her head out the door a moment later. "Ben, is everything all right? Did something happen at work?" Her eyes are puffy, her lips are chapped, and her skin is a shade of pale.

"Alexia?" It's all I can say, but it's enough.

"Ben, I know." She holds up a hand. "He came over before Danielle's to pregame. But he got too drunk too fast, and I didn't want to drive." She shakes and starts to cry. "We got into a huge argument and then he finished the bottle. He's still passed out now."

I reach out and pull her close. She feels like a bag of bones against me. I have the urge to pick her up and put her in my Jeep and bring her to the condo and set her in front of the fireplace with a bowl of soup. She rattles and stills, and I hold her close.

Alexia pulls away and wipes her tears. "I'm sorry, it's been a long night."

"It's fine. Really. Are you okay? Did he . . ."

"No! I'm fine!" she cuts me off.

"Do you want me to get Chantel to come over?"

"No. Jesse will freak if she's here when he wakes up."

That sounds about the last thing anyone needs so I don't argue.

"Are you sure you're okay? I could get someone else to come over." I'm thinking Ginny, but I keep that to myself.

"No, no. It's fine. He's just being Jesse. And with all that's happened to him, I guess he deserves to blow off some steam."

"What? He busted up those mailboxes. He did that to himself."

Alexia scowls. "He only did that because he was framed for the other shit. You know that."

My mind lurches. This line is in utter opposition to her previous logic. "But you said he was stupid for what he did. That you couldn't be with him."

Alexia looks over my head. "Yeah, well, some things are easier said than done."

"But Alexia, you deserve better."

She looks at me now, her eyes rimmed with tears. "You always say what you're thinking, Ben. The truth. You see people for who they are. I always liked that about you. But this time, you may be blind to the truth." With that, she closes the door and I feel like falling apart.

—

The first snowfall hit last night. Only an inch or so, but enough to make me think of what a pain in the ass winter will be: deliveries in terrible conditions, a freezing house warmed like a log cabin, and, if I go along with them, frigid dares. I'm sure O. P.'s going to take advantage of this terrain. Or, more aptly, Ricky. Maybe I'll die of hypothermia?

I dress in the cold, putting more layers on top of my current layers and head downstairs. The fireplace is roaring and I sit on the hearth. Mom and Dad are awake, and both look at me and then immediately down. Dad coughs and folds the newspaper across his lap. "Is there something you want to tell us, Ben?"

The warmth I felt drains out of me. Here it is. They figured it out. "What do you mean?"

Mom sighs. "Don't play dumb. We know."

Now my brain pulses like a cell tower. I don't respond, but wait for the words I figured would come well before now.

"Where is your report card?" Dad asks like I'm a four-year-old, and once I process what he's said, I feel like rolling around on the ground like one.

"My report card?" The words giggle out of me.

"Yes," Mom says. "Why's that funny?"

I almost laugh. Almost. But I bite my tongue and put on a

surprised expression. "Honestly, I hadn't thought about it. I don't know where it is. I figured maybe you guys got it. It came in the mail, right?"

They look at each other and in their confusion I see my opening.

"Maybe because of the move it didn't come? Maybe it went to our house?"

"Ben, this is our home." Mom means for this to be a strong statement, but it falls apart at the end.

Dad looks at me for a moment and nods. "I wouldn't be surprised. Can you check at school?"

"Sure. And when I pick up John, we'll swing by the house and see if it happens to be there."

Mom says, "But . . ." and doesn't finish.

I stand up, feeling like I've dodged another bullet, and get some breakfast. While I'm staring at my cereal and devising a plan to keep the report card hidden, Dad stands up and says, "Wish me luck."

"Huh?"

"My interview. It's today."

I totally forgot. He told me when I got home that night after dealing with Jesse and Alexia. What was that, two weeks ago?

"That's right. Good luck!"

"Not that he'll need it," Mom says.

"True, but I'll never turn any away," Dad says.

I like that statement and I hope like hell my luck keeps holding out.

—

"But why are you checking? You know it's not there." John tilts his head and looks at me like roadkill. We're parked outside my house, the former one.

"I know. But I'm interested in who moved in. You haven't seen anyone, right?"

"No."

Which is weird. "Right, so, it'll only take a sec." I hop out and head up my old steps. It feels odd, like I'm visiting a relative's house.

I peek in the window and the house is empty. No furniture, no moving boxes, nothing. It's exactly as we left it. The mailbox is equally so. I take another look and climb back in the Jeep.

"Did you see *anyone* move in?"

John's texting and only half listens to me. "I told you, no."

I wait for him to finish.

"What?"

"Jesus. Have you seen anyone at the house?"

"Just some guy the day after you guys moved out. He had keys and everything. I think changing the locks. But that's it."

I think about this, but have no answer, so I drive on to school, as if maybe the answer will emerge there.

Lockers are decorated like presents, and kids are sucking on candy canes and talking about what they're getting. I have no clue what Christmas will be like. My parents have no money. I don't really want anything, anyway. But I've still got Chantel to con-sider. I don't know what *we* are, but I should get her something.

We turn the corner and Ricky does not look pleased.

"What's up?" I ask.

"I've been thinking." Ricky's voice is low.

"Careful with that, it's not your strong suit."

He ignores me. "We can't go seeking revenge. We made him pay already. That's enough."

A spark fires off inside me. After seeing Alexia as she was, I reached out to Ricky with this plan. He was fine with it then. "So it's okay for Holmes to do what he's doing to Alexia?" I ask as calmly as I can.

"No. But that really has nothing to do with us. It's coinci-dence. Besides, she's not your girlfriend. Why do you care?" Ricky stares me down.

"What if someone were beating up Trev? He's not really one of us. What would you do?" The question's not fair and I feel like a dick for asking, but he pushed me to this point. Some weird noise comes out of John's throat, and Ricky's face goes white.

"I hope he'd kick his ass." Trevor's voice is meek, but we all turn to look at him.

He looks around. "One time, freshman year, I was walking home and Jesse was out with his crew. I think they were drunk. There were four of them." Trev looks at the floor. "They jumped me. Called me all sorts of names. You know. Punched me and kicked me. When I thought it was over, Jesse picked me up."

Ricky's fists are clenching and unclenching and everyone is dead quiet, listening.

"Yeah, so, he told me I was his little bitch now and then pushed me over to a fire hydrant. Told me to bend over and grab it." Trevor pauses and I don't want to hear what he's going to say next. I hate Jesse for what he's done to Alexia, what he'll keep doing if we don't go ahead with the plan, as crazy and as stupid as it is. But I know I'll hate him even more after this, even if it is about Trev. Because in spite of what I said, he is part of us.

"So I did, because there were four of them. And before I knew it, my pants were down and Jesse was behind me. 'This is what I do to my bitches,' he said, and then he spanked me so hard my eyes watered. The other guys stared, laughing, and Jesse hit me again. They all took turns and one of them took pictures, emailed them to me and told me not to say anything or else they'd tell people I paid them to do it." He stops again. "They knew what I am."

No one speaks. We look around but not at one another. Trevor shrinks back into himself and I want to apologize, but it's too late, the moment's passed.

Ricky looks from Trevor to me, his eyes simmering. "Count me in."

I look him in the eye and he's as furious as I've ever seen, but I can also see Trevor, and the smallest of smiles crosses his lips. I feel a mix of anger and contentment. Maybe we are crazy and suicidal, like Ginny thinks, but deep down, we're still decent. And no dare will change that.

CHAPTER 22

Right now I really wish I'd paid better attention in physics. We covered electrical currents and the whole Ben Franklin story. My teacher even laughed after making some joke about how the inventor was equal parts genius and daredevil. So it only figures that it's the middle of the night and Ricky is pulling Christmas lights and tasers out of a box.

"Doesn't this, like, make you shit your pants or something?" John holds up one of the tasers and shines his headlamp on it. The headlamps as well as the decorative lights and tasers are courtesy of O. P. As are the stupid Santa hats and beards we're wearing instead of our usual masks.

"Nah, it'll make you twitch, but that's about it." Ricky's answer sounds like he's convincing himself.

Trevor strings the lights around the small pine tree Ricky has chosen, and Ricky clears away the dusting of snow at the base of the tree.

I watch and am starting to connect the dots. "Explain this."

Ricky stops and picks up a taser. "Fine, but are you two going to make a whole scene out of this?" He's talking to John and me. We look at each other and I shrug.

"Depends on what we're up to," I say.

"Fuck. You do realize that you can't have it both ways—safe

dares and lots of cash. We have to . . ."

"Shut up with all that and just tell us the plan," John says.

Ricky either doesn't feel like arguing or doesn't want to get punched again, because he gets to it. "It's simple. We turn ourselves into an electrical current using the taser. You'll stand on this spot without your shoes, and we'll tape the end of the lights into your hand. One of us will taser you and, bam, we'll have a light show."

Right, and we'll broadcast it to everyone and make more money. I feel my feet rooting into the ground.

Trevor finishes with the lights and grabs his camera. "Who's going first?"

John and I answer at the same time, "Ricky!"

"Whatever. Fine." He takes off his shoes and stands in his socks on the cold, wet ground. "Can't have the current ground," he says. "Ben, get over here."

I stay in place. "No. I'm not sure about this one, Rick. I think we might be going too far. Messing with electricity isn't bright."

"Nice pun, Benny boy. Now help me out."

I shake my head. "You're not listening."

Ricky sighs. "Aren't we past this? Or are you really choosing *now* to throw a tantrum?"

"What, is there a better time for you? I'm sorry."

"Yeah, *before* the dare, not just as we're getting set." He turns his hands, palms up. "Come on."

I don't bite on his plea. "Answer one question. Did O. P. tell you to forget the passwords this time?"

Ricky's face pinches. "Does it matter?"

"Of course it matters!" John says. "Shit, Rick, we're going to get caught. That can't happen. I need the money."

"*You* do? Ha! Why do you think we're doing this?"

And as he says it I can tell he wants those words back. He might as well have his hands covering his mouth.

"I can easily set a password. There's really nothing to it," Trevor says.

Ricky eyes him and juts his chin, then looks at me and squints. "We are not putting up any more passwords."

"So we're in this for the money? That's it? And *you're* calling all the shots?" I ask.

"Why do you have such a problem with that?" Ricky asks. "John, do you care?"

John looks at me, then away. "About the money, no. I think it's pretty obvious that this thing isn't healing well." He holds up his arm. "But you being a dick isn't cool."

Ricky opens his mouth to answer but turns to me. "How am I being a dick? After this we're taking care of Ben's problem."

"Don't call it *mine*! We all threw Jesse under the bus, and now that's come back on us through Alexia."

"Fuck you, Ben! You're being a goddamn pussy, like always."

"That doesn't even make sense. Besides, pussy or not, Jesse aside, I would have done my research and realized that O. P.'s a joke, some guy who doesn't even advertise our links. Did you know that, Rick? You go to O. P.'s site and there's nothing. No mention of us. What's that all about? Huh, fearless leader?"

"How the hell should *I* know?" He pauses. "That's his business. Not ours."

That pause is all I need. "I'm calling bullshit! You know that's ridiculous. Who spends that kind of money and doesn't look for every opportunity to promote? Even Chuck does that."

Ricky's dancing now, hopping foot to foot. "What are you saying, Ben?"

"I'm saying something's not right with this whole deal. I want to talk to O. P. again. I have questions. And I'm sick of asking them through you. Write me out if you want. But after this, you get me connected or I will never spend another minute with you." It feels good getting these words out. They've been a long time coming.

There's a moment of silence, but then Ricky asks, "What about Holmes?"

The question is downright dirty. Fortunately, Trevor agrees. "You take that back, Rick, or I'll taser you right now and I won't let up."

"What?" Ricky asks.

"These guys do everything you ask, even after realizing it is only about the money, not the lie you sold them on. And now the one thing Ben's asked you to do, the one thing you *should* do, you use as leverage? No, you don't get to do that." He looks at me. "If he refuses to help, I'll go with you."

"You know I'm there, Ben," John chimes in.

We all look at Ricky, who looks pathetic without his shoes,

and for so many other reasons. "Okay," he says.

I breathe deep to steady myself. Trevor walks up to me. "Ben, we'll make this work." He claps my shoulder and nods. I follow his lead. "Now, please tape this plug onto Ricky's palm. It's retrofitted to absorb the shock and not burn out. John, grab a taser."

It takes me a second to move, because too much has happened. But my body's getting used to moving without my brain, and I do as Trevor has asked. The plug is huge and I want to ask how much current we're about to take in, but Ricky does not look at me as I wrap the tape around and around.

Once the tape is secured and John has armed the gun, Trevor motions for us to turn off our headlamps and flips on the night-vision lens. He counts down and points to Ricky, who starts pitching like he always does, as if nothing has happened between us. But a shit ton did, and it's not over.

Ricky unbuttons his shirt and nods to John, who aims the red dot of the laser guide on his chest.

In the dark, the dot is haunting. It's too much like the movies I've seen where the next moment is punctuated by gunfire. I want to yell for John to stop, but at the same time I want him to light Ricky up. It's beyond twisted, but something else is equally clear— I'm not nervous. That feeling of excitement that I used to have has returned full force. This, for money or not, is going to be awesome.

John fires.

Ricky screams, a sound like someone getting beat upside the head, but the lights don't come on. John looks horrified, as if he wants to let go, but he doesn't. He's either waiting for the lights or is too scared to think. I can't see what's happening to Ricky, but it sounds awful. I step forward to end this, or to get a better view—I don't know which—and the lights pop on.

Ricky is on his knees, head jarring like some bobble-headed Santa Claus, arm outstretched like it's caught on a wire fence. The lights are so bright against the night that we all stare at them. They're the same giant bulbs we used on our home, which aren't on the condo this year.

Ricky lets out another snarl and Trevor yells, "Enough!"

John flings the gun to the ground and a second later the lights die away. We all click on our headlamps and charge to Ricky. He's on his side and his eyes are rolling in his head. Spit's oozing from his mouth, and he twitches a few more times. Trevor hands off the camera to John and madly pulls at the electrodes embedded in Ricky's chest.

Ricky twitches and shakes for another second and then stills. He blinks and looks up. "Did I die?"

Trevor shakes his head. "No. Maybe? But you're here now."

Ricky smiles back at him. "I'll take that."

I'm moved by the scene, and it's about the last emotion I expect to feel. Chantel and I don't even have this kind of closeness. Alexia and I used to. And there's something horribly wrong in that. Not in Ricky and Trevor, but with me. It's time for me to be done with my fear and figure out what I want. Who I want.

—

The lights worked every time, and John and I ended up in pretty much the same position as Ricky. Except we had to shoot John twice. He's so damn big. Fortunately, I was recovered and jumped in to help Ricky. John didn't shit, but pissed his pants.

Normally we would have busted his balls. But we couldn't do much of anything. I don't know because I've never been tasered before, but I think I'm still messed up from it. We're at the mall, John and me, and I keep walking into the railing on the second floor. I can't seem to move in a straight line. I hold on to the rail and ignore the pissed-off shoppers. Christmas is a week out, and they are all power-shopping and do not want to be interrupted by some strung-out kid.

"Is the store up here?" I turn to John who looks happy to be taking a break. He leans over the rail next to me.

"Yeah, up ahead. Hey, am I walking as messed up as you?"

"Can't tell, I'm focusing on staying upright. You know?"

"Yeah. Ricky get the video up?"

I check my phone, and there's still no text from him. I don't blame him, though. Just trying to function in normal life has been rough. "Nope. By tonight, I bet."

John grunts and hoists himself up. "Come on."

We trudge on and find the perfume kiosk. It's the only gift I could think of. What I lack in originality, I intend to make up for in expense.

John and I lean over the counter, side by side, peering into the glass and trying to make sense of all the options.

"You need some help?" The woman behind the counter asks.

I look up too fast and fall into John. The woman frowns. "It's a medical thing," I lie. "My ear."

"Oh, I'm sorry."

I wave off her comment. "What's the hottest fragrance this year?"

"Who are you shopping for? Your mother? Someone special?"

Even in my muddled state I find it sad that she didn't expect me to have someone in my life besides my mother. Then again, I'm no model, and I just told her I have an ear disorder. "Girl-friend," I say.

John laughs. The woman ducks to grab a bottle. "What are you laughing at?"

"Chantel, your *girlfriend*?"

"What else should I call her?"

John shrugs. "It's your relationship, but I don't think you're that exclusive."

The woman's back, holding a bottle, but I ignore her. "What's that supposed to mean?"

"See for yourself." He turns my head and directs it toward the pretzel shop.

Standing before it, nibbling on a chocolate-dipped churro, is Chantel. The churro is being held above her mouth by some guy, who's not close to seventeen, but not old enough to be her dad. He smiles as she reaches with her teeth. He teases it away, but then relents and gives her another bite. She presses her lips with a napkin. I feel as if I might hurl.

The perfume saleswoman coughs and I turn. "This is one of our most popular." She models the squat yellow bottle and sprays the air. I sniff. I don't know why. I guess it's automatic after having seen my mother and sister do the same countless times. Because what I really want to do is grab the bottle and throw it at the goateed guy's head.

"How much?" I mumble and don't hear the response. Not that it matters. I made $4,500 for the "Thanksgiving Massacre." That's what Ricky titled it for more hits. Who knows what we'll get for "Christmas Electroshock Therapy"?

"Sounds good." I hand the bottle back.

"Would you like it gift wrapped?"

"Please," I say and turn to John.

He shakes his head. "I don't know, Ben. That doesn't look good. Sorry."

I'm angry, but I'm also disappointed. Not because Chantel and I aren't exclusive. I don't know if I ever felt we were. No, I'm upset that so much got in the way of that happening. Or I let it? Or she led me on? I don't know the root, and there's no way in hell I'm going to figure it out now. But I'm also relieved, because this is exactly what I was hoping for during our last dare.

I pay for my whatever's gift and point toward the exit.

As we shuffle on, I look back. He strokes her cheek and she giggles. The weight of the perfume pulls on my arm, and up ahead John bumps into a railing.

CHAPTER 23

"**T**hose guys at your school are goddamn crazy!" Chuck greets me as I walk into the shop.

"What?" Playing dumb today is easier than usual.

He waves me toward his "office," this closet of a room. "Come, see." Chuck got a computer after Thanksgiving's rush and has finally figured out how to use it.

I follow him in, and, indeed, our YouTube channel is up. Trevor scored the opening credits with "Rockin' Around the Christmas Tree," and the video plays out with each of us and the corresponding tree lighting. What I didn't expect are the close-ups. I have no recollection of Trevor doing that. He must have gotten down on one knee to get the angle. It was worth it, though, because all of our twitching is a stark contrast to the multicolored glow behind us.

Each of us has a Christmas song clip accompaniment, too. Mine is "Deck the Halls." I like the idea of kids all around town hearing that as they decorate their own trees or sit around boring family get-togethers, cracking up.

"Unbelievable, right?"

I shake my head. "I told you they were nuts."

"Yeah, but there are levels of insanity. This," he points at the screen, "this is deranged."

I agree, but really can't say much. It may not take a professor to see what is obvious. I shuffle out of the office and Alexia's at the counter. Seeing her knots up my stomach. We're taking care of Jesse tomorrow night.

"Hey, Alexia."

"Oh, hey, Ben." She jumps a little, but more startled than scared.

I don't know what to say since we haven't really spoken after I dropped by her house.

"You okay? Seem like something's up." She turns to me and everything about her is so genuinely nice. I'd like more of her in my life. There is no question of that after what I've seen. But knowing and doing are two completely different ideas.

"It's nothing. Have you and Chantel been hanging out much?"

Alexia sighs. "She hasn't really had much time for me. She was like my Siamese twin when Jesse was, you know, but now, I thought she was off with you all the time."

That hurts. If she's been gone that much, I have an idea who she's been with. "Right. I thought so. How is Jesse?" I don't even know why I'm asking this. Must be the taser.

She turns away. "Fine, good really."

I feel like pulling up her sleeves to make sure, but I say, "That's cool."

Alexia shoots me a look like she used to when I first started here. Like some slug she found in her salad. Or some one-time friend she wanted to remain that way. "Guess so." She moves away and counts empty boxes.

I slump back against the counter and can't help feeling like an ass. I hum "Rockin' Around the Christmas Tree" but it doesn't help.

—

Of course Ginny's car is in the driveway. Why wouldn't it be? She's home for break and will want to grill me about my suicidal tendencies. I just want to go to bed.

I walk in and the house is dead quiet. The fire's burning, but none of my family is around. "Hello?"

The fire pops in response. I walk upstairs. The fire's going up here as well and I'm momentarily happy. But where is everybody? My parents' room is dark, but Ginny's light is on. I knock. Nothing. I knock again. "Ginny?" Still nothing. "I'm opening the door."

She's on her bed, earbuds in her head, iPod at her side, laptop in front of her. I flick the lights and she jumps. "Jesus Christ, Ben! The fuck are you doing?"

"Saying hey. Where are Mom and Dad?"

She powers off her music and settles back on the bed. "Out to dinner. Didn't you hear?"

I search my useless brain and come up empty. "Hear what?"

Ginny tilts her head. "You kind of look like shit."

I sit on the chair near her door. "You see our video?"

She nods.

"It doesn't wear off right away."

Ginny shakes her head and pierces me with her look. "Benny, come on. Enough's enough."

"Yeah, yeah. What's the deal? What didn't I hear?"

She grimaces, obviously ready to lecture me, but she stops herself. "Dad got the job."

"What? Really?" I'm not sure if I'm excited or doubtful.

"Yeah. He starts next week. They went out to LongHorn's to celebrate."

This is fantastic. "Do you think he could buy back our house?" I startle myself with this one, even put a hand over my mouth.

Ginny looks confused. "Man, your brain is messed up. What?"

"No one lives there. I stopped by and it was empty."

She moves to the corner of the bed, into her "chatting" pose. "That may be, but people do renovations to homes before they move in all the time. And Dad's only had his job for a little while, so it's not as if he won the lottery or anything. I don't think they're financially prepared to do anything but put us through school." She takes a deep breath. "Speaking of which, did you tell them about your SAT scores? Show them your report card?"

I process her point about the house and have to admit it makes sense, so I answer her questions. "No. To both."

"Good. But have you been studying?"

"Yeah," I lie. She opens her mouth to say something, but I interrupt. "You finish your shopping?"

"Yeah, Christmas is in a week."

"I know, but it was hard this year, right? I didn't know what to get Mom and Dad."

"I hear you." She pauses. "What about me?"

"Oh, that was easy," I say, and Ginny perks up. "A guest appearance in our next dare."

She frowns. "Get Out There, that's your sponsor, right?"

Butterflies erupt in my belly. "Yeah, why?"

Ginny grabs her computer. "I think you should be concerned."

"What do you mean?"

She clicks the mouse a few times and turns the computer to me. Get Out There Adventure's website is on the screen. Nothing looks out of place, but the butterflies all die and my stomach drops.

"What's going on?"

She takes a deep breath. "Here's the deal. I went to the site to buy you a Christmas gift. I was thinking one of those ultrawarm sleeping bags because you've been complaining about how cold it is at night. Figured it would be ironic that it came from your sponsor's store."

I'm following her, knowing full well there's going to be a significant BUT coming in this story.

"I started searching the site. What did you say the name of your guy is?"

"O. P. Why?"

"So I *was* right. I couldn't find anyone listed on the site by that name. Same when I Googled."

My brain's processing and I'm trying to formulate a conclusion to all this, but it's not coming together.

"So I emailed. They said that they don't have anyone with that name on staff."

I take in what she's said, but it's like trying to cram clothes into an already full hamper. The thoughts spill onto the floor like so many dirty socks. "So? What's your point? Maybe he isn't using his real name with us?" I know that sounds stupid, even for me.

"My point is that if you really are being sponsored by someone from this company, you should know who he is."

"What do you mean, *if* we really are? We're getting paid." I say this, but I'm pulled back to our last argument with Ricky. I want to talk to O. P. now more than ever.

"Benny, that doesn't mean anything. Have you seen the checks?"

I stare at the floor because I don't know what else to do. In Ginny's face are too many accusations. I haven't seen the checks; Ricky gives us our cut. So if what she says is right, which is still an *if,* but still—who did we sign a contract with? And why is he paying us? I grab my head and squeeze because it feels like I'm getting tasered again. Except I know this time there's no one there to flip the switch and shut this thing off.

CHAPTER 24

Ru avoiding me?

R u mad?

Why won't u return my texts?

Why didn't u pick up? I just called.

Come over later?

I ignore all of Chantel's messages because I don't know what to do with her right now. I want to confront her about the guy from the mall, but I'm not prepared for the answer she'll give me. I'll either come out looking like some stalker, asshole boyfriend—if I even have that status—or she'll let me know it's some other guy she's with. Either way, I lose. And right now, I've got to keep my head straight.

"Is that Chantel blowing you up?" John asks.

I tuck my phone away. "Yeah. Unfortunately." I look at John and he gives me a knowing nod. "What time does the lot close?" I know the answer. We've been through this a dozen times. I just need help focusing.

"Nine, and Jesse's the closer. All by himself," Ricky answers. His voice is scratchy, like he's been at a concert screaming his head off. I wonder how things are at home. I should ask, but when and how am I going to do that?

The lights start popping off at the front of the lot. A car with a tree strapped to the roof drives off. It's 9:05, time to roll.

"Masks, boys," Ricky says and pulls out his own.

We each retrieve the plastic elf faces that he picked up for us. Mine is super tight and in an instant condensation builds on my lip. Ricky turns and looks at us. "You know the plan. Simple grab and tackle. No one says a fucking word from here on out."

I wish I possessed the ability to plan this, but I was either too scared or too smart to run the reconnaissance. Ricky didn't mind. Trevor helped, and now here we are about to move ahead with a plan that is all about vengeance.

My heart races. I've been in a couple of fights, but nothing serious, nothing like this. But I'm worried. Not about my fighting skills—it's four on one—but the aftermath. We may put him in the hospital, and I don't know how I feel about that. But then I think of Alexia. And of Trevor. Still, if we do this, are we any better than him?

And I have to wonder, would I have ever considered this possible before I started these dares?

The rest of the lights blink off, and the only illumination that remains comes from the little booth where Jesse has a register and a small heater. He's counting the cash as our boots crunch over the snow. He looks up when Ricky taps on the window, and for a second, he stares. That second is all it takes for Ricky and John to pull him out of the booth and send him sprawling into the snow.

John tugs my arm and points at Jesse. This is my fight, but I'm stuck, can't move. Ricky's not. He takes two steps like he's kicking a field goal and then splits the uprights with Jesse's head.

Jesse falls onto his back, and I turn away. I'm sure the point we're trying to prove has been made with that one blow, but the sound of fists on flesh rises behind me.

I stand apart from the guys, cloaked in darkness and surrounded by Christmas trees. My family comes here, but we haven't yet this year. There's no way I'm coming back after this.

Someone grabs my shoulder and spins me, then punches me square in the nose. I fall to the ground, blood pouring out. I brace for more, but my attacker moves on, drops John, who is standing back while Ricky and Trevor are wailing away on Jesse.

Blood fills my throat and I hack to clear it. I rip the broken mask from my face and see Trevor kicking Jesse. He and Ricky don't know what's coming at them. I scream, "Ricky!" but it's drowned in my throat. John sits up and his mask is gone. His eye is swollen shut. What the fuck happened?

I get to my knees in time to see the bat. It flashes under the lights before it is swung, taking out Ricky's and then Trevor's legs in one swoop. They cry out and fall to the ground next to Jesse.

Ricky and Trevor hold their knees and scream, while Jesse hoists himself up. He's blood-soaked and disheveled, but looks outraged.

"John, let's go. Get help."

"You aren't going anywhere, bitches. Stand up."

I don't need to turn around to know who is at my back. Danny Blackman's voice is distinct, deeper than any teacher's. Which means the one with the bat must be Chris Carsdale.

I look over at John and he's got his hands raised like a gun's to him. Carsdale has a bat to his chin. I scramble up and move toward my friends, but am forced right back down by a boot to the ass.

I stand, sure that a bat's going to crack my skull, but none does. John appears at my side, and he helps me up. We move to Ricky and Trevor. They're still holding their knees but are crying out less. Jesse is on his feet, wiping off his face. He looks at us, and I'd rather risk running through Carsdale's swing than face him.

"You all must have a death wish." Jesse looks at the guys on the ground. "Stand the fuck up!"

They don't move, so Danny and Chris hoist them up and pin them against a wall of Christmas trees. "Stand with them," Jesse barks to John and me. We move.

The guys' eyes are wide with fear and none can stand straight. They lean on one another, and this feels like an execution line. Danny hands Jesse a bat. He paces before us and smacks it into his palm.

"So the four of you asstards thought you could take me out?" He laughs. It's beyond disturbing because he's covered in blood and seems not the least bit bothered by this fact.

"What I want to know is why." He stills and looks at each of us. "Sure, fudge-packer, Trev may have some beef, but I haven't done shit to him in a while. Or are you three really so tight that you'd help him out, anyway?"

I breathe through my mouth, feeling very much like an animal—scared, stupid, and utterly at this asshole's mercy. The only safe connection is Trevor, but we can't do that to him, make this about his history, even if that's what Jesse thinks. But the only other card is Alexia, and we sure as hell can't play that one either. We're screwed.

"Pretty much," Ricky says, and his voice is strong and makes me feel slightly better.

Jesse stops before him and leans the bat into his chest. "So you're a little fag, too?" He spits. "Never would have expected that." He pushes the bat in deeper and steps back. "That the same for you two?"

Jesse's looking at John and me. We don't move. "That's right." Jesse removes the bat from Ricky's chest and moves toward us. "Big boy here's been too busted up for any action, so who knows? But you," he points the end of the bat at me, "you're into that sweet, sweet Chantel."

Jesse looks over his shoulder. "She is a good time, isn't she, boys?"

Danny and Chris nod and grin like the ghouls they are.

"Yeah, we partied over the summer. *All* of us. You get me, Ben?" He steps directly before me.

I feel sickened and am ashamed because I feel this way. I don't know if he's lying or telling the truth, but the fact is, I can imagine Chantel doing that. She used me for one night and then kicked me to the curb. Or did she? Didn't this asshole get in the way of everything because of what he did to Alexia? Shit, what about Alexia?

"I get you," I say. "I know all about you, you spineless asshole."

Everyone stills and Jesse tilts his head. "What did you say to me?"

"You heard me, but I'll repeat it if you'd like." I've lost my mind.

It's that simple. The adrenaline rush is so similar to that of the dares that I'm not thinking straight. Jesse has a bat pointed at my head and I'm calling him out. Dad may have been right to get me away from Ricky all those years ago.

Jesse smiles. "Now I understand. Little Benny wanted to hurt me because I hurt Alexia."

"Fuck you, Jesse. Either put us all in the hospital or let us go, because listening to you is a worse punishment than death." Trevor does not lisp once.

Jesse rushes to him, gets right in flis face. "Who the fuck do you think you're talking to?"

"You're Jesse Holmes, and I'm Trevor Culin. Seems like you've forgotten."

I may be losing it, but Trevor is completely gone.

Jesse raises the bat. "Exactly. And soon, when I split your head open with this bat, you won't remember anything."

I cringe at what I know is coming, but John bolts. The bat is midswing when he gets there and blocks just like he's done so many times on the court. The bat flies out of Jesse's hands and skips across the ground. I dive for it, and see Ricky do the same. I get to it first and stand.

Everyone is frantic, crouched, waiting for the next move. John's holding his bad arm, probably messed up again from what he did. Ricky's watching the bat and nodding at Jesse. Blackman and Carsdale have moved to Jesse's side. Trevor stands tall.

"Guys, go."

"Ben, what? It's only a bat. You can't take all three of them on," Ricky says.

"Goddamn it, Ricky, shut the fuck up and do what *I* say! Now!" My scream echoes and everyone is still again. But a moment later, John, Ricky, and Trevor walk past me to the car, Ricky whispering, "Don't try to be a hero."

Now, it's only me.

"So what's your move here, Ben?" Jesse asks, not as brave as before, but not entirely scared either.

I'm shaking inside, but I know I can't let him see it. "There's no move, Jesse. I'm not like you. But I will say this, if you touch Alexia or Trevor again, I'll find a way to take you out."

"I've seen who you know. I'm not so fucking scared, but thanks for the warning. I'll be sure to, uh, pass it along to Alexia."

I grip the bat and step forward. I could reach him from here, could get his leg or his temple, somehow mess up all his athletic plans. But I might not connect. Danny or Chris might jump in the way, like John. Shit, poor John.

"Believe me, don't believe me, that's your call. But I dare you to try me. You have no idea of what I'm willing to do."

Jesse looks at me and a spark of something new alters his face. He sees me, but it's not me. Holding the bat, realizing what I've said, I see it, too. I'm not the same person anymore.

I turn away, not afraid, and join my friends.

I climb in shotgun and Ricky looks at me. "Everything cool?"

"We'll see," I say. "But let's go before they get any ideas."

Ricky takes off and Trevor leans over the seat. "Thanks, Ben."

"Any time, Trev." I mean this.

"I thought you would like to know we have a little security."

I turn in my seat and look at him. He holds up a voice recorder and presses play:

"You're Jesse Holmes, and I'm Trevor Culin. Seems like you've forgotten."

"Exactly. And soon, when I split your head open with this bat, you won't remember anything."

Trevor turns the recorder off. "We're safe." He smiles and I'd love to return it, but he didn't see what I saw in Jesse's eyes.

"For now."

—

We've dropped everyone off, Trevor last, so I'm walking since the condo's just over from his development. But I wait for Ricky to return. He looks worse than I feel.

"Is he okay?" I ask.

"Yeah, just a bad bruise. Nothing's broken, I don't think."

I nod. "He sure stepped it up tonight, didn't back down from Jesse at all."

"Yeah, I'm proud of his stupid ass."

"You think Jesse's going to tell the cops?"

Ricky sighs. "No, not his style. Besides, we've got Trevor's recording. Slip that to him in an email. Guarantee he stays away."

I feel like saying something about what I saw in Jesse. But how do I describe that? "That's a good plan, and since we're already conferencing with O. P. we should probably let him know, in case."

"True, but I doubt Jesse will pull another copycat."

He's right. "Yeah, but just to be safe."

"I guess so."

"When we talking to him?"

"I don't know. He hasn't gotten back to me." Ricky looks away, and I don't like the move.

"So *you* tell *him*."

Ricky looks at me now. "He calls the shots, not us."

"Bullshit! *We* call the shots. You realize we signed and none of us are eighteen. He's got no power. I'm out unless we talk." I say this, but after what happened with Jesse, I don't even know if I believe it.

Ricky grabs my shoulder and spins me. "One, quit using that line, it's an empty threat. And two, you can't be out. Not after all this."

"I can't? Watch me." I turn again, expecting him to get me in a headlock this time. That was a dick move on my part. Instead, I hear him plead behind me.

"Please don't do this, Ben." For possibly the first time in my life, I realize that Ricky is on the verge of tears.

I step back to him. "Rick, I'm sorry. This is too much. I know getting back at Jesse was my idea, but that doesn't mean I can't see the writing on the wall. Tonight did not go as planned. And more than that, big picture, I'm worried about O. P. Have you ever been to his site? We're never mentioned or linked. I'm not even sure he works there."

"Yeah, yeah, you figured all this out because you're so fucking smart. You see everything. You understand everything." He shoots me such a dirty look, he either ignored what I said or it hurt that much. "How's everything with Chantel working out? Huh?" His eyes are brimming and his face is flushed. "We all heard what Jesse said."

I look away. "I don't know. I think she used me, but I have no idea why."

"I'm sorry about that. Shit, I know the feeling. But don't use this as an excuse. Don't go running because you're scared, Ben. That's what you always do."

"What the hell are you talking about? I'm not scared; I want answers."

"No, you don't. You want shit to go the way you want it to, because you're scared of everything. Like with Chantel. You're with her because she's the second best option to Alexia. And now you're talking shit about O. P. because all the pieces aren't neatly in place. Because you believe that we—or you—should be running the show. Guess what, we're not."

Ricky takes a deep breath and moves closer to me, dropping his voice. "You would know that if you ever read the contract you begged me for. You think it won't hold up because we're not eighteen? There's a clause in there around that point. Yeah, that's his money if we walk. He can ask for *all of it* back." He lets that point settle before moving on.

"There, that's your life. It's a fucking mess and you can't run from it because you're a scared little boy, too afraid to recognize who you are and what you want." Ricky's voice is hoarse, but his words are sharp.

"Ricky, I . . ."

"Don't, Ben. I can't handle another excuse. Tonight was way fucked up and it's because we did something to help you and to help Alexia. Don't confuse that in all the little excuses you're creating."

"And to get back at that asshole for Trev." Now I cut him off. "Don't forget that."

Ricky steps closer to me, and he looks so drained I don't know how he's standing. "I know, Ben. I do. You and me, we're not that different. We were boys in middle school. You, me, and John. Shit changed and we went our separate ways. But you can't dismiss that we're back together for some reason bigger than us. I know I blew smoke with the legacy shit. But maybe this is it. Not the way we planned, but so what?"

I nod and feel my own face flush. Ricky puts his hand on my shoulder.

"Don't bail on us, Ben. We need you. And you need us."

He's right, about so much I've been too afraid to admit to myself. "That's the truth." I pat his hand, and turn toward the condo.

I feel like I'm back at square one, Law One. This *me* Ricky's talking about is the same one Ginny asked about motivation. And I didn't know, but maybe now I do? Or is this me, still in Law Two, perpetually moving forward, now gaining speed? Or is this a perfect example of the Third Law and all my actions coming back to haunt me?

CHAPTER 25

"**D**id you hear what happened to Jesse Holmes?"

Wide eyes, slack jaw.

"He got jumped by some gang and they stole all his money."

Wider eyes. "No shit?"

"Did you hear what happened to Jesse Holmes?"

"Yeah, jumped by like a gang."

"No, it was the mob. The owner didn't pay them enough, I guess. Jesse took the hit."

"No shit?"

"Did you hear what happened to Jesse Holmes?"

"Didn't he like bust up a bunch of mailboxes?"

"Huh? What? No, he got the shit kicked out of him."

"Probably screwed someone's girlfriend."

"No shit?"

I hear these conversations and dozens more. It's all the school is talking about. Not once did I hear anyone say anything about us. Which is good, I guess. Somehow they've looked past John's black eye and my busted nose. I told my parents I slipped on the ice. Same story I'll use around here if anyone asks.

Ricky is at his locker but Trevor isn't with him.

"Where's Trevor?" I ask.

"He's sick." Ricky keeps his expression flat, so we understand what he really means. "You hear all the rumors?"

"Yeah, just now," John says.

"Anything about us?"

"Nothing," I answer.

I look down the hall and see Alexia's tear-puffy face. And next to her, Chantel. Ricky clears his throat. I step away and go to the girls.

Alexia turns away when I approach, but Chantel is all over me. "Hey, where were you? I thought maybe you'd come over. My parents put up the tree. . . ." She stops. "What happened to your nose?"

I don't look at her, but watch Alexia. She snaps around and gives me a cold, calculated look, taking in my face.

"Uh, well." I act caught off-guard, but really I'm prepared. "My dad got a new job and we were out celebrating. I slipped on the sidewalk."

Alexia's face falls, and I feel awful because it was clear, if only for a moment, that she believed I was somehow connected.

"My poor baby." Chantel strokes my neck, and I resist pulling away. This isn't what we do. This isn't who we are. But I don't want a scene.

"Sorry about Jesse," I say to Alexia. "Really."

Alexia bobs her head and holds a tissue to her face. Chantel hangs on the space between us, and I forget about her and concentrate on what I really want to say and to whom. "At some point, he won't be there for you. But I always will."

Alexia pulls the tissue from her face and stares at me. Chantel's mouth hangs open. "What the hell, Ben?"

I size up Chantel, think of a dozen things I could say, but don't, because they reflect right back on me. "Alexia's been my friend longer than she's been yours. Relax." I grab her hand and squeeze and then head back to the guys.

"Everything good?" Ricky asks.

"All depends how you look at it," I say.

—

Chuck grabs me and holds me at arm's length. "Doc, the hell happened to your face?"

I give him the lie and say it loud enough in case Alexia's listening.

"Shit. Don't scare the customers," Chuck says.

I punch in. Alexia's behind the counter, taking calls and acting fine, like her boyfriend wasn't beaten last night.

"Hey, I've got like three deliveries in your old neighborhood." She stops. "I'm sorry, I didn't mean it that way."

I don't need her to be more of a mess, so I laugh it off. "No, it's fine. Let me see the tickets." I grab them from her and check the addresses. All down my street. Former. I look up and see how dark the circles are under Alexia's eyes, and whatever cute remark I was going to say is gone. "You all right? I mean, I know you can't be, but still."

She turns away her eyes are filling. "Yeah. I thought he was someone different. You know? But all those rumors . . . He said he got robbed. But when I asked him why he didn't call the cops, he started yelling at me, like it was my fault."

My stomach folds and I fear for Alexia. Jesse's going to be out for blood. And my connection to her may mean trouble. I rub her back because I don't know what to say, and she lets her chin fall to her chest.

"Ben, I'm scared. I've been with Jesse long enough to know his moods. I've never seen him this dark."

I rub in wider circles, wishing I could wash this all away, but knowing I am to blame. Alexia lets out a small sigh and turns to me.

"Ben?" Her face is wide open, eyes searching mine.

"Yeah?" I manage to say, even though I'm confused. Something about her seems as if I can help. As if she needs *my* assistance and mine alone. I remember this face.

"Hey, there's no mistletoe in here, you lovebirds!" Chuck says, oblivious to the moment. Alexia collects herself and looks busy with the remaining slips. Chuck grabs mine out of my hand.

"Looky here. You're headed back to your old digs, huh?"

I don't answer. There's no point.

"What happened to your place anyway?"

It takes me a second to regroup. "We sold it," I manage to say and want to punch Chuck in his gut for interrupting.

"No shit? What happened to the deal? Because no one lives there. The bank owns it now."

I wait for the joke, for whatever stupid line Chuck's going to insert, but it doesn't come. He just stands there, smelling like sweat and staring at me.

"How do *you* know?"

"You kidding me? This isn't my only gig. Real estate is where it's at. You buy, flip, resell, or these days, rent. Best damn use of your money. Fact is, if I can get a good price on your old place, I might buy it, thanks to you."

He's got to be joking with me. But I saw the house's emptiness with my own eyes.

"Benny?" Alexia asks.

Chuck slaps me hard. "You'll be fine, Doc. A little fresh air will do you good. Get on those deliveries and see if there's one of those brochures for your old place."

He leaves and my legs feel watery. If he's telling the truth, I'm pissed. If that house, my home, is on the market, we should be getting it back. Dad's working again. I've got some cash. It could happen in spite of what Ginny said. Maybe there is a way for me to restart? I grab my orders and charge out to the Jeep.

Like a few months before, a FOR SALE sign sits on my lawn. I grab it, and the cold metal singes. I try to pry it from the ground, but it's frozen in place, so I leave it be and walk up my front steps and have a seat. I love this porch. Playing out here with John, watching sunsets with Mom, waiting for Dad to come home from work. Even playing with Ginny. I look around. Not much has changed since I was a kid, but I damn sure have.

I take a deep breath, not to get calm, but to absorb the air from my home. *My* home. Where I belong. I think a moment and know exactly what I need to do.

Christmas songs are playing on the radio. Mom's humming while she wraps gifts in front of the fire. Dad's stringing lights on the tree with Ginny. It's like walking into some painting, except for the ugly floral print and raspberry carpet. I go to unzip my coat, but look at the tree again, and flash back to the lot.

"You okay, bud?" Dad holds a strand of lights, limply. Ginny looks up as well.

"Yeah, yeah. I, you know . . ." I almost say, *I was just at the house and it's for sale, and wouldn't that make an awesome Christmas gift?* But instead I offer, "Tired. That's all. Long day."

"I hear you. But it's nice to have a long day again." He goes back to hanging the lights. Ginny shoots me a concerned look. Mom sighs and pats the box she's finished wrapping.

I hang my coat on the rack and kick off my boots. I'll talk to Ginny later, but for now, I'll go get warm by the fire.

I start to nod off after having moved from the hearth to the couch, where I'm staring at the fire. Dad and Ginny asked if I wanted to join in the decorating, but I offered suggestions from where I sat. Mom wrapped and I let the music pass over me while I sifted through all that we're jammed up in.

I stand up, yawn, and stretch.

"Time for bed?" Mom looks at me over her glass of wine.

"Yeah. I'm beat."

"Come give me a kiss before you go." I plant one on her cheek. She seems to radiate the same warmth as the fire.

"Are you happy here?" I don't even know why I'm asking.

She tilts her head and thinks for a minute. "It's corny, but my mother always said, 'Home is where your heart is.' And so, yeah, I'm happy here." She turns to me. "You?"

I shift and look away. "Yeah, I guess. It's just . . ." And I almost say something about the house, but what would be the point? I'll let her have this.

"It's not the same," Mom finishes for me.

I nod, grateful for her insight.

"Ben, even if we were there it wouldn't be the same. You're leaving at the end of the summer, and Ginny's on her way toward finishing up her undergrad. Might as well make the change now."

"I hear you," I say, squeeze her shoulder, and make my way upstairs, where thankfully the fireplace is roaring.

I'm almost asleep, to the point where I'm reviewing the day and feeling the weight of it pass through me, when Ginny darts into my room.

"Shit, it's still cold in here."

I have to force myself to speak. "Yeah, cold."

"Were you sleeping?" She sits on the edge of the bed.

"Almost." I click on my bedside lamp and we both squint at the light. "What's up?"

"You tell me. You walked through that door like someone asked you to bury a dead body."

Ginny and her ability to read everything. I guess she's always had this gift. "Not a body, but a house."

"What? What the hell are you into now?"

I prop up on my elbow and squeeze my eyes. "It's not like that." I collect what I'm going to say before speaking. "Our house is for sale again."

"Our old one?"

"Uh huh."

"How do you know?"

I explain about the delivery and Chuck. I leave out the part about sitting on the front steps.

"Damn," Ginny says and bites a nail. "That'll sting when they find out."

"Yeah, it will." I imagine both their faces. Awful. "Is there any way you could look into what happened, find out what the price is and what the deal is with the bank?"

Ginny's eyes narrow. "Why, what are you thinking?"

I sit fully upright and rest against the wall. "I was going to ask you to keep looking into Get Out There. Ricky didn't want to hear anything about O. P. And since you're at it, maybe check on this. Who knows? Dad's working now."

She nods, a slow, filtering motion. "Okay, but we've had this conversation before. It's not a tangible option."

"I know. But looking into it can't hurt. Come on, you're not the slightest bit interested in what's going on?"

"Yeah, I guess I am." She looks me over. "Huh?"

Her one word sounds like the summary of a dissertation. "What's the *huh* for?"

She smiles, and when she does, she looks so much like Mom it's unnerving. "Because of all this shit with the dares, I've been looking at you as this, I don't know, stupid-hormonal-teenage-boy-with-his-head-up-his-ass."

"Thanks. I guess."

"Well, you are. But there's more, too. Benny Bear's still in there." She rubs the top of my head. "Still the same, but different. Good." She pauses. "Except *I'm* still worried. I don't care what Ricky thinks. I'll pull the plug on your operation myself if you do anything riskier than shocking one another. Also, your grades, they suck ass." Ginny pulls a piece of paper out of her back pocket and hands it over.

I know what it is before opening it and do not want to look. But I do. My interim is as shitty as I expected. Still close to failing everything but English and PE. I sigh.

"I got it out of the mail today." She shakes her head and stands. "If you're concerned about them, maybe you'd better take care of that first, and then maybe we can figure out the house."

"Yeah. I guess so." My voice is heavy from sleep and embarrassment.

She goes to the door. "If I leave this open a crack, you won't be so cold."

"Here's hoping." I snap off my light and lie back down.

Ginny lingers as if she's going to say more, but she doesn't.

The fire crackles in the hall and I settle into my pillow, accepting that all is not in my hands, and for everyone, it's better that way.

CHAPTER 26

I awake Christmas morning to a text from Chantel: **Merry Christmas. Hope to see you later ;).** I don't reply, but shudder against the cold. I've kept the door propped open, but the dying fire is no match for the draft of these windows. I stand and pull on a sweatshirt and warm-ups, find my slippers, and head downstairs.

Of course I'm the last one awake, but they haven't unwrapped anything yet and are sitting by the fire drinking coffee.

"Merry Christmas," I announce and they respond in unison. I fill up my own mug and join them, sitting next to Ginny on the love seat.

I sip and take in the stack of presents. Or should I say the lump. In years past, Ginny and I have had pounds of presents, piles we'd have to work to finish unwrapping, only so we could play with the ones we really wanted. This year, however, I'm lucky if there are five gifts under that tree, and nothing looks more significant than a sweater.

Mom, noticing my look, sits up and extends an arm toward the tree. "It's not the most extravagant year we've had, but it sure beats some of the early ones, huh, Joe?"

Dad looks into his mug. "Yes, it does. Like 'Gift of the Magi' a couple times."

I feel ashamed.

"Here we go." Mom hands over gifts to Ginny and me, and then both my parents sit back and watch us open them. Same as we always do.

I was right about the sweater. It's a nice cable-knit black one. Dad says, "To keep you warm on those deliveries." I think I may wear it to bed. Other than that, socks and underwear and a gift card, and I'm out. Ginny gets the same, except her sweater is pink. We both say thank you, and I'm glad to hear the effort in Ginny's voice matches my own.

My parents normally exchange their gifts to each other, but instead they stare at us. Then Dad realizes. "Oh, right. Your mother and I aren't exchanging this year." Pain spreads across his face.

"Right." Ginny and I both hop off the couch and distribute our gifts. My parents don't look us in the eyes, and I feel somehow like I'm handing presents to charity cases.

We sit back down and open Ginny's gifts first. She got me a College Survival kit, filled with things like earplugs, a shower tote, and a collapsible hamper. I wonder when she bought it, because if she still has hope for me making it away for school, she might not be as bright as we believe.

"Isn't that adorable," Mom says.

"Wish I'd had one," Dad says.

I say thank you but Ginny gives me one of her lifted eyebrow stares.

She bought my mother perfume and my father a portfolio. He chokes up.

"I knew you'd get back on your feet," she says and he gets up and hugs her and it's so damn sweet I hate myself.

They move onto my gifts and Ginny actually gasps. "No shit? Where'd you get this?"

She's holding up a copy of some rare book by this guy G. Stanley Hall. Apparently he's important in adolescent psychology. There's a book dealer in town who orders a calzone every Friday and helped me find it. "I have my connections," I answer, and Ginny punches my arm. She's shocked, and it's awesome.

Mom opens her gift, this cashmere sweater I've seen her looking at in one of her many catalogs. "Benny, this is . . . perfect." She holds it up to Dad and he nods, but then looks at me quizzically before opening his own present.

He stares for a long moment but holds up the monogrammed desk nameplate. It's mahogany and has a slot for his business cards. He shakes his head and chokes out a thank you. They all stare at me and I feel hot and uncomfortable.

"Ben, how did you? The expense? Where did you get the money?" Mom's stroking her sweater, and I don't think she realizes it. Dad's staring at his nameplate, but Ginny looks up from the book she's been leafing through.

The answer is of course from the dares. These purchases didn't make a dent in what I have saved, but I can't say that. "Good tips, I guess."

Dad bursts out laughing. He realizes the abruptness of it and puts a hand to his mouth but continues to giggle. "All this time I've been out of work I should have been delivering pizzas."

Mom and Ginny laugh along with him and Ginny punches me again, giving me eyes that reveal she knows where the cash is from.

"Christ, I could have bought the house back if I went and worked for Chuck." Dad laughs harder at his joke and I don't mean to, but I say it.

"You could get the house back now. It's for sale."

All laughter stops. The only noise comes from the crackle of the fireplace and the low din of the Christmas music in the background.

"What did you say?" Dad's voice is low and almost ugly.

"The house. It's back on the market." I turn away from him but looking at Ginny doesn't help. She stares with more intensity than Mom.

"What? How do you know?" Dad's edged closer on his seat.

"I was making deliveries and saw the sign." I leave out the part about Chuck. I don't think it will help the situation.

Dad looks into his lap and then runs his tongue over his lips. "How long?"

"What do you mean?"

"How long has it been on the market?" Dad snaps, and all the festivity is drained from the room.

"Joe, let's not do this now." Mom reaches over and grabs his arm.

He doesn't notice. "How long?"

"I saw the sign last week."

"Last week? Jesus, why didn't you tell me?"

I can feel Ginny's eyes boring into the side of my face, probably wondering how I'll handle this. But in spite of my grades, I'm not stupid, just distracted by life. "I wasn't sure you'd want to know."

"Why wouldn't I want . . ." Dad stops short. We all know what he was about to say, and we all know why I didn't tell him. He closes his eyes and shakes his head. We each look in different directions. A moment later he stands. "I'm going for a walk."

Mom reaches out to him. "Joe, don't. Not now. It's Christmas."

"I won't be long. Besides, we aren't doing anything else, are we?"

His words cut us all, because, no, we aren't. Normally we might install the newest video or electronics or whatever big gift we received. But there are no big gifts this year.

He re-emerges wearing a face of determination. I know exactly where he's going and can only imagine his reaction. Maybe he'll have more success with the sign.

The door closes behind him, and Mom moves to the window to watch him go. She turns back to us and I expect anger, but her eyes dart instead, pure worry. She grabs her mug, moves to the liquor cabinet, and pours in a hefty amount of sambuca. She settles back on the couch and stares at the fire. Ginny nods toward the stairs and Mom doesn't look up at us when we move away.

Ginny's room is much warmer than mine and I'm jealous, but there's no time for that.

"What did you did you do that for?"

"I didn't mean to. Really. It just popped out."

She gives me a dirty look and sits on her bed, crosses her arms over her chest. I take a seat on the floor.

"Shit, I was getting somewhere too," she says.

"With the house or the other?"

"The house. I still don't have anything on whomever is paying you. But obviously you're making money." She looks down at me. "Seriously, how much did you spend?"

"Couple hundred," I mumble.

"Jesus, Ben. That's more than our gifts combined."

I feel ashamed. I just didn't think. I know we've been up against it, but we downsized and Dad started working again. How long does it take to get out of debt and start earning? Shit, I don't really want to know the answer to that. "So, the house?"

Ginny sighs. "Yeah. Right. It's been foreclosed. Apparently whoever bought it never made any payments and the bank didn't waste any time. It foreclosed and is now trying to unload the house."

"Why didn't they call us?"

Ginny looks at me like I've hurled on her floor. "Really? How often do you think people who just sold their house want to buy it back?"

I shrug because I have no idea, but these days, maybe more than she thinks.

"Exactly. So the house will either get sold at the asking price or . . . it will most likely go to auction."

"Huh?"

"People aren't buying. Especially not down in the village. They want homes up here, in the new section. So the bank will wait and then turn the house over to auction and take the best bid, granted it's enough."

"Like on eBay?"

"Yeah, kind of."

"When does that happen?"

"Hard to know. Maybe in a couple of months." She shakes her head. "Why, you thinking about putting in a bid?"

Ginny smirks and I want to smack her. Does she not realize what I'm pulling in? Give me a few more dares and I'll have some serious cash. "How much would it take, you know, to bid?"

"You serious?"

"Yeah."

She blows air out her mouth. "Ten to twenty percent of the mortgage up front. The house will sell at most for two-hundred thousand, so twenty to forty grand."

She's done her homework. I think how long that might take. If we do well over the next two or three dares, I could have twenty. We'll need more hits, but I'm sure Ricky will be on board. I guess I've made my decision about O. P., too.

"I could swing that. Couple of months."

Ginny squints at me like I'm something that's blossomed out of her carpet. "For real? How much do you have now?"

"Close to twelve grand."

Her eyes bug. "You're seriously making *that much money*?"

I nod.

Ginny runs her hands over her legs. "Then I guess it's possible. But what about school? You won't have to worry about student loans. Pay for your college. Do you know how happy that would make them?"

She's got a point. I close my eyes and imagine telling them I've saved up and will pay for college—that is if that's what I want. We celebrate that fact, but we do so in this condo. Then I imagine telling them I've got them the house back. They lose their fucking minds. "I don't know if I want that."

"Ben, don't be an ass. Please, you doing this could be a step toward being responsible."

"Stop."

Ginny opens her mouth.

"No! Stop!"

She looks at me, eyes pinched.

"Let me do what I'm going to do with my money."

"That's selfish, Ben."

"How? I'm helping either way."

Ginny stares for a moment and turns away. We don't talk for a bit, but finally Ginny says, "You're right, it's your money. I'll keep an eye on the house if you want, talk to the bank and ask to be kept updated."

"Yeah. That sounds good. Thanks."

She wants to say more, but maybe because it's Christmas, or maybe because I'm finally being fully honest with her, she lets it go.

—

Dad came back a little over an hour after leaving, red-faced and dazed. By then Mom was a bit tipsy and she collapsed in a heap of tears in his arms. He dutifully hugged her and set her on the couch. He walked away mumbling and has been in their room since. I've heard him on their computer, probably reconfiguring their finances spreadsheet. I've seen it before, but I'm sure it looks so much more different now. More money going out than coming in. God, I wish I could tell him, but I can't. Not now. Not until I have the cash in hand and we can make heads or tails about the house.

"Dinner!" Mom calls and I set down the magazine I was flipping through. She's been cooking for most of the day and the condo smells like our home used to. But like on Thanksgiving, instead of the dining room, we have a space in the corner near the tiny kitchen, where the table sits on the ugly carpet and the chairs have barely enough clearance.

I move to my seat. "Looks fantastic!" And it does. She went all out making the traditional feast. But it's awkward in this setting.

Even more so than Thanksgiving.

Ginny emerges and sits. "Smells great, Mom." She's super chipper but Mom keeps looking at their bedroom door, which is still closed.

"I'll go," I say, and before she can tell me no, I'm knocking on the door. "Dad, it's me. Time for dinner." He answers but it's muffled by the door. "What?" I ask. He repeats himself, but I still don't understand. Fuck this. I push the door open.

As expected, he's hunched in front of their computer on the little card table he uses for a desk. He whips around in his chair. "I said I'm not coming. Go, eat!" He turns back around and I squeeze the doorknob.

I'm so pissed at myself for starting this, but it's not my fault it happened.

"Dad, it's Christmas. Leave it be for now. Mom's worked hard, you know?"

He laughs, but it's not a cheery, Christmas jolly sound. No, it's bitter and Grinch-like. "I'm sure she has. On a meal we can't afford, *but that she had to have, because it's Christmas.*"

He never talks about her like this and I feel like backing away and leaving the beast in his cage.

"And you with your gifts and news about the house. Don't go telling me to *leave it be.* My own son's got more things figured out than I do." He's turned around now and springs from his chair. "Here," he points at the computer. "You think you can do better? Have a seat. Crunch the numbers. Help me figure it out."

"Dad, that's not what I meant. I just wanted to buy you all something nice and figured you'd want to hear about the house."

"Of course I do! You think I like living here after I worked so goddamn hard to keep that place in shape? Fuck, no!"

He takes a deep breath and I'm glad, because he's more upset than I've ever seen him and I'm afraid for what's next.

"But now, to think that it's out there, just beyond my reach. That's adding insult to injury. I worked my balls off for twenty years and what did I get? Nothing. They teased me with the idea of some transfer and then tossed me out. And now I'm clawing back, like when I first started. But when I first started I could make that house a reality. Now . . ." he takes another breath and his face falls. He seems to lose all his energy and sits heavily in the chair. "Now there's no way, and I hurt all over. I never saw this coming, Ben."

I've got nothing in response. I can't speak, can't move. Don't know how to react. Cry? Yell? I can't make this any better in this moment than he can, but I feel like I need to. So I cross the room and put a hand on his shoulder. I don't say anything. I stay there and wait. He takes his time collecting himself, breathing slow and holding it for a long time. Then he says, "I'm okay."

I release my hand and he stands, rubs his eyes.

"I tried ripping down the sign," I say.

He holds out his palms. They're red and bruised. "I succeeded." He grips my neck and we walk out together.

I text Alexia and wish her a Happy New Year but don't receive a reply. I'm not surprised. Based on her Facebook statuses and Tweets, Jesse's trying to rekindle things, but it also seems as if her dad's getting in the way. Awesome.

My own father's been quiet but stable. I know he's turning over the facts, looking for an answer. Ginny's intelligence isn't a random occurrence.

I walk over to Chantel's because we're supposed to have an evening "just for us." We exchanged gifts on Christmas, but her house was packed with relatives who mostly ignored us. They were all rich businessmen talking about investments and opportunities. I wanted even less to do with them than they did with me.

But tonight her parents are at a party, so I get to see where we stand. I ring the doorbell.

She answers, wearing an outfit that accentuates her breasts in a way that forces me to stare.

"I guess I've gotten your attention." Chantel takes my coat.

"Uh, yeah. Sorry." I'm blushing.

"Don't be." She takes my hand and walks me into the living room. She has a fire roaring in her gas fireplace and champagne on ice on the coffee table.

We sit on the leather and I feel like it's trying to hug me. Chantel leans against my side. "Ben, I'm sorry things have been so crazy. I hope you haven't given up on *us*."

I don't know what to say, because I have, but then again, I'm here. "I haven't."

"Good." She kisses me on the lips and bounces to the champagne. After popping the bottle, she pours two glasses and hands me one. "We should toast. You do it."

"I don't really know what to say. Here's to whatever the future may hold."

Chantel frowns. "Ben, that's too dark. It should be light and fun. Here." She kneels on the couch. "You do the same." I do, and now we're face-to-face and I'm so uncomfortable and it has nothing to do with the couch.

"Let's link arms. It's adorable."

We do and I'm pressed into her now, the effervescence of the champagne fizzing beneath my lips and her staring into my eyes. I could give in to this. She is beautiful and this is undoubtedly the most romantic thing I have ever done. But . . .

"To us," she says and I have no choice but to drink. She leans in, her sweet breath on my face. "Kiss me, Ben."

I open my mouth, to kiss, to speak, but I see him, the man from the mall, and not in my mind, not as some hallucination, but in a picture frame on the mantel.

"Who is that?"

Chantel frowns and turns around. "Who?"

I disentangle from her and cross to the picture. I bring it back. "This guy."

She looks at it and then back up at me. "My Uncle Paul. Why?"

I so want to see a lie in her eyes, something to tip me off that this is bullshit, that she forgot to put away a picture of her lover, boyfriend, something. But it's not there. She's telling the truth.

I turn my back to her and stare at the fire.

"Ben, what's wrong? Do you know my uncle?"

"No, I don't. Sorry. It's nothing."

She hands me back the picture. I return it and see his face again.

"Chantel, is he the only Paul in your family?"

She sips her champagne and answers, equally bubbly. "No, he's got a nephew, Paul. We call him P. J."

I know what her answer will be, but I still ask, "So what do you call your uncle?"

"O. P.," Chantel says. "Old Paul. He doesn't like it because he's not that old, but we do it anyway."

I drop the champagne to the marble floor and it shatters, the splintering the only sound I hear against the rush of blood to my head, as too much improbability clicks into place.

CHAPTER 27

'm not sure why I do it, but I enter the guidance office and head
to the wall of applications. They've got them for all the local
private colleges, the universal one used for all the state schools,
and then the one for the community college. I grab the latter and
don't look up as I pass by my guidance counselor's door. I'm sure
she wants to talk to me since I've skipped out on every appointment she's tried to schedule. I'll end up with detention just so we
can get face-to-face.

I head to physics and we discuss potential energy. There's grav-
itational potential and elastic potential. I know all about potential.
There's potential that O. P. is Chantel's uncle, which means what,
exactly, I don't know. Because he may not be. Could be a coinci-
dence? They happen. But something tells me that's wishful thinking. And if so, then what is Chantel's role?

She's had her own questions since that night. I told her I
didn't feel well and took off, but she's not buying it and I know
we're going to have to talk. A week of stall tactics hasn't gotten me
anywhere.

I head to my locker before going to lunch and John rolls up.
He's still favoring his good arm, and I think it's sad that at seventeen he has a "bad" appendage. "What's the deal?"

He looks at me as if he doesn't understand the question, but we both know he had an appointment over break. He's got answers.

"Tell me, man. We'll deal."

"It's over, Benny. I've got some nerve damage from the surgery. Or because of taking that bat. My fingers don't work right."

"So, because of the nerves, you mean?" I don't finish, but John answers.

"Yeah, no one's looking at me for next year. I'm beyond damaged goods."

I lean against my locker and take a deep breath for him. I cannot imagine how painful that must be. Not only the physical, but the mental and emotional. I'm witnessing firsthand what it's like to have a dream shattered. I may be able to help my father, but I don't know about John.

"I am so sorry." I can't think of anything better.

"Me, too."

He's choked up and I want to end this conversation before I make things worse. "Come on." We head toward the cafeteria.

Alexia and Chantel are in line.

"There you are. I've been texting you all morning? What's up?" Chantel waves me over, and I go to her and let her hug me. She looks me over and grabs my cheeks. "What's wrong, Benny?"

I don't answer because I am afraid of what I might say. There's no way I'm confronting her about her uncle until I'm sure. I'm not even telling the guys. But I do notice the new necklace Alexia is wearing. I wonder how much closer this brought Jesse to her, and how much her dad was okay with it?

I follow John to our table and Ricky asks, "You ready?"

Trevor watches Ricky. John and I wait anxiously. Because of the holidays—or so he says—O. P. didn't mail the check. None of us saw the number of hits because we were too messed up, and Trevor was too busy editing.

"Do you think it's possible that we reached twenty thousand?" Ricky's voice has a game-show announcer quality. We shrug.

"Higher?" He continues and cocks his head to the right while turning his hands, palms up.

"You're killing me," I say.

"Yeah, out with it," John adds.

Ricky laughs maniacally and looks directly at me. "Thirty thousand."

The figure hangs over us, and the math is so simple, and at the same time so painful. Seventy-five hundred is a lot of money, but doesn't get me to twenty thousand. I need one more dare before the auction.

"I hope you boys got big plans for your wad of cash because it's about to get bigger. Next stop, the Winter Formal." Ricky smiles. John shakes his head like he's clearing it, and Trevor looks momentarily scared.

My stomach convulses. This is the first time we'll be pulling off a dare in public. I'm equally petrified and excited. This kind of stunt could give us killer exposure. Sure, what we're doing is fun to watch, but when shit gets crazy at some unexpected place with lots of unsuspecting people around, that gets attention. In our case, will it be too much? Shit, with everything as upside down as it is, what do I really care?

—

I punch in and say, "Hey," to Alexia and look for slips.

"We've only got two orders. Looks like it will be a slow night."

I can't help but stare at the necklace.

She sees me, tugs the gold in her fingers. "This was for Christmas. Along with a lot of apologies."

"You accepted both?" I don't mean for it to be an accusation, but as soon as I say it, I know that's exactly what it is.

Alexia looks at me with her gorgeous eyes and they gloss with a sheen of tears. "I know you think I've got my shit together, Ben, but really, I don't."

"I'm sorry, that came out wrong."

She turns away. "Don't be. It's not your fault. It's his and it's mine. Mom always says it takes two to tango."

"Yeah, but if the guy makes you dance, does that logic really apply?"

She's quiet for a moment and I watch her collect herself and think. When we were young, she always took a moment, staring off into space, chewing gum or holding a stuffed animal or in the middle of a leaf pile. I always laughed and waved my hand in front of her face. Not now. Now, I wait.

"You see things differently than me, Ben, so maybe I'm wrong, but I don't think logic applies in relationships."

I shrug. "You're the expert on that. I don't really have any experience."

She turns back to me. "What about Chantel?"

"What about her?"

"Really? I . . . she seemed . . ."

"That's it right there. That's how I feel. I thought so, too. Guess we were both wrong."

Alexia purses her lips. "Like I said about logic, huh? I haven't seen Jesse since he gave me this." She flicks the necklace. "Spent New Year's alone. He's with his friends almost every night."

Two ideas solidify. One, Jesse Holmes is a tool for leaving a girl like Alexia hanging—along with his other failures as a human being. Two, if he's been busy with his boys that could mean he's scheming. We'd better have a plan.

"If you're single for the Winter Formal . . ." As much as I want to finish, I can't.

Alexia smiles, and it's the first whole-face grin I've seen on her in forever. "Right back at ya."

My face reddens and my mouth falls open, but before I can respond, Chuck's bellowing, "Doc, get in that ambulance and save someone from hunger."

Alexia and I are all business then, and I'm out the door and so thoroughly lost it's almost comforting.

—

The house is subdued when I return. Mom's watching TV, Dad's in their room, and Ginny's in hers. I say hey to Mom and she asks about school and work during a commercial, and when the questions are over, I'm free to leave and go crash in my room. I head up the stairs and hear a frustrated growl come from behind Ginny's door. I hesitate but then knock. "Fun times?"

"Fucking awesome!"

I turn the knob and push in. She's on her bed, laptop on her legs, papers everywhere she can reach and beyond.

"Don't touch anything."

I wasn't planning on it. I spy a clear space in the corner and sit with my back to the wall. It feels good. "So what's the deal? Paper not going as planned?" I can't remember the last time I put any effort into something I've written.

"I wish it were that simple." She shakes her head and looks over the piles and at her laptop and then at me. "You want to hear?"

"Sure?"

"Some of it may be over your head, but I'll try to dumb it down."

"Thanks." I feel like kicking the closest stack of papers. She misses my sarcasm though, and carries on.

"So we set out to prove that risk-taking activities, the kind of bullshit you guys are doing, is a result of adolescents' desire to achieve adult status. Basically, you act like an ass to prove you're an adult."

I let this sink in. "That's not it at all."

"Exactly!" Ginny throws up her arms and almost topples her

laptop. "I've been watching you guys, and it has nothing to do with that. It's all about . . ." Her face turns upward and she stares at the ceiling for a second. "No, you tell me. Why? Why are you doing this?"

"Really? Come on? The money."

She frowns. "The money didn't come into play until after. Therefore, it may keep you doing what you're doing, but it wasn't your prime motivation."

Shit, she's good. I look at the carpet, this worn raspberry-colored disaster and think back to August and what Ricky said to get us so fired up. Then, of course, to how things have morphed, and our last conversation.

"It was a few things, really. You know how Ricky, John, and I always used to do stupid stuff. It was kind of an extension of that, only on a bigger scale, bigger result."

Ginny's staring at me, but jotting down what I'm saying at the same time. "Which was?"

"To be awesome. You should understand this. You're awesome because of your brains. Some people are because of sports. Through the stupid shit we do, because people love it, we get that feeling."

"But it's more than that, right? You could feel good about doing community service? Why this daredevil life-risking, whatever?"

"Don't overanalyze it, Ginny, it's fun. Community service is not fun. Sure, you think what we're doing is stupid, and it is, to a degree."

She looks at me, and I know I'm not off the hook. "To what degree?"

I lean back, so full of shit that I'd like to say, but can't, so confused with my trajectory that I'm beginning to wonder if I ever was really on course. Like Ricky said. But I'll answer this, because I can.

"To the degree that we get to throw caution to the wind, to say fuck it. I'm sorry, that's not PC or what people are supposed to think, but look at Dad. He did all the right things all the time and look where it got him."

Ginny raises her pen to ask a question, but I ramble on.

"I can't live like that. He stopped me years ago because he was afraid. He was right, because that's who he is, what he does, makes the tough calls. I respect that. But I'm not that. I'm seventeen, and yes, I want to live to see seventy, but not if it means I have to sacrifice my desires. I'm allowed to want. And I want this."

Ginny writes some more and looks at me. "Damn, Benny, that was pretty deep."

I feel like flipping her off because I think she's teasing me, but her face is set and she's nodding like she does when things start clicking. She's figured something out, and I can see the lightbulb.

"Well, I hope I helped." I stand. "I have to go plan my world domination now." Ginny starts rifling through the papers around her, and I walk out of her room.

I stand in the hall and listen to the crackling fireplace and wonder what she's going to come up with. I want to read her paper now. I want to know what she thinks because maybe that will help me figure out what to do after this all falls apart. Because in spite of all I said, yeah, I want this, but that doesn't mean I deserve it, or will get it.

CHAPTER 28

The house is cold when I wake up and I feel like I should stay in bed. I filled out the community college application last night. Who knows what inspired me? Maybe it was seeing Ginny working so hard at something that may be pointless, but at least it's something she's into and can do in the future. I'll be delivering pizzas if I don't find something besides monthly suicide attempts.

I crawl out of bed, and Ginny's downstairs, reading yet another paper and drinking coffee. The coffee looks like a good idea. I mumble, "Morning," as I pass her and she gives me a quick, "Hey," but doesn't take her eyes off the paper.

I put an English muffin in the toaster and drink coffee while I wait. There's nowhere to sit in the little kitchen so I lean against the counter and look out into the still black morning. I can't wait for spring.

"Hey, I meant to tell you, I got the details from the bank." Ginny starts into the conversation like we'd left off with it last night.

"Okay." The toaster pops and I butter my breakfast.

"It's going to auction at the end of the month."

"*This* month?"

"Yeah, which is two weeks, in case you've forgotten," she says and looks into her coffee mug.

"But I don't have enough money yet."

"I know." She sighs. "Maybe you want to consider saving that money for school instead."

I think about the application I completed. I could pay for both years right now, but that's not what she means.

My parents pop out of their bedroom, and it's obvious that they've just finished a conversation. Both their lips are sealed but they have the same conspiratorial look.

"Good, you're both up. I thought I was going to have to wait." Dad sounds more upbeat than he has since Christmas.

Ginny and I look at each other and shrug. Mom laughs. Too hard. Shit, she's nervous.

"Sit, please." He's talking to me, but Mom sits at the dining-room table while I grab a seat next to Ginny at the counter. "As you know, I've been upset about the house. I didn't know the owners failed on the mortgage so soon, and I certainly didn't know it was going to auction."

I try not to choke on my muffin.

"So, I've spent the past couple of weeks getting our finances in order so that we can get the house back." He doesn't look at us.

Mom lets out a little cheer that is so weak it's pathetic.

Dad steps forward and puts both hands on the counter. "My plan, unfortunately, will affect both of you."

Ginny stops drinking her coffee and looks at me out of the corner of her eye. There's only one possible way this is going to hit us both. Even I've figured that out.

"Gin, darling, we're going to need to free up some cash, so I'm going to have to ask you to take on more of your student loans. I've got a plan mapped out, but you'll need to go to financial aid after break and take care of the paperwork."

Ginny's doing her best to compose herself, but her lip's trembling and her jaw's wobbling. She nods at our father and he turns to me.

"Ben, the same applies to you. Once you have been accepted we'll need to look at your finances very carefully, but I'm afraid you'll be in the same situation as Ginny."

It pains him to say this, but as much as I feel for him, I also want to laugh. He doesn't need to worry about me. I got this.

"I think it's the right move, Dad. Sometimes we have to sacrifice." Ginny sounds like she's reading the words off a teleprompter, but I also know they're as much for me as Dad. She's telling me I've bought her silence. She could spill the beans right now and I'd be fucked. Dad has the house figured out, I'm not needed there. But I sure am if she's going to have to pay her way through the remaining ten years of school she's planning on.

Mom chokes out a sob and even Dad wells up. I say, "I couldn't agree more."

Mom bolts out of her chair and rushes to us. "I don't know what we did to deserve such good kids, but my God . . ." She doesn't finish, but pulls us into her blubbering mess and squeezes tight. Dad walks over and joins the embrace. Mom cries on Ginny's shoulder, and he leans in to kiss her cheek. Ginny looks up at me. Her eyes are as hard as her jaw, and I nod to let her know I understand. She nods back, and the deal is sealed.

I drive down our old street on my way to pick up John, and stop before our house. The FOR SALE sign is back in place but I don't have the urge to take it down. No, it's all good. Dad will take care of his business, I'll tend to my own, and come spring I'll be back on that porch.

John's waiting outside when I pull up, in spite of it being twenty-something outside. He hops in quickly.

"Go, man, go." It's like he's just held up a bank.

I gun it, and once we're a block away he settles into the seat.

"Figured he was gonna follow me out and keep yelling."

"About what? What happened?"

"The scholarship. It's official. We got letters from every school. No one wants me." He says this very matter-of-fact, but also very quiet.

I pull into the school's lot and park. "Shit. That sucks."

John looks out his window. "I don't know. This is going to sound weird and all."

"I can handle weird. Go ahead."

"It's, you know, all I've ever talked about was getting a scholarship to school? How basketball was my dream?"

I say, "Yeah," and feel pained because I know I'm partly to blame for him losing that dream.

"Ever since I hurt my wrist, like *the very moment*, you know what I've been thinking?"

"You wanted to kill Ricky?"

"No, Ben, it's not like that." His voice is quiet again and I feel like a dick for making light of this.

"Sorry, I didn't mean anything."

He waves my words away. "I know. What you said makes sense. Who wouldn't be pissed? But that's the thing, even then I wasn't. I had to act like I was, play the part and all." He turns to me and his face is jumpy. "I realized I've been playing *that part* forever. The basketball star. As soon as I busted my wrist I was happy. I was relieved that the pressure was gone."

John's eyes bulge and he seems out of breath when he finishes. I nod because there's nothing else for me to do. I didn't know he felt like this, and hearing it all makes me feel slightly better about how things have worked out. But still. "Man, I'm so sorry. I had no idea. I don't know how you hung in there so long if you hated it."

"It's what I know. And it was expected."

I can get my head around that. "So what's the deal with your dad?"

John wraps his thumb and index finger around his forehead and squeezes. "He wants me out of the house. If I refuse to find another school to take me on scholarship, he won't pay for me to go anywhere else, and he won't let me live at home."

The bell for first block rings and neither of us move toward the doors. "You'll have enough to go to the community college, and my dad's trying to get our house back. So if that works out, you can live with us."

John looks at me. His eyes are puffy. "You serious?"

"Yup. He's using Ginny's and my college funds, but whatever."

"Shit, she must be pissed." John sits up and it's good to see him not consumed by his own problems.

"Yeah, but she knows how much we're making and how I'm not going away to school, so . . ."

"What do you mean you're not going away?" John cuts me off.

"Uh, yeah, I guess I haven't said much about it. I fucked up my SATs and my grades kinda blow. So, you know, I'm looking into community college."

John's face knots into confusion. *"You? Not going to college?"*

"I'm still going, just not where I intended."

"Your parents okay with this? Especially your dad." John tilts his head forward, as if weighed down by the words.

"Haven't told them. But, really, what are they going to do? They told me I have to foot the bill."

"But where are you going to tell them the money came from?"

"Tips. Fat fucking tips."

—

At lunch, I come out with it. "So we've got an issue," I say.

The guys lean forward. "Let's hear it," Ricky says.

I explain about Chantel and her uncle. We all sit back and

look around.

"So what does this mean?" Trevor asks.

"It means we conference with O. P. ASAP," I say.

"And say what? *We know who you are?* How does that help us?" Ricky says.

"Seriously? Are you really asking that question? The very guy who we've signed off with has put his niece onto me. That's beyond creepy."

"You really think it's like that?" John rubs his face. "Like some kind of setup or something?"

"I don't know, it seems like it has to be more than a coincidence," I say.

Ricky shakes his head. "I hear your point, but one, Chantel hasn't ever said anything about the dares, right?"

I nod.

"Two, when she was talking to you about her uncle, did it seem like she was in on all this, like she even knew?"

I think of her face on New Year's as I hurried out the door. She was lost. "No, she didn't. But come on, this is weird, right?"

"I think *weird* fits," Trevor says.

"Agreed," Ricky says. "But that doesn't mean anything. You might just be getting paranoid, Ben. It's what you do."

I'm pissed at this point, but have no argument. Even if I did, Ricky continues anyway.

"Regardless of what is or what isn't, we need to think about what we're going to say. We can't launch into *that*. You know?"

I do know. And I'm sure part of it has to do with Ricky worrying that our sugar daddy is going to disappear. I feel the same, but damn, this needs to be dealt with because I literally do not know what to do with Chantel. This whole whatever we have was strange before. But now? I guess there's only one way to find out.

I look at Ricky. "Agreed. Set it up and we'll see how it goes. I promise not to lose my shit."

He gives me a long look. "Yeah, you're good now. I can feel it. We'll deal with this pervy shit, if it's that, and then move onto something fun."

I hope like hell we can get past this to that, but keep my mouth shut.

"Where have you been?" Chantel plops her tray down at our table and I jump in my seat.

"What's up?" I manage.

She pops the cap off her bottle of water. "What's up? Um, I don't know, I've only been texting and calling for the past couple of days."

The guys look at one another and then pretend to eat.

"I've been busy. Sorry."

"Ben, what's the deal? You've barely talked to me since New Year's. Did I do something?" Chantel's face is splotched.

I feel awful. She seems so genuine, like she's always been. And if she doesn't know anything, then what I did was a total dick move. I decide not to lie. "Family stuff, really. I don't want to go into it, okay?"

Her face softens. "Ben, I'm sorry." She grabs my hand, and I don't unlace our fingers. "You can talk to me. You know that, right?"

If I look anywhere but at the bench right now, I might come undone. Who knows what the guys are thinking, and all these images I've had about Chantel are evaporating by the second. "I do," I say.

"Good, because we need to talk about the formal. There's no way I'm missing *that fun*."

Everything slows with that. I don't know if it's because my brain's so full that the processing is taking longer than usual, but it feels as if someone's set the room to pause while I catch up. And I do. I catch what she said. Or more importantly, *how* she said it. The inflection on *that fun*. No one says that about the dances here. McNeil's got breathalyzers at the door and chaperones that prowl the floor searching for "inappropriate touching."

I clear my throat and hear Ricky do the same. Maybe I'm not paranoid? "What do you mean?" I ask Chantel. My voice is deadly, just like Ricky's. Even Trevor glances over for a second.

Chantel looks blank for a moment and gives me the slightest head shake.

"No. I mean it. Tell me the *fun* you were talking about. I'd like to know." Now my voice has an edge and I realize I need to control it before we have a scene here. I promised Ricky I can handle this shit. I need to show him I can because I want the reins for that conference with O. P.

John sips his drink and openly stares at us, like he's watching tennis.

Chantel says flatly, "Being there with you. That's what I meant."

She's an awful liar. I guarantee some third grader could have done a better job of convincing me. But she sits there, grinning, and I have to wonder: Am I seeing things I want, or am I uncovering some truth? Is Chantel lying? Does she know about the dares? Or am I so hypersensitive that I am, again, looking for someone else to blame?

CHAPTER 29

I t's snowing. The flakes are fat and stick to the ground like batter on a grill. We haven't had a real storm yet, but this white mess is moving like we're just getting started. I head into the condo and shake off. Ginny's by the fireplace, reading a textbook, highlighting away. She looks up when I come in and right back to her book.

I kick off my boots, hang up my coat, and head to the fridge. I grab an apple and take a bite. The crunch echoes through the house.

"Gin, where are Mom and Dad?"

"Funny," she says to her book.

I move to the couch. "No, seriously. Where are they?"

She closes her book around her highlighter. "Have you really forgotten?"

I nod and bite my apple.

She looks at the fire, tilts her head, and turns back to me. "They're at the auction."

"Isn't that tonight?" It's not even 4:00.

"It is. But there isn't just our house on the block, lots of others, too. And with the weather they wanted to get there and not miss anything."

I imagine the scene down at the courthouse—my parents,

Chuck, and whoever else is interested. Ginny's shaking her head at me.

"What?"

"Nothing. I was going to say something, but never mind."

"No, say what you're thinking."

"Ben, don't start. I don't feel like arguing right now. I'm working on this paper and am concerned about Mom and Dad. You could get your head out of your ass, okay?"

"What the hell are you talking about? I'm busy, too. It may not be school work, but I'm making more money than you ever have."

"Wow, I'm so impressed. You're doing stupid illegal shit so that you can feel like your life has more meaning. I'm amazed."

I look outside, at the snow falling, and know I need to leave, to get to Pizza and More. There's no time for this argument.

"Text me if they get home before I do. I want to know how it went."

"You know how it's going to go, Ben. But I'll still text you."

I almost raise a point to argue, but she's right. Dad's chances are slim. I wonder how close they are to mine?

Ten minutes later I'm pulling into the parking lot. The roads are bad, but the Jeep is steady. At least something in my life is. My lights flash over Alexia out back, smoking a cigarette.

I step out of the Jeep and walk to her. "You okay?"

She exhales. "Really? That question?"

I put my palms up. "Sorry. It's . . . I didn't realize you smoke."

"I don't," she says and takes another drag. "But my life isn't supposed to be like this. You know?"

"How so?" I ask.

She shakes the snow from her hair. "Come on, Ben. You know why we moved. Dad got the big promotion and we got the house and the better neighborhood. Least that's how it seemed." She takes a drag. I wait. She's beautiful even smoking a cigarette. I don't know how. "But it's been shitty. He's never around and when he is he's pissed. Mom can't stand him. And now with the way the plant's going . . ." She stops, looks at me. "You know. It's not getting any better."

I look up, watch the flakes drizzle down, and enjoy the crush of silence that comes with snow. "And there's Jesse and that mess."

"Yeah. And that." She stops, but wants to say more. I can sense it. So I wait, but the moment passes and she takes a drag of her cigarette.

"You going tomorrow?" I ask because I don't want her to go inside. I want her to ask me whatever's on her mind.

"The formal? No. Jesse said he's got other plans." She shakes her head. "Whatever. I'll be at home with a gallon of ice cream and some shitty movie. You and Chantel, though? She seems excited."

"Um, yeah, we're going, but we're meeting there."

"Oh, I'm sure she loves *that* plan. What's the deal?" Alexia's forehead wrinkles. Also adorable.

"I think we're through, but I didn't want to do that before the dance. That's not right." The answer emerges, and everything is silent except for Alexia's gasp.

"Ben . . . shit, I'm sorry."

"It's like you said with things being crazy at home. Same here, and I can't . . ." I grasp for the words. "She deserves someone who's got time for her." That's honest, I hope.

"Or you need someone you want to make the time for." Alexia nods and looks at me sideways.

"And there's that," I say. Shit, she can see right through me. However, at the same time, I can do the same with her. "So is that the deal for you with Jesse? You have this *need*?"

Alexia takes a drag and flicks away the cigarette. "I know I seem pretty cliché, Ben. Jesse's all popular and I'm trying to stay that way, but I guess he's what I know."

This is so sad it's unbearable. "So you stick with him because he's comfortable? Because from what I've seen, that's not comfort."

Alexia's head snaps my way. I brace for her to go off. Instead, she sighs. "I know. Maybe I'm too weak, or he's too strong, or it's something else altogether. Fuck, I don't have a good answer. Sorry."

"Don't apologize. It's your life. I guess I just wanted to understand."

Alexia's quiet for a second, but then she says, "But you already do, Ben."

Her words cut two ways. One, I do know, because the only things that have really changed about her since we were kids are her address and her group of friends. Two, I also understand more than even she does. Because I'm partially responsible for how Jesse has been behaving. I lit a fire and he got burned, and I knew—even if I chose to ignore it—that he would come looking for the source. It's only a matter of time until he does, and in the meantime, he takes out his frustration on her. All of that is my fault.

I shouldn't be so quick to judge. I am not Jesse Holmes, but I am also not the innocent Ben I pretend to be.

"You're right, I do, and I'm sorry for the way things are," I say.

"That makes two of us."

When I nod I realize that the look I saw from her is back. "What is it?"

She turns away. "Nothing. I was just thinking . . . It's stupid." She pauses. "I'm sorry for what's going on with you and Chantel. I'll keep some ice cream handy. She loves Rocky Road." Alexia looks at the falling snow, and I know I could walk inside, leave her be, and that would be that. But I can't. I need to know.

"Thanks. Really, I'm sorry about hurting her, but she's out of my league anyway."

Alexia laughs. "You said it, not me."

I step closer to her. "But, hey, you were about to say something. Go ahead. I can take it."

She stares at me for a long moment, and it's almost uncomfortable, like when Ginny's reading me, but then Alexia relaxes into herself. "Don't laugh," she says.

"I promise." Although I'm not sure I can keep it.

"I've got a dare for you."

"Really?"

"Really. You ready?"

"Uh, sure."

"Kiss me."

"What?"

Alexia looks away and I feel like an asshole for not scooping her up and laying one on her. "Sorry, I just wanted to make sure I heard correctly. Your dare is for me to kiss you?"

Alexia nods but still isn't looking at me. My heart crashes.

"You didn't need to dare me to do this." I grab her gently and she turns her head. Those enormous eyes are taking me in, and in them I see her pain and her fear. I don't know if this will take that away, but it sure as hell is worth trying.

I kiss her and her lips are softer than Chantel's, more delicate. She shudders against me, from the cold or this moment, I don't know, but I pull her close. She opens her mouth and presses with more force. We kiss and I think of nothing else—not our dares, not the shit at home, not Jesse. I feel her and this kiss and it gives me more of a thrill than anything I have done up until this point.

Alexia pulls away and stares at me. She's breathing a bit deeply and her face is flushed. "I should have dared you a while ago."

"Like I said, I didn't need it, but I am so glad you did."

We kiss again and separate when Alexia giggles. "Thanks, Ben."

"Anytime." I lace my fingers through her hand.

"Promise me you'll be careful tomorrow."

I know she means the dance, the parties after, but the irony is almost too much to bear. "I will," I say, and our moment of suspended reality is gone, and who knows what will be?

—

It's been a slow night so we're closing early. Alexia's already gone. I don't know what the moment we had means, and I'm trying not to overthink it because I've wanted that kiss since forever. But still. My phone chimes with a text, and I grab it, expecting Ginny.

Can u b @ Trev's by 8? It's Ricky, and I guarantee this is about O. P.

On my way.

I drive and replay the kiss over and over. It was awesome, but in the back of my mind Jesse Holmes lingers. I don't think Alexia will say a word, but if he ever finds out, shit. And then there's what I admitted to Alexia about Chantel. At least I know Alexia will be there for her. That is if she's even upset. She truly is way beyond me, which is why we need this chat with O. P.

I pull up and find Trevor outside with his garbage can.

"You don't have a butler or something for that?"

He ignores me. "I've been waiting for you and I needed a ploy to talk to you outside." Trevor's all business and he's making me nervous.

"Why's that?"

"I've been doing some research."

At those words my happiness fizzles.

"Get Out There Adventure is not owned by, nor does it employ, anyone named Paul. Hardly anyone works there, really. Regardless, it's owned by J. W. Steele, who is loaded, and listed with the Better Business Bureau as owning multiple websites."

"Does Ricky know?"

Trevor shakes his head. "No. I don't know how to handle that. He really needs this money. And John, too. But we can't keep doing this. It's not safe. If what you think is true, this man used his own niece. That makes my skin crawl. A lot like Jesse does."

I hope my instincts are correct, but at the same time, I don't. "Are we still conferencing with him?"

"Yeah." Trev looks at his watch. "In like five minutes."

"Then let's go."

Trevor goes to say something, but stops himself and says, "I trust you, Ben."

"Trev, the feeling's mutual. Thanks."

I follow him inside, where Ricky and John are set up like before.

"You ready, Ben?" Ricky asks and nods toward my seat.

"Absolutely." I look over at Trevor, but it's as if we never spoke.

A moment later our screens are filled with O. P., or Old Paul.

Ricky thanks him for meeting with us again, and all around kisses his ass. All the while my head is boiling with how we've been used.

"So this is our dilemma," Ricky turns. "Actually, let me have Ben explain." Ricky slides over for me to pull up my chair. I do and I sit and I stare for a moment too long. Ricky elbows me.

"Right, so our problem with this dare." I pause. I think of all the problems I've created by perpetuating this lie. The one this asshole began, the one I then took and made my own. I don't know who I'm more upset with, but I sure as hell know who I'm taking it out on. "The problem is, Paul, that we're sick of being your pawns. I don't know why you're doing this, if it's some sick way of getting pleasure by fucking with people, but we're out."

Ricky shoves me out of the way. "Sorry. Sorry. I don't know what the hell Ben is talking about but that is NOT how we feel."

"Put him back on," O. P. says, and now Trevor looks at me, the smallest smile on his face.

Ricky whispers, "I don't know what the fuck you're doing, but . . ."

I don't give him the chance to finish. I sit and O. P. grins at me through the monitor. "So, what do you know?"

I hate the smugness. I hate the arrogance. I hate everything about this dick because he is the embodiment of all that is wrong in our society. But I won't give in. For all his scheming, I'm still smarter.

"I know you used your niece to get to me. I don't know why, but that doesn't matter because more importantly, I know you need us."

O. P. laughs. "Really? Why's that?"

"We don't need you."

Now he sits up straight and leans in toward his computer.

Ricky's making a choking sound but I ignore him.

"How's that?"

"That contract means nothing. You don't own Get Out There. You don't own anything but some websites. We can take our dares and do with them what we please and post them on YouTube and make ten times more money."

"You're correct. My partner owns Get Out There, but hold on, what makes you think I won't tip off the authorities to who you are?"

"Contributing to the Delinquency of a Minor. This coercion, through these chats, it's been recorded. All we need to do is put it on a flash drive and walk into the local police station. Do you really want to play this game?" Yeah, for once, all year, I've done my homework.

O. P. is silent. Ricky is as well. John whispers, "What the hell is going on?"

"That's not what you want, though, is it?" O. P. asks.

"No." My heart's hammering, but otherwise I feel fine. No deep breathing necessary.

"So where do we stand?" O. P. asks, and it may be the first time he sounds genuine.

"You'll help us with our next dare and that's it, we're done with you."

There's a long moment, a pause that seems as if FaceTime might have frozen and the air is as saturated with silence as outside, but then O. P. answers. "What do you need?"

—

Dad's sitting alone by the fire, drinking a glass of whiskey. He sets it down when I come in and by the look on his face I know the outcome of the auction. Ginny never did text me, and I'm guessing this is why.

"There he is." His tone's light, but he's forcing it.

"Hey, Dad, what's going on?" I step out of my boots and hang up my coat.

"A number of things. One, we didn't get the house back."

I hold on to my coat. How is there anything more than that? I let go and cross the room to him. "I'm sorry."

"So am I," he says. "But it is what it is, and maybe for the best?"

Now I know the alcohol's talking because there's no way he actually believes any of that, but I understand having to accept and move on. I wish I could have helped earlier with the finances. But there is the future I secured.

I sit. "Did Chuck bid?"

Dad shakes his head. "Not on ours. But others. I think he picked up one."

Chuck's crazy but him not bidding on our home makes me respect him a little.

Dad takes a sip of whiskey and he sets his glass down. Then he touches an envelope on the end table.

I freeze. The envelope is from my school. The return address is clear. Shit, this is what's more. I take a deep breath to calm down, but my stomach feels like a washing machine.

"Ben, I'm sorry I've been so *absent*. What with the job and then the house, I feel like I haven't been around at all, even when I've been here." He picks up the envelope, but doesn't pull out the contents. "Do you know what this is?"

I can only assume it's some letter about my shitty GPA. "Maybe?"

His eyes pinch and I know that was the wrong answer.

"Why haven't you shown us any of your grades?"

The blood drains from my head. I nod at the envelope. "I bet that explains it."

His face pulls serious. "Why didn't you say something? If you were struggling this much, we would have helped."

"But like you said, you've been busy." I feel like a piece of shit for throwing it back at him. I know that's not the case.

He closes his eyes and sucks air through his teeth. "I know, I know, but your mother, or Ginny, we could have helped."

I don't say anything. The fire pops.

"So what do we do now? What's your plan to bring these grades up? No college is going to accept you with these."

He's right. And I know it. But I don't care. My sister's brilliant and I should be following in her footsteps. But I'm not.

"I'm not doing anything about them."

Dad looks at me sideways. "What do you mean? Do you think it's too late, because it certainly isn't too late. I can contact the school and we can work it out, chalk it up to the stress of all you've been through."

"But that would be a lie." I cut him off and his look lets me know that's the last time I'll do that tonight. "That's not why my grades have tanked." My heart's racing because as much as I'm being honest with him, I don't even think I've been this honest with myself.

"So why? Tell me."

I look into the fire and try to get the words straight. But I'm tired and don't know if I mean what I say, but it's too late to figure it out. Perfection has never been my thing, anyway.

"I've been hanging out with Ricky again."

"Jesus, Ben, You're throwing your life away for him?"

"No, it's not like that. Please listen."

Dad rubs his hands together. "Shoot."

And it builds inside, all that I need to say, and I'm ready to let it go. "I'm sick of who I am, who I'm supposed to be. I'm not Ginny, with my life all mapped out. I'm not you, either. I don't want college just because I may end up with a shitty job."

"What do you want? To hang out with Ricky and get arrested? Because I'm sure that's where you're headed."

I put my hand on his arm. "Dad, I know your life sucks so bad that you want *something* to work out. That's how I've been, needing everything in place and worrying until I'm sick when it's not."

He looks at me and I can't tell if it's anger or pity I see, but he doesn't cut me off.

"These past couple of months, I let that go, and I'm better for it."

"Really, because your grades show the exact opposite."

"Do you honestly think I'm talking about grades here, Dad?"

He works his jaw and looks away. "No, I understand your point, but someday you'll be in my shoes, you'll know what it's like to have a family depend on you."

"You're right. But now I'm in my shoes, and I'm telling you that if you let me figure this shit out, let me be whoever I am, I won't *ever* be in your shoes."

Dad winces. "Wow, Ben, that hurt."

I hang my head. "I know, and I'm sorry, but it's true. We all know you've always done as you're told, for us. I love that about you. But I'm not so sure that works anymore."

"What? Being honest and decent?"

"No, Dad, compromising too much of yourself."

"It's easy for you to say. You've never had to compromise who you are."

I swallow. "Yes, I have. And in a way that's fine, but to the point where I don't know who the hell I am, it's not."

"How does anyone know who they are at seventeen?"

It's a great question. "How do we ever know who we're supposed to be at any point unless we test ourselves and see? I have a feeling you'll be different when all the dust from this settles."

He shoots me a wistful, son-of-a-bitch, look. "How'd you get this thoughtful?"

I'd love to tell him the truth, but that's not an option. "I've been taking your advice. Trying to see that next turn before I get there."

He stares at his feet and then nods. "So these grades? College?"

"We'll see what's what. I can always get into community."

He stills for a long moment. "I hear you. I don't know if I agree, but I do hear you." He claps his hand on my shoulder. "You are your own man, Benjamin. I'm proud of that. But don't think for one second that we're not here for you."

"I know."

"And trust me, I'll have to talk to your mother about this. And Ginny. It won't be pretty." He extends his hand. "Deal?"

I take it. "Deal."

Dad holds up the envelope, cocks his eyebrow toward it, and chucks it in the fire. We watch it burn and it's nice to know he's on my side.

I say good night and head upstairs. Ginny's standing by her door. "No shit, huh?"

I point toward the stairs.

"Yeah, I was listening. It's what I do."

I shake my head. "And?"

"You're taking the easy way out, but maybe that's what you need to do?"

"What? How? I told him the truth."

"No, you didn't. You gave him some bullshit line about finding yourself. If you were so interested in that, you'd be doing everything you could to get out of here and do just that."

"What, the only place you can *find yourself* is at college? Is that what you're doing? Is being a parrot for some professor really who *you* are?"

She knots her forehead and looks as if she's going to punch me in the face. I feel like shit for upsetting her, but as I'm about to say her name, she unleashes.

"*I am not a fucking parrot!* When I finish this paper you'll read it and you'll see yourself for what you really are: a scared boy who's afraid to grow up. Go on, do your dare tomorrow, believe that you're a big man for it and then come back home and realize that's all you have, a little game of playing pretend. You thought you could save the house. Ha! Nice job with that! You think that running away from school is the answer. How's it going to feel when you're delivering pizzas to all your friends while they're home from break?" She steps closer to me and her face is crimson. "Do me a favor, grow up. I dare you."

She slams the door and I stand before it for I don't know how long. Her words stack up against the arguments in my head, and I know I've lost.

I feel cold through and through and it has nothing to do with the temperature in the house. I thought I had it figured out, facing up to who I am, where I'm going, what I want. And Dad let me off easy because he's worn out. I used that to my advantage. What does that say about me?

I don't know if I want to know the answer, but I'm sure I'll find out. Tomorrow it looks like all of Newton's Laws apply.

CHAPTER 30

I straighten my tie as the limo is beeping outside. I grab my phone, pull on my suit coat, and head downstairs. Mom grabs me around the shoulders. "Don't you look handsome. One picture with me before you go." She plants me in the center of the fireplace and puts her arm around me. "Ginny, grab the camera. It's on the table."

Ginny slides out from beneath her schoolwork, and when she grabs the camera her expression is as blank as stone. We haven't spoken since last night. "Say cheese," she says and Mom squeezes me. The camera flashes, and in an instant I'm out the door, pulling my black overcoat around me.

Ricky, Trevor, and John are already inside, and now's our time to finalize our plan.

—

We pull up amidst a swarm of limos and cars, climb out, and head toward the gym. McNeil is with the other teachers and chaperones, administering breathalyzer tests. We file into the line.

"Hey, Ben?"

I turn and Chantel bounds over to me. She's looking for a hug, so I give it, but having her in my arms only reminds me of Alexia, and I'm embarrassed in a dozen ways.

We all pass the breathalyzer test and enter the dance together.

A disco ball spins and the bleachers have been covered. The DJ is playing a decent mix, and the darkness is welcoming. I case the room, looking for the exits that I've never cared about before.

Chantel slips her hand into mine.

I look at this and then her. "Can we talk?"

Ricky shoots me a look. "I'll be quick," I say and pull Chantel backstage.

She's looking at me with an expression so similar to Alexia's it's disarming. I don't want to do this, but with all we're about to, I have no choice.

"I know about your Uncle Paul."

She looks confused. "What do you mean?"

"His plan, how he set us up, how you're involved." I lean in. "I know everything."

Chantel pushes me away. "Ben, what the hell are you talking about? You're scaring me."

"Don't act like you don't know." But even as I say it, just like at her house on New Year's, I know she's being honest.

"I swear, Ben. I don't." She's tearing up. "If you don't want to be with me, that's fine, just say it. You've been so distant lately, but I know you love Alexia. I understand. You were friends first and all, have some chemistry or whatever, but don't do this to me. Don't make up some lie. Tell me the truth." And now she's crying and I'm baffled. Unless . . .

"Sit, please." I help Chantel move to a step. She looks up at me and I wish I had a tissue or a time machine.

"Ben, what's going on?"

I sit next to her and sigh so loud I'm surprised by it. "I'm going to tell you something, and based on how you respond, I'll be able to answer that question."

She's still confused but nods. "Okay."

I clear my throat and breathe deep. I was not prepared for this. "Ricky, John, Trevor, and I are the Daredevil Crew."

Her eyes widen. She begins to laugh.

"I swear on my life, it's the truth."

"What? *You?* And Ricky . . . and . . ." Either her mind's blown or she's an amazing actress.

I put up a hand. "You probably have a thousand questions, but we don't have time."

"Why?"

I close my eyes. "We're inside the next dare."

She screams and I have to put a hand over her mouth. I shush her and she shakes her head. I release her and she stares wide-eyed. "Ben, tell me this is a joke."

"Not even close."

Chantel looks at the ground. "Okay, give me a minute."

As much as I don't have the time, I give it to her. It is truly the least I can do.

"So, if that's the case, if what you said is true, why were you asking about my uncle?"

"It's a long story that, again, I'll tell you, but not now."

She nods, but her look is not blank. There's humming consideration behind her eyes. She may not be certain about us, but possibly she's thinking through the potential of her uncle's involvement. Maybe he's done other shit like this in the past? "Okay. So what now?"

"I need to keep you out of this."

"Because of Paul?"

I hesitate. "Yes."

Her face sharpens. "Shit! I guess I'm not surprised. He asks about school every time I see him. He usually doesn't care, but not lately." She stills for a moment. "I'm sorry this happened, Ben, whatever has. I really do like you. Maybe after all this is over?"

This is more painful than I thought it would be. And my inability to answer says it all. Chantel nods and her eyes glaze over.

I lean down and I give her a deep kiss. "Good-bye. And really, thank you. I promise to still explain. But don't be surprised if your uncle stops asking you about school." I smile to try to lessen the blow, but that's impossible. Too much and not enough have been revealed.

Chantel stares as I step back, her eyes watering. "Ben, I meant what I said about Alexia. I understand."

I don't know if that matters because Alexia seems perpetually lost in her dance with Jesse Holmes, but it's nice to know that her friend believes something exists between us. "Thanks. Do me a favor, check on her. She's going to be lonely tonight."

Chantel tilts her head. "That makes two of us." She blows me a kiss. "Be safe."

I turn and head for the guys, my mind a scrambled mess. Ricky's waiting. "You good? Because we've got to get set up."

"Yeah, talked with Chantel."

"How'd that go? She yell at you for calling her uncle a perv?"

"She doesn't know."

"What?" John asks.

"Seriously, no clue."

We all stare for a moment, silent.

"Fuck, I guess we'll figure that out later." Ricky shrugs.

I nod and we head down the darkened hall lit only by the red exit signs, and turn right, placing us behind the gym, near the music rooms. Ricky stops and we all stand under the seeping red light.

"The mob will hit at exactly nine," Ricky says. "The DJ's been paid to play the song then, and that should trigger it."

"How does everyone know?" John asks.

"Didn't you see it on Twitter?" Trevor answers.

John shakes his head.

"All the rating of songs? The one that keeps getting a ten, that's it."

The song runs through my head. It's the latest meme, and everyone knows the moves. We're going to create one hell of a mess.

"What if this doesn't work? What if McNeil cuts the song after the first beat? The moves are pretty dirty. And we're inside, not out. How the hell are we going to get away?"

My voice bounces off the walls and then everything grows silent.

Ricky steps to me. "Ben, we're going to be fine. This is the last one we need to do this way. From here on out, we decide."

He sounds so much like he did in August, I chuckle. "Like it was supposed to be from the start?"

"We can't go back, but we can start again."

There's some brilliance in this and I slap Ricky's back. "Exactly."

Ricky claps his hands. "Once the mob hits, we move. Ben's right, they'll be doing everything they can to cut the music, hit the lights, and shut the floor down. That's when we lock them in."

Ricky lets this idea hang in the air. I don't know if it's because he's trying to get comfortable with it or because of how insane it sounds saying it out loud. "Inside that room are keys and fifteen cans of spray glue. One for each door. If you turn the bolt and fill the door's keyhole with glue, in fifteen seconds it hardens and freezes it shut."

"And then the dare is really on?" I ask.

"Yeah. Let's see if O. P. got everything." Ricky opens the door.

In neat stacks on the floor are helmets, vests, gloves, and ropes. I've seen these before. We all have. At the local rodeo.

"Holy shit," John says.

"Yup. That's how it'll feel getting on the bull," Ricky tries to control his voice, but something's making it waver. He clears his throat. "We lock the dance in, and then the trucks roll up and dump the dirt in the foyer. The pen will then roll up with the bull already saddled and we go for our eight seconds."

Ricky finishes speaking with the emphasis of a balloon deflating. Trev looks at me and I shrug.

"The vests all have cameras, so we'll use that footage instead of the handheld." Trev stops abruptly and turns to Ricky, who is sitting on the ground. "Are you all right?"

Ricky looks up at us. "Yeah, yeah, just put your vests on and give me mine."

I slide into the protective gear and feel like I'm suiting up for the electric chair. There is no way this can end well, and I think for the first time, Ricky is having doubts. So am I. All the other dares, the danger was on us. But not this time. What if the glue doesn't work and people charge the doors and get trampled by a bucking bull? Or the doors hold and people get crushed against the metal, trying to watch?

I hook my fingers back under the shoulders of the vest. We can't do this. It's too much. We have gone too far.

I start speaking but my phone vibrates with a text. I want to ignore it, but at this point, who knows who it could be?

There's a picture. It's of Alexia, crying, standing on top of Jesse's car. The text below reads: **Meet us and save her. I dare you.**

Out of the corner of my eye, I see Ricky pull straws from his pocket. "Shortest goes first, and on up until the last."

I find my voice. "Stop! Fucking stop!"

Ricky holds the straws like a bouquet and the guys all stare at me.

"Look." I hold out my phone and the guys gather around.

"Is that Alexia?" John asks.

"That's Jesse's car." Trevor adds.

"Ben, what the hell is going on?" Ricky asks.

I read the message aloud. "He's daring us to come save her."

"It's a fucking trap. I guarantee it. He probably Photoshopped that shit."

It's possible, but what if this isn't some stunt?

Ricky steps to me and puts his hand on my shoulder. "Ben, we've got like five minutes before our dare goes down. Come on, we'll deal with that after."

He may be right. This may just be Jesse's way of fucking with me. I look at the picture again. It doesn't looked Photoshopped. But even if it did, what's more important, this dare—which I know hasn't pushed the envelope, but lit it on fire—or leaving her to chance?

"I'm going," I say and stare at Ricky.

"What? You'll get your head cracked. Be smart. Stay here. We'll do this and then if you want, we'll go see what's what." Ricky's back together, his typical self, and I look past him. John and Trevor look like I feel.

I swallow and shove Ricky with all the strength I have. He stumbles but stays upright. "*I'm* going. These dares mean nothing

now. And this one . . . not happening. There's too much to control. Too much at risk. You know I'm right."

My phone vibrates again: **Ten minutes and we surf. U
coming?**

"What is it?" John asks.

"They're going to make her car surf." I look up from my
phone. "He'll kill her, Rick."

Ricky looks into my eyes for a long moment and I can see the
struggle. We'll make a killing with this dare. The hits will be off
the charts, but that's not what it's about anymore.

"Guys, keep your vests on. If we're going to save Alexia, I want
it on film." Ricky grabs my neck. "This dare's yours. Lead it."

—

The limo driver wasn't at all happy. He'd just settled in with his
book when we rolled up and gave him the address—a street over
from Jasperg—and he mumbled about "stupid fucking teens." We
strategized during the ride, but since we really don't know what's
ahead of us, there's no great plan from Ricky, no advice. We're flying by the seats of our pants.

The driver pulls over. "Here we are."

We pile out and stand on the shoulder of the road. It's cold
and dark, with only an errant streetlight, but up ahead their voices
are clear, along with taillights.

"Am I bringing you back to the dance?" The driver's head's out
the window. The guys look at me. Ricky shrugs.

"No. We'll take care of that."

He looks us over. "What the hell are you doing?"

"A senior ritual." I'm trying to keep it light, but he cocks his head.

"Like some kind of prank?" He pauses. "Shit, are you those kids, those idiots from YouTube?"

"No, we're not." It's not a lie. We're not the Daredevil Crew anymore.

"Shit, that would have been awesome." He does a U and heads down the road.

"So what now, Ben?" Ricky asks.

"I'll go in alone. You guys hang back near the woods. I'll give you a sign when I need you."

"What's the sign?"

I think for a second and up ahead the gunshot crack of a beer can pops. "Newton. I'll scream Newton."

I don't wait for questions. I walk and keep my eyes on the shadows moving around the red lights ahead. Two cars, so Jesse's boys must all be here, and somewhere, Alexia.

"Is it go time?" It sounds like Chris Carsdale asking.

"Couple of minutes."

Danny and Chris are directly ahead, maybe twenty-five yards. I put up my hand for the guys to stop. They do and move off the road, carefully picking their way into the cover of the woods.

"I sure hope that fuck shows. This'll be awesome."

"It will be even if he doesn't," Danny answers. "All of us and only her. You know he's got a plan B."

Chris laughs and a chill runs up my neck. I don't know if I'm more frightened or pissed off. I tighten the vest around me and check that the camera's on. "Let's stick to the original plan, assholes."

The beer that was just opened is dropped. An instant later headlights pop on. I'm blinded. I turn away from the light and shield my eyes. When I turn back I see Alexia inside the car. She's been gagged. Jesse steps out and hangs on the driver's door.

"Ben, so glad you showed up. Woulda been real boring if you didn't."

"I'm sure the three of you could have kept one another company." I'm surprised at how calm I sound.

"Big mouth for such a little boy all by himself. I'm surprised the rest of your douches didn't come. Too busy?"

"Something like that."

"See, that's the thing about loyalty. You can't ever really trust people unless they're scared of you." Jesse laughs. "It was nice of you to try and protect her. But never send a boy to do a man's job."

I don't know if he's drunk or so full of himself he thinks he's untouchable, but I'm happy as hell his mouth's as loose as it is. The mic on this vest better be working.

"So why are you here? Or is kidnapping a girl a manly thing? I didn't get that notice."

Jesse waves for Chris and Danny to crowd me.

"The manly thing is doing whatever the fuck you feel. And

right now we're going to fuck your shit up and then make you watch Alexia surf that fucking car. The one back there, that looks like Ricky's. Yeah, I figured you out. Had a hunch, then watched you all real close. It was a gamble, but it seems to have paid off."

He smiles so wide it doesn't seem physically possible. And I know because of that I should be shitting my pants. But I'm not afraid. This is what I wanted.

Jesse continues. "We'll wear your masks and get it on film. And when she's in the hospital, you can try to weasel your way out. Good luck with that."

They advance and my heart leaps into my throat, but I manage to scream, "Newton!"

Jesse turns but Chris punches me hard. I fall back onto the road but have enough sense to roll away. Feet are charging over the blacktop, and through the light of the headlamps the guys are visible, tangling with Danny and Chris. At least we outnumber them.

I look for Jesse, expecting him to hit me from my blind side, but I'm alone in the middle of the street. The ignition firing jolts me worse than that taser. Jesse's in the car with Alexia. He undoes the gag and is already wearing a mask that looks like ours. Alexia screams.

I sprint to the car and Alexia sees me. She's being tossed on the roof. "Ben! Help!" I'm ten feet away, and the hit comes from the shadows. I'm drilled and skid like roadkill.

"You're not going anywhere," Chris Carsdale hisses into my ear while he lays on me. "Now you watch, you little bitch. Best show you're ever gonna . . ."

He doesn't finish because Trevor kicks him in the ear. Chris grabs his head and screams like a girl. "It's gone!" His face is drenched in blood, and Trevor may have taken his ear off. But Trevor doesn't care; he just reaches down and hauls me up.

"Get that motherfucker!"

Jesse's behind the wheel and I reach the door as he's pulling away. I wrench it open and run alongside. Alexia's screaming from the rooftop, but I don't know what she's saying. I'm concentrating on how to get in. Jesse sees me and swerves, but I hold on to the door and the roof and stay balanced. I have one chance because he's picking up speed. I dive and crack my forehead against Jesse's dash. But I'm in.

He steers with one hand and punches the back of my head with the other. I get an arm up to block and connect with a punch of my own, somewhere in his neck. He stops punching and grips the wheel with both hands.

I freeze. What do I do now? I can't grab the wheel or pull the E-brake. Alexia's on top.

Jesse breathes deep and fishes around his lap, pulls out the camera. The screen lights up and this feels oddly like our other dares. Jesse turns the camera on himself. "This is Ricky Puckman of the Daredevil Crew bringing you our latest dare. We've got a real crazy one in store. It's back at the scene of our first, and we now have the help of Alexia Bellamy." He points the camera toward the windshield and then back to himself. "As you can see, we're going forty out here on Jasperg Lane and Alexia's on top of the car. Ready to watch?"

Jesse lowers the camera and covers the mic. "You better take that fucking wheel, Ben, or she's dead." With that he rolls down the window and slides out. The car slows, and I wait for it to stop. This dumb fuck. But his hand appears and he jerks the wheel. "Need some gas, Ben!"

Fuck. I hop into the driver's seat and take control. Jesse lets go and I can hear him talking to Alexia, coaxing her into standing up. If I stop quickly, she'll fall. If I slow down, Jesse will grab the wheel and rock her off. What the hell can I do?

"Ben! Stop the car!" Alexia screams.

I grip the wheel and try to think, but the road keeps unfolding, with rows of dead cornstalks on my periphery. Alexia pounds the roof and Jesse screams, "Stand up, bitch!"

There's no way out of this. I can't save her. She has to save herself, but that doesn't mean I won't help.

"Alexia, hold on!"

"What are you doing?" Jesse's hand reaches in and grips my hair. "I'll knock you out before you fuck this up."

"Go ahead," I say, and pull off the road and into the field.

Jesse grips harder and starts pounding my head into the door. My eye smashes against the frame a dozen times, and fills with blood. I can't see out of it. We slow way down, but the car bounces in the ruts. I can hear Alexia slamming into the roof. Jesse keeps cracking my face into the frame, but I ignore the pain and focus on what's important. I'll hit the brakes when we're slow enough. It's the best I can do.

Jesse lets go of my hair and grabs the wheel. He whips it and we swerve uncontrollably. Here's my chance. I crawl up onto the seat and crouch. Jesse screams, "Gas, Ben, or she flies off."

I can only see half of what I should, but his hand is visible, clenching tighter around the wheel. I spring.

I fly into him and out the window and there's an audible crack over the thudding car and Alexia's screams. I hold on to Jesse's neck and we propel from the car and hit the ground. A stalk sticks into my head, and Jesse is already screaming. I roll off and watch the car continue and finally come to a stop.

Alexia is no longer on the roof.

I slide off Jesse and look down. His arm's split in half and he's screaming, but I'm not helping him. Blood pours out of my eye and I can barely see, but I stagger along the field and call out for Alexia. There's no answer.

"Alexia!" I scream and taste more blood in my mouth. I'm dizzy but have to find her.

I plod as best I can, scouring the field, and then I see a lump. I move to Alexia and fall by her side. She's breathing, but there's a stalk in her side and blood on the ground. I lie next to her and stroke her hair and say I'm sorry.

"It's my fault. All of this. We set Jesse up, and I should have known better. And now . . ."

She sighs and all goes black.

CHAPTER 31

shift and my head throbs. I lift my hands to touch it and they're tethered. Must be the cornstalks, but that doesn't make any sense. I try to rub them away and pain shoots up my right hand.

"Benny, no. No, don't do that."

I open my eye at Mom's voice. She's inches from me, smoothing my hand, which lies on top of a bed. I pull back and look around. Through the dizzy wave I see Dad and Ginny sitting in the corner, the space between them cluttered with monitors and medical equipment.

I lie back, closing my eye, realizing one is bandaged. I can't make sense of why this is, why I'm in the hospital. "What happened?"

Mom squeezes my hand harder. "Oh, Benny, it doesn't matter." She slides across the bed and hugs me like I'm a three-year-old and had a nightmare. She cries, and I try to hug back but have no strength.

The door opens and people shuffle in. I peer at the visitors, a doctor and a police officer. The cop's eyes do not leave mine, but the doctor swoops in and starts checking the monitors.

"I'm going to need Mom, Dad, and Sis to leave. Need to check Ben's vitals, okay?"

They stand and Ginny waves. Dad pulls Mom from me and

shoots the cop a look. "What about him?" he asks.

"Officer Smith has some questions. He needs answers so he can finish his job." Doc whoever tilts his head and shrugs. My Dad nods, looks at me, and drags my mother out into the hall. Ginny follows and does not look back. The door closes and Officer Smith takes out a small notebook.

"Ben, do you think you could tell me what happened this evening?"

I close my eye and then open it. I'm dizzy and confused, but need to answer his questions. "I don't know what you mean."

There's a pause, filled by the beeping monitors. "The dare you were involved with this evening, with Jesse Holmes and Alexia Bellamy?" The officer's voice is gentle, but direct.

I feel a laugh bubble inside. Why would I be doing *anything* with those two? They're a couple. I used to be a friend of Alexia's, but so what? I open my mouth to ask the cop what he's talking about, but an image fills my mind: Alexia on the roof of a car, Jesse driving. I was there? Yes, I was there.

One of the monitors beeps furiously and I break into a sweat. I'm flooded with memories now, and I realize everything we've done, and that we've been caught, but am afraid to remember anything about tonight.

The doctor places a hand on my chest. "Lie back, Ben. Easy now. I don't want you to start bleeding from your wound." I grab his wrist.

"Is she okay?"

The doctor, whose nametag I can now see—Stein—pats my hand and removes it from his arm. I have no strength whatsoever. "Who, Ben? Who is *she*?"

Officer Smith readies his pen and my head throbs so hard I have to shut my eye. Again, it's only one. Is that the wound? Regardless, I see Alexia on the ground. The blood. Her sigh. "Alexia Bellamy. How is she?"

"I can't tell you specifics. But I can say she's with us and is being treated."

I'd love to yell, to demand he tell me more or I'll rip out my IV, but it's exhausting enough to accept this and say, "Okay."

"Please, Officer Smith, make it quick."

I hear the cop flip pages in his notebook. "Ben, just answer yes or no."

"Okay."

"Did you have an altercation with Jesse Holmes and his friends this evening?"

"Yes."

"Did that altercation end with a vehicular accident involving you, Jesse, and Alexia Bellamy?"

"Yes."

"Were you the one operating the vehicle at the time of the accident?"

I start to say yes, but stop myself. That's not really how it happened. I was driving, but not in the normal sense of the word. "It's complicated."

"Just a yes or a no, Ben."

Doctor Stein hums to himself as he works over me. I have no idea what the hell he's doing or what anyone else has said about what happened. I don't know if there's a story I'm supposed to be selling. It's only me and my throbbing head and my one eye and Officer Smith and his fucking questions. I want Doc Stein to knock me out. But not until I know what's happened to Alexia.

"No, then. Because it wasn't just me. Jesse had the wheel."

The officer sighs, a deep breath out his nose. I wait for him to ask for explanation, but he moves on. "And were you involved in a dare that was scheduled to go on at your school dance?"

Shit, what doesn't this guy know? I force my eye open. Officer Smith is staring down at his notebook, which is probably filled with facts about tonight and about us and all we've been doing. He might as well be holding a shovel to dig my grave.

"You tell me how Alexia is doing, and I'll answer your question."

Smith frowns. "I'm not about to . . ."

Doctor Stein hums so loud now it's ridiculous. He looks around. "I'm sorry, I didn't mean to." He checks my chart and says, "Officer, I'll give you another minute and then you need to let Ben rest."

Smith opens his mouth to speak but doesn't. He shuts his notebook and frowns. "She's in stable condition after having surgery to remove a cornstalk that she was impaled by. It didn't hit any major organs." He crosses his arms over his chest. "Now, back to my question."

He already knows the answer and he gave me the one that I wanted to hear. The rest doesn't matter. "Yes. I was part of the Daredevil Crew."

I expect Officer Smith to slap a handcuff on my wrist, but he just nods once and says, "Thank you." He turns on his heel and is out the door.

I feel like crying. What did I do? What have we done?

"Sleep, now. You'll feel better when you wake up." Doctor Stein's voice is gentle and so reassuring that I settle back onto my pillow and in an instant feel as if I'm drowning. I do not resist.

—

The sun slants into the room and touches the foot of the bed. It's a moment before I realize I'm staring at it, which means I'm awake. I blink to shake off the sleep and something deep within the left side of my head burns. I examine the room. Half of the room. I have to turn my head to see the clock displaying it's after 7 a.m. It's dizzying and I have to lie back. I open and shut my eye and the same throbbing emerges on the left side.

In this moment, I know. I understand that I've screwed up in a way I never imagined I would. My life is a hot steaming mess.

I hit the CALL button, and a nurse appears, and behind her, my family. She turns to them. "One minute, please." It's not a request. She shuts the door in their faces and comes to me.

"Ben, good morning." She smiles bright and that makes it all hurt more. They only do that for the doomed. "Are you okay?"

"It hurts," I say and point at my head, not that I can see my hand.

She purses her lips. "Mmm-hmm. That makes sense. Anything else bothering you?"

I force myself to ask. "Why does it hurt?"

Her look tells me. It's a moment of pure shock, one I imagine we induced in so many people as they watched our videos. "You don't know?" Her words are hesitant.

But I do. I've paid enough attention in school. Maybe not this year. But I know. "Is it because the muscles are still working along with the remaining eye?"

She puts a hand to her mouth and nods.

I'm half-blind. Somehow, last night, I lost sight in my left eye. "Okay," I say, and let the nurse resume her business of checking my vitals.

When she's done, she squeezes my hand and says, "Doctor Stein will be along shortly. You want your family now?"

"Please."

They pile in, Mom and Dad examining me from head to toe, asking if anything hurts, if I need anything, and then Mom crying uncontrollably when I tell her I know what happened. Dad comforts her, and Ginny, who is sad but not crying, approaches the bed, carrying her laptop.

"So, you're quite the hero."

"What?" It feels like Ginny's joking, but everything is surreal at this point so I can't be sure.

"Maybe *hero* is a bit much. But last night . . ."

"Ginny, enough!" Mom snaps.

Ginny looks at her and then at me. "Give him this. Come on."

"Please, let her explain. I don't remember much."

Mom sits up out of Dad's embrace. "But you remember us? Who you are?"

That last one's a difficult question, but I say, "Yeah, it's last night that's fuzzy, I think."

The door opens and Officer Smith enters. "Good, you're awake." He nods to my parents and pauses at my sister's laptop. He turns back to me. "Ben, do you remember me?"

"If I say no, will I get out of trouble?"

"I'll take that as a yes. But to answer your question, it's a lot like the way you answered me last night about who was driving. Do you remember me asking that?"

"Yeah."

"It's complicated." He again looks at Ginny's laptop. "Are you connected through the Wi-Fi?"

"Yes,"

Officer Smith reaches for her computer. "May I?"

Ginny hands it over, and as the officer finds whatever page he's looking for, shakes her head and mouths, "I'm sorry."

Officer Smith sets the laptop on the bed's railing and turns the screen to me. It's our website, and on it is a new video labeled, "The truth."

"Just watch." Office Smith presses PLAY.

The video begins with Ricky, not wearing a mask, explaining about what happened last night. He then waves, and Trevor and John come on camera. "We needed to make this video so that you would all understand what went wrong last night and why we even started these dares in the first place."

I sit up and as much as it hurts, force myself to watch as scenes from our dares play out and Ricky narrates about the initial idea for a legacy and then the change with O. P. He includes footage from our interview with Ginny, and, thankfully, leaves out whatever the connection we believed about Chantel. He describes what happened with Jesse and his friends around Christmas, as well as what's been going on with Alexia. He clears his throat, details the plan for last night, and tells of the text I received.

"The rest," he says, "will speak for itself." Footage rolls. It's from my vest and of Jesse describing what's about to go down. And then it splits as I scream Newton, cutting to the guys fighting. It catches back up with me on the ground and Trevor telling me to get Jesse.

It's all me, then, getting in the car and getting bashed around. The road streaming past is visible, and Alexia's screams fill the room. The swerve off-road is jarring and how I've lost my eye is obvious. It is smashed to a pulp by Jesse's hand.

Then there's my leap, and the ensuing crash is devastating. Then there's quiet and there's Alexia.

"We wanted you all to know. We are sorry for the damage we

have caused, but we also hope this will help the officers, Alexia, and Ben."

The video closes and I look at the numbers. It already has twenty-five thousand views.

My parents are horrified. They look like they've just identified my body in the morgue. "So it's true, all this time, you've been behind the dares? You and John? And Ricky?" Dad's voice is low and pressured. He turns from me to Ginny. "And you knew? And you didn't say anything?"

Ginny looks down and nods.

"Why? For *school*?"

Ginny looks up. "Dad, it's not that simple. . . ."

He holds up his hand and cuts her off. "No, it's not." Dad turns back to me. "Answer my question, Ben. Let's start there."

Officer Smith arches his eyebrows in anticipation of my answer.

Shit. There's no use hiding. "Yeah. It's how Ricky described it. We're the Daredevil Crew." I look up. "I'm sorry."

Neither of my parents speak. I doubt they know what to say. Officer Smith clears his throat. "Thank you, Ben. It's a start. There's going to be an investigation. Some of your dares, especially the one on Halloween, may have broken a few laws."

Mom gasps.

Officer Smith continues. "Then there's this O. P., Paul Swenson. We're investigating his role. He's already been charged with contributing to the delinquency of a minor. That money you earned, I wouldn't spend it."

My head is throbbing and not from my injury. I should have seen this coming from the very start. Maybe I did and looked the other way. And for what? It's not as if my life was terrible before. Did we really need to go this far? Maybe for the money, but what are we going to do now?

I sit up. "What about Jesse?"

Officer Smith looks me in the eye and there is a glimmer of respect. "Kidnapping. Fortunately for us he's eighteen and Alexia isn't. And then there's the assault charge. For you. I hope he gets a tough judge. At least for now he'll be in county once he leaves here."

"He's here?"

Smith smiles. "Something like two rods and a dozen pins. You almost took his arm off."

I know by the way he says this I'm supposed to relish the fact, but I don't. There's nothing to be happy about in all of this. "Alexia?"

"I don't know much, only what I told you last night. I'm only dealing with the criminals."

His words fall around me like a cell. He's dealing with me, isn't he? "My friends?"

"All brought in for questioning, like you will be as soon as you're released. This conversation helped, but . . ." he looks at my parents. "Between you and me I'd get a lawyer, just to be safe. We're more interested in Swenson and Holmes than we are your son. But the evidence is available online. People will want to see them pay. We can't have a repeat of this." He snaps his head to punctuate his statement.

Smith stands, looks around the room. "Folks," he says, and then looks at me. "Feel better, Ben." He's out the door and, oddly, I want him back. Because now I have to deal with my parents.

I've fucked it all up. Instead of saving money, now my parents will need to spend more on a lawyer. Instead of working hard to get into college, I now have a police record.

"I'm not going to lie, Ben." Dad leans on the bed. "I am very disappointed in you and your sister. But mostly you. I don't understand how you could think your life is of such little value to chance it for recognition? Money? That conversation we had, I thought you were being honest and taking my advice. Seeing the next turn." He pauses, I think understanding just how this sounds. His voice drops with his next question. "Was that a cover for all of this?"

"Yes, and no. I meant everything I said."

He grips my shin. "I thought I—we—raised you better. I know recently it's been rough, but that doesn't justify . . ." He stops, stares at me. "I want more for you, Ben. *This* is not your path."

He's right. I don't know what that means going forward. But I do know I can't answer him, because if I speak, I'll turn into a hot mess of tears, and I can't bear the pain.

Mom leans in and hugs me tight. "My baby." She releases me and rubs my face with her fingers. "Do you want to talk?"

I shake my head. "Sleep." It's all I can manage.

"We'll give you some time." She kisses my forehead, and they stand. Dad shuffles out. "A couple of hours and we'll be back," Mom says. Ginny stands next to me, her face white and on the verge of tears.

"Not that you want this now. But I'm going back to school tomorrow. *They're* making me. So I figured you should have it." She squeezes my hand. "I'm sorry. Maybe I should have stopped you." Her voice quavers.

"Don't. I chose this. You know that." I squeeze her hand.

"But still. Shit. Forget all the lecturing I did." Ginny dries her tears with the back of her hand. "You're messed up Benny Bear, but you've got a good heart." She places her paper on my lap. It's painful to read the title: *Dare Me: An Exploration into the Self-destructive Adolescent Male Psyche.*

She joins my parents in the hall.

I set the paper on the nightstand and curl up on my side. My head races with all that's happened, all the ways it's gone wrong. Is there one thing I did right?

Alexia? I don't know. Because, really, it was my messing with Jesse that put her in this position. And I know why I wanted him to be our scapegoat. The realization makes me gag. I turn over and stare at the ceiling.

Alexia's in the hospital. We damaged property, scared the shit out of people, and should have died a half-dozen times. Probably would have if we'd made it to ten.

It's basic physics. Or maybe karma. *For every action . . .*

And here I am. I can accept what I've done to myself, it's my penance. I can even understand what Jesse did, because he behaved as he usually does, just at a higher level, because of us. I can accept what may happen to my friends. We deserve this. It's our punishment for thinking we were above the law, outside the system. No one is, even if we like to think so. This world has its hold on us, and those bonds cannot be broken.

But Alexia. I'm responsible for what happened. All of her pain is on me. The boys apologized for everything else. I need to handle this one.

I slide out of bed and almost fall to the floor. But after a moment of steadying myself, I grab my IV stand and use it as a crutch. My head throbs and the suction pads on my chest tether me in place. I unplug the monitors and pull the pads from my body. I'll explain later. Or not.

I'm wearing those socks with the grip on the bottom and I squeak when I walk. My ass is hanging out the back of my gown, and my head's wrapped in gauze. I'm a zombie Q-tip, but I don't care, because down the hall, a door to a room is open and a flower shop full of arrangements and balloons is tucked inside. Alexia's.

I knock on the door, and her mother looks up. Behind her, the privacy curtain is drawn and my insides curl on themselves.

"Yes? Can I help you?" Alexia's mom says.

We've haven't seen each other in years. Considering that, and how I look, it makes sense that she doesn't recognize me. "I, uh, I wanted to see if she's okay."

Alexia's mom frowns. "How do you know my daughter?"

How do I answer this? *I'm an old friend. We work together. I might love her.* I manage, "It's me, Ben."

Her face lifts and her eyes bulge. "Ben? Ben Candido? As in Ben from last night?"

I brace for her to swing something at me, but instead she rushes and pulls me into an embrace. "Oh, sweet Jesus. Thank you, Ben. Thank you, thank you, thank you."

I let her squeeze and stay quiet. I don't deserve her thanks.

She releases me from her hug, but holds me at a distance. "Look at you. What happened?" She points at her head.

I shake mine. "I'm going to have a little trouble seeing." It's all I can manage.

She squints at me, confused.

"My eye's gone."

She holds her hands to her mouth and looks like she's going to break down. I don't want, nor do I deserve, her sympathy.

"It was a long time coming," I say and then have to sit.

We are quiet for a moment. While Alexia's mom collects herself, my head steadies and I gather the courage to ask, "How is she? They haven't told me anything."

Her mother bites her lip. "She has a punctured lung and a lot of scrapes and bruises. Nothing worse. So we're lucky." She takes a deep breath. "But I'm worried about inside. I don't know what that boy did to her."

I want to kill Jesse all over again, and at the same time I hate myself all over again for letting this happen. I go to apologize but Alexia's mom places her palm on my back. "Would you like to see her?"

"Please."

She guides me to her bed and pulls back the curtain. She's asleep, and looks peaceful.

My head spins and I, again, sit abruptly.

"Are you all right?"

"Fine," I say. "Don't worry about me. Please."

"If you insist."

I examine Alexia. Her face is puffy from the drugs or the injuries or both. Her hands are stuck with IVs. Her chest is wrapped like my head. Still, she's beautiful to me. I grab her fingers and remember the other night. They're warm, and I take that as a good sign. I squeeze and whisper, "I'm sorry."

I know I'll have a shit load more of that to do for so many people, but right here, right now, is the most genuine time I'll say it. Because I am sorry for what happened to everyone, all the problems I've caused, especially for her.

I thought we were going to be the shit. Then I thought we were going to be loaded. And all along I thought we were going to die. None of that happened.

Yet in a way, the last did. All of us, from my friends to Jesse and his crew, my parents, Chuck, and Alexia. We're all changed from this. So maybe I was right. Maybe we did die. Not literally, but figuratively. There's no way I'm ever going to be the same. I'm scarred and have caused scars. Maybe Ginny's paper will tell me why? But I don't really need it to. Deep down I know.

It was all about the dares. They pushed us to be more than we were. Possibly more than we should have been. Maybe we should have been satisfied. Or maybe it's completely normal to want to change. Or, in my case, to see who I really was?

Regardless, I chose. We all chose. In some way we all wanted this. Not this end, but we set this course in action, stepped on the acceleration, and are now accepting the consequences. That's life, plain and simple. Here and now.

Legacy doesn't matter, and money is good, but certain things have to be earned. Like respect. Loyalty. Love.

I love Alexia. I think I always have. But I don't deserve her.

And of all the outcomes, that is the most painful. The way I abused her trust and sought to be the white knight saving her, that was ridiculous. Alexia never needed me. Not in the way I believed. She has always been stronger, even if Jesse pulled her so far down. Some things take on a life of their own, in spite of who you are. I've certainly learned that. Alexia needed someone to help her, not take over. Why couldn't I see that until now?

I sit back and watch Alexia, and do not care how long it takes for her to wake up. I will be here and I will tell her the truth, all of it, so that she can move forward. So that I can, too.

Daredevil or not, my life has meaning, value. I don't know what that is or how much, but I'm done with that game anyway. It's time to set forward on a path in which the consequences are ones I can live with.

ACKNOWLEDGMENTS

This story is about our culture, our desire to be seen, and what we are willing to risk for that visibility. It is not a glorification of the daredevil, but rather an examination of why.

Therefore, I thank my agent, Kate McKean, for understanding this premise, for offering insight as I shaped it, and for believing I could make this work. I am still amazed that I found someone who appreciates the craziness of my mind and of my stories.

Lisa Cheng also deserves much credit. *Dare Me* landed on her desk full of life, but a bit disorganized. She teased out what was worthwhile and what needed trimming. It was, at times, a laborious project, but one made infinitely better by her sensibility and intelligence.

My wife, Carrie. What can I say besides thank you for loving me? Without your acceptance of who I am and where my passion lies, my stories wouldn't exist.

Grace and Kaygan, my daughters. So this one isn't as rough as *Tap Out*, but don't go breathing a sigh of relief. I'm still your dad, and I still have plenty of stories to tell. But know that you inspire me.

Not only to write, but to appreciate life in the way only children can, with boundless enthusiasm.

To my family, who has always known that my life is a constant dare, and that the thrill of the ride, while jarring, is so worth it.

Mark Ayotte. I'll keep writing if you keep reading, because you're batting a thousand.

To my friends, who stood with me on those bridges and jumped. Thank you for your willingness to see just how far we could take it. I've yet to find my limit.